SEAN MAPLE

A Conflict of Interests With
MURDEROUS INTENT

novum ▲ pro

www.novum-publishing.co.uk

© 2021 novum publishing

ISBN 978-3-99107-139-6
Editing: Hugo Chandler, BA
Cover photo:
Helen Hotson | Dreamstime.com
Cover design, layout & typesetting:
novum publishing

www.novum-publishing.co.uk

For Clotilde and Anne-Marie

I want to thank Bianca and the team at Novum for their support.

DISCLAIMER

This is a work of fiction. Any similarities or resemblances to any person living or dead are not intended and are purely coincidental.

PROLOGUE

A Most Solemn Occasion.

The priests and the acolytes' pace and turn on the altar as the distant faces of the choir mouth their devout responses. It is as if she is a remote witness rather than a figure central to the solemn rite being enacted here. The fine black mesh, the veil that hides her swollen eyes, intervenes, a screen, a barrier that brings into sharp relief the vivid, richness of vestments, flowers and gleaming brass, like staring in through a keyhole, a secret onlooker. Still dazed, still shocked in her empty loneliness; she turns her head; regards the flag-draped coffin; a confusion of runaway memories outstrips her efforts to fix her mind; wilful recollections that run on beyond control; an endless loop of intimate distractions.

Uniformed and plain clothed police officers, rigid grief in each pale face, eyes downcast, line the front pews, here to honour their comrade and to bid personal farewells.

She grips the hand of her precious son as the priests intone the Requiem Mass; the acting Chief Constable delivers his eulogy; distant words fade indistinctly at the rim of her consciousness; decay amongst the aged stones and rafters.

A lifetime of churchgoing ensures that she observes the ritual, mouths the familiar responses, and crosses herself. But her mind is not engaged.

As the broad west doors swing back, cold, October light swamps the sombrous interior, a rude inundation, flushing out dark odours of tallow and incense, blanching the musty dimness, purging all but the furthest niches and corners with its curious brightness.

Pallbearers step forward, hoist their burden, and execute their awkward, shuffling turnabout then step off, leading the solemn procession. She follows, tall, impressive in her apparent dignity, the pale child pacing bravely at her side and many a mourner in that packed congregation wipes away a tear to see them pass by.

It is as she smells the newly opened earth, leans forward with her handful of soil, and sees the narrow coffin far below in that sheer sided pit, that the bitter finality overwhelms her. The tumbling earth bounces like far off drumbeats as she turns into the warmth of her mother's embrace. Her father hugs the boy and, feeling so helpless, rests a hand on her back.

★★★

Ringing reverberations of the iron bell toll the solemn hour as the Guard of Honour elevate their weapons. The salute cracks out and large, black birds rise suddenly from the towering yews; a cacophony of beating wings and coarse, protesting cries counterpoised with the echoing gunshots. The echoes fade in diminishing ripples; lamentations that die away: lost among the stark outlines of a multitude of headstones: the old leaning and lichen-clad, the recent startlingly cold in their white, marble purity. The vociferous birds fall back in ragged disorder to settle, concealed, silent again within the evergreen foliage.

A witness in the high tower might see the concluding rites: the dwindling of that tightly knit gathering of mourners as smaller groups drift away along the gravel path until only the melancholy families are left standing over the open grave.

★★★

CHAPTER ONE

Young Terry Driscoll waited anxiously in the toilet cubicle. So familiar was he with the arrival and departure times at each stop, he could judge with accuracy when the train was nearing his station. He travelled the route five days a week and on Saturday mornings if there was a school match.

Terry was an above average performer at most things but when it came to games, he was exceptionally gifted. Tall and naturally athletic he could hold his place in any of the school teams; but hockey was his passion. At thirteen he was the youngest member of the school team, played on Saturday afternoons for a local club side and had been invited to take part in the forthcoming junior county trials. Terry was a popular boy, but lately he'd found himself out of favour with a group of the senior boys and he had no idea why.

He sat with his bag on his lap, holding his hockey stick between his knees, swaying to the rhythmic motion of the train as it rattled on its way. Oblivious to the noise and discomfort, he pondered on his chances of escaping the attentions of Justin Simms and his gang of yobs. He had chosen the carriage that would stop nearest to the station exit and he knew that once through he could outrun them easily. The question was could he get onto the platform with a head start? Not for the first time, he debated whether to stay hidden until the train pulled out of the station, get off at the next and then telephone his mum to fetch him in the car. This idea was attractive but the thought of having to explain why and all that this would lead to, convinced him that it was not a realistic option.

Picking on Terry had become the gang's regular sport because it had been such a success the first time. They had seized the unsuspecting youngster, punched, and kicked him unmercifully, and tried to force his head into the toilet pan while they flushed it. He had fought with a strength and vigour that surprised them but in so doing had only prolonged his own discomfort, thus increasing the delight of his tormentors. Terry's friends all lived closer to the school than he, so they didn't need to use the train and the bullying had isolated him from some of them who were fearful in case they came in for similar treatment during the school day.

Simms and his gang had refined the game to the point where they would sometimes surround and thoroughly frighten him and then let him go to jeers, catcalls and a casual slap but on other occasions they would beat him up and dare him to tell anyone. Friends were sympathetic of course but could offer no solution other than to urge him to complain to the school's management. In short, Terry's school days had become a misery and thus far, having taken Simms'. threats very seriously, he had told only his closest friends.

He checked his watch and saw it was time to make his move. He did not think they'd seen him enter the toilet as there had been none of the usual kicks and bangs on the door or attempts to call him out: but he knew that they might well be waiting. There was no way of telling how punishing these encounters might turn out, so he always expected the worst. Reaching anxiously for the lock on the door, he eased it open, looked both ways, then stole out into the corridor.

He saw at once that he had miscalculated.

The train still had quite a long way to go before it would reach his station. It must have reduced speed along the last stretch and, being preoccupied with his thoughts and unable to see out through the opaque toilet window; Terry had been unaware of this. Sensing someone behind him, he turned, and his heart sank.

'Wrong!' crowed Simms in an exultant falsetto as he grabbed Terry's collar and wrenched him away from the toilet door. 'Get that window down,' he shouted as he forced Terry back against the wall and held him there by the lapels of his blazer. One of the gang lowered the window and stood back. Simms dragged him sideways and he became aware of the rushing cold air as he was forced closer and closer to the open window. He resisted fiercely, but the bigger boy had a man's strength. He could not believe that they would push him through, but he was unable to speak because Simms' bruising knuckles were digging into his throat.

'Chuck him out. Chuck him out,' chanted the gang and he felt strong hands gripping his clothing and pushing him out and into the chill turbulence beyond. When his upper body was out, they held him balanced there, the sharp-edged window frame digging painfully into the small of his back. Through his tears he looked into the grinning faces.

'Please, please,' he begged but his entreaties and tears were whipped away in the violent maelstrom, the buffet, and the roar of the train's clattering progress. If Simms heard him, he chose to ignore it.

'Wotcha doin' out there, Sunshine?' He shouted. 'Ain'tcha got a ticket then?'

They held the boy there for long agonising seconds, raising and lowering his legs as they sang at the tops of their voices:

'Rock-a-bye baby, on the treetop

When the wind blows the cradle will rock.

When the bough bends, the cradle will fall.

Down will come baby, cradle and all.'

Terry's heart lurched in his chest as, on the word, 'Down,' Simms raised his legs and pretended to let go. His upper body began to drop lower as he grew weaker and fatigue began to set in. Terrified, he tried to turn his head, fearful of striking a bridge or some other trackside object.

'Let him in Jus'. He's had enough.' This was Ray, a big lad who had suddenly become aware of the malign intent in Simms' expression: suddenly become aware, as he exchanged anxious glances with his mates, that this escapade had entered a realm of frightening possibilities. It was one thing to pick on a younger boy and rough him up a bit – but this was something way beyond nosebleeds and split lips: they were rattled by Simms' vicious treatment of the youngster. Simms glared darkly at them.

'You bloody well pull him in!' he snapped.

The distressed boy was hauled in quickly and one of his tormentors moved to raise the window. 'Leave it,' bellowed Simms, hauling the terrified boy up from the floor. 'See this?' he sneered, holding Terry's bag up before the snivelling boy's pale, dirt streaked face. 'See it?' he repeated, shaking him fiercely. Terry nodded weakly and Simms flung the bag through the open window. 'See this?' he repeated, holding up the hockey stick. Terry lunged to grasp it but doubled over in agony as Simms punched him hard in the solar plexus, pulled the stick from its case and tossed it after the bag. He dragged his winded victim to his feet and leered into his face. 'One-word Sunshine and you'll be next: out you'll go. Got it? Wipe your snotty face, you bloody little creep.'

He forced the cowering boy to the floor, kicked him in the back then ran down the length of the carriage. The gang followed but they were driven by shame, they ran to distance themselves from their unfortunate victim, not to stay close to Simms: Simms who no longer held their trust. Their habitual swagger was gone; all bravado had drained away during those fearful minutes at the window when they had sensed that Simms had been close to letting Terry fall.

Passengers, disturbed at the sudden invasion, looked ruffled and muttered about such uncouth behaviour but no one challenged the boys in their headlong dash along the aisle.

The train drew into the station and Terry, hanging back to watch Simms and company leave, began to make his painful way to the exit. Every step he took sent a stab of pain into his lower back and he was forced to stop several times and rest. The attendant who checked his season ticket was shocked at his dishevelled state but said nothing. God only knows what goes on, on that train, he thought to himself, watching with some sympathy, as Terry shuffled away across the car park.

As he limped out of the gateway and onto Station Road Terry heard Simms' mocking tones yet again.

'Looks as though you've lost your walking stick Sonny.' Simms, alone this time, stood over him. 'Remember,' he whispered, 'not one single fucking word or you'll be straight out the window. Now off you go to Mummy. Jolly hockey sticks eh.' Terry felt a cold hatred welling up in his chest, but he was too frightened to say or do anything that might provoke his tormentor to hurt him anymore.

As he set off for home, hobbling in pain, he became aware of a disreputable figure shuffling along next to him. His nervousness increased when this unsavoury character came close and laid a hand on his sleeve.

'Just a moment old man,' said the stranger.

Terry stopped, astonished at the cultured voice, so at odds with the man's appearance.

'What do you want?' he asked. 'I haven't any money.'

'No! No! No!' the man cried, obviously put out by Terry's remark. 'Here take this.' He held out his walking stick towards Terry. 'This will help; like this see?'

He placed both of Terry's hands on the stick and showed him how to move it forward and then shuffle up to it before moving it forward again.

'That's right,' he said, encouragingly. 'Support your weight with your arms, then move forward with small steps. Move the stick forwards and repeat. How's that?'

'Much better thanks,' Terry replied, grunting from his efforts.

He concentrated on the stick, using it Zimmer fashion, and made good progress, his back pain being much reduced. At first, he was embarrassed at the way passers-by stared at them, but he was grateful for the old man's help and their overt disapproval soon ceased to worry him.

His new companion kept pace, offering encouragement the whole time and at last they arrived at Terry's house. He opened the gate and saw Terry to the front door.

'Here we are old man,' he said, holding his hand out for his walking stick. 'Home at last.'

'What's your name?' Terry asked.

'Mummy always calls me Matty,' replied the old man.

'Thanks ever so much for helping me Matty,' Terry replied. 'If you wait a minute Mum will give you something.'

'I appreciate the thought chum but that won't be necessary: glad to be of help.'

He walked back to the gate, let himself out and gave Terry a wave.

'Cheerio old man. Take care,' and he was gone.

Terry ached all over, but it was his back injury that really worried him and his inability to straighten up and move without that terrible pain was frightening. He opened the front door and fell to his knees inside.

'Terry?' called his mother. 'Where have you been? It's nearly ten past six.' Receiving no reply, she stepped into the hall. 'Dear God,' she cried, putting her hands to her face.

Terry was lying stretched out on the floor his dirty face tear stained and drained of colour.

'Mum,' he whispered.

She ran to him, dropped to her knees, and cradled his head in her lap.

'Who did this to you my darling boy?' Terry, eyes tightly shut, shook his head. 'You must tell me. You're badly hurt. Now who was it?' Terry maintained his stubborn silence. 'It was that Simms boy wasn't it.' She said this with such conviction that Terry nodded eventually.

'It's my back that really hurts Mum,' he gasped. 'I can hardly walk for the pain. I've never had anything like it. I don't think I could've made it home on my own. This old tramp lent me his stick and helped me along. He was great. But he didn't talk like a tramp. He was really posh. He said his name's Matty. He talked like an archbishop, but he was pretty smelly.'

Gently, his mother lowered his head to the floor, fetched a cushion and settled him more comfortably.

'I know Matty. I'll tell you all about him one day. Now you just stay where you are while I telephone the doctor.'

As soon as she had made the call Maureen hurried back to where Terry lay on the floor.

'He's out on a house call but they don't think he'll be long. You comfy there? Another cushion?' she asked, settling next to him.

'I'm fine Mum. Lying flat like this has eased away most of the pain. Tell me about Matty.'

'You don't want to hear about all that now. I'll tell you when you're feeling better.'

'Honestly, Mum, I'm fine; come on, he's such a funny old bloke.'

'Well his family was very well off once. They were business-people. They had servants, a chauffeur, and a big Daimler – and other cars as well. They had a big estate called Kingsfield Park – a big house with stables and horses and everything – they were really well to do.'

'What happened?' Terry asked.

'I can't tell you exactly. It was all before my time.'

'How d'you know about it then?'

'Because people were still talking about it when I was a child. Anyway, they ran into financial difficulties, so everyone said. There was a scandal too. Matty's mother had a fling with one of the staff and his father found out about it and threw the man out, literally – they had a fight. There was talk of a blackmail attempt, but I don't know the ins and outs of that. Well things got worse and worse. All the horses were sold, the staff was let go and they sold off most of the land. Then one night, the big house caught fire – Matty was about your age at the time. They found him wandering in his pyjamas. He'd found his mother and father dead in the stables and was in shock. It seemed that Matty's father shot his wife and then turned the gun on himself. The shotgun was on the floor. The odd thing was that the gun was one of a pair, but they never found its partner. The police made extensive enquiries, but it never came to light. They were very distinctive English guns handmade especially for Mr. Cobbett; that's Matty's surname, and folk were convinced that no matter how hard up he was, he would never have split them up. They were worth so much more as a pair. Your grandfather saw them once when he was invited to a shoot and said what fine guns they were – drove the family mad going on about Mr. Cobbett's pair of Woodwards. Anyway, one gun and the case disappeared, and I don't think they ever got to the bottom of it. Poor Matty was put into care and never really got over it. He'd been close to his mother. He must be well over sixty and he still says, "Mummy calls me Matty." Kingsfield Park was all sold off for building, but nothing's been done out there. Arthur Simms bought the house and a few acres. Evidently, he had plans to rebuild the house and put holiday chalets in the grounds but none of that ever happened either. I don't know if Matty ever got anything out of it. You wouldn't think so to look at him. All he seems to have left is his posh accent. I'm glad he was there to see you home safely though.'

She smiled, reaching out to push the lock of hair from his forehead. Terry returned the smile and they held hands, waiting for the doctor.

★★★

CHAPTER TWO

Thursday morning

The school secretary looked up from her keyboard checked the security monitor and called, 'Come in,' as she operated the remote-controlled door lock.

The door released with a heavy 'clunk' and Maureen Driscoll, looking pale and overtired walked in.

'Good morning,' said the secretary. 'Can I help you?'

'I've come to see the headmaster,' replied Maureen.

'Not without an appointment I'm afraid.' The secretary continued, 'You've no idea what a busy man he is these days; what with targets; tests; policies for this; policies for that; meetings here; courses there; County breathing down our necks, he hardly gets a minute to himself you know. It's just one thing after another, on and on and on it goes.' As she delivered her well-rehearsed litany of woe, she reached across for the large desk diary and said, 'Now, where are we? Let's see. Hmmm, Monday, Tuesday, Wednesday, ah, how about next Monday at four twenty? Name?' Receiving no reply, she looked up and was most disconcerted to see that she had been talking to herself. The woman was gone. 'Well really!' she exclaimed. 'Some people!' She was still huffing indignantly when her telephone rang, and she was hard put to compose herself sufficiently to answer it.

★★★

Mr. Wilkinson, the Headmaster in question, was addressing the school assembly. 'Now I'm moving onto a most persistent problem. Litter!' He cried, looking down at the rows of disinterested pupils. 'Yes, I know what you're thinking.' Here he goes again. Off on his favourite hobbyhorse. 'Well let me tell you, I …' he paused, becoming aware that eyes were turning away to his right, in response to some kind of disturbance. He turned and was extremely annoyed to see a pale faced woman walking across his stage towards him. He caught the eye of a deputy and jerked his head sideways, clearly meaning, 'Get rid of her.'

As the deputy reached to take her elbow, Maureen smiled and said through clenched teeth, 'Don't you dare lay a finger on me young man.'

She stepped forward, stood next to the fuming Mr. Wilkinson and addressed the pupils. It was a huge hall, and she raised her voice to carry to the older students at the back.

'I'm Terry Driscoll's mother.'

There was an immediate guilty response among the older boys, several heads went down as they lowered their eyes, unwilling to meet Mrs. Driscoll's accusatory stare. Justin Simms stared straight ahead and showed no reaction whatsoever.

'I've just come from the hospital,' she continued. 'Terry's had a reasonable night, all things considered. He's got some nasty bruises, a rib that might be cracked and a back injury that, fortunately, is not as serious as it appeared at first. He had some nightmares and has had a lot of discomfort and distress, but I was there to calm him, and the pain control helped a great deal. All being well, he should be allowed home this afternoon. I don't know when he will go back to school. I'm seriously considering another school. I'm not having this sort of thing happening again.'

'I want to tell you older boys, you easily led brainless boys that you are heading for serious trouble if you continue to associate with that bullying thug, Justin Simms; Justin Simms, the big brave chap who hung my Terry out of the train window and then threw out his bag and his hockey stick.' There was a gasp of astonishment at this and the discomfited boys at the back of the hall looked even more wretched. Simms, however, continued to stare straight ahead seeming to be unaware of Mrs. Driscoll's scathing attack. 'Well Justin?' She continued, glaring down from the stage, 'Are you proud of what you've done? Tell us how you terrorised a boy of thirteen.' Suddenly Simms locked eyes with her in an impudent stare and it was Maureen who in the end was forced to look away. 'Remember this,' she went on. 'Simms is trouble. Do not follow him like a bunch of silly sheep. Show some backbone. You don't have to go with him.'

Had she addressed them in this way before the train incident, she would have met with that insolent boredom affected by those eye-rolling teenagers who regard adult opinion as an irrelevance. But these guilty-looking boys did appear to be showing genuine remorse. 'Just remember my Terry's in hospital because you helped to put him there,' she said, and turning to acknowledge Mr. Wilkinson she left the stage. He, signalling to the deputy to take over, ran after her.

'I say, Mrs. Driscoll,' he called. She turned and waited. 'I'm so sorry,' he began. 'Really I'd no idea.'

'No, you never have. That gang of yobboes have done more or less what they like since they've been at this school.'

'Let's go to my office. My secretary will make us a nice cup of coffee and we'll decide on the best way to sort this out.'

'I've just come from that silly, primping woman. I am not at all happy about this, Mr. Wilkinson. It's not just the train, and I do realise that as I have only just found out about Terry's ordeal myself, you can't have known that it was going on. He was too frightened to tell anyone. Nevertheless, I feel that you should have your finger on the pulse. These bullies can't be left to inflict their unpleasantness on those who can't stand up to them. What are you going to do about them?'

'You know we can't do much about what happens on the train,' he replied. 'It's a matter for the Transport Police.'

'You mean that you don't have a policy in place to cover this sort of thing?' Her sarcasm was lost on him. 'Surely you could liaise with them?' She went on, 'and come up with some kind of strategy. This incident should tell you that it's all gone pretty well out of control. Perhaps the media will take an interest? Perhaps they could send representatives to attend the next meeting of Governors?'

Exasperated, she turned away and headed for the exit, the sound of her heels echoing in the long corridor as they struck their angry rhythm on that hard, shining floor.

Mr. Wilkinson, uncharacteristically lost for words, watched her go. He was a worried man.

★★★

By the time she had driven home, the short interview with the pompous headmaster had been pushed to the back of Maureen's mind. She walked into the house, rang the hospital, was advised to ring back in an hour so; made a cup of coffee and sank gratefully into an easy chair. Her mind was in something of a spin. She had been reluctant to face up to it, but she thought she knew exactly why Simms was targeting Terry.

Nine years ago, her late husband, Detective Inspector Frank Driscoll, had seen the culmination of months of painstaking work when Arthur Simms, Justin's father, had been convicted for the murder of a policeman and sentenced to life imprisonment. The trial had been long and difficult, and the Queen's Counsellor retained by Simms' defence had resorted to every means at his disposal to discredit the police and, in particular, Inspector Driscoll himself. He, however, had remained unruffled in the face of considerable pressure and Simms had been found guilty on a majority verdict. Simms and his family had reacted with such riotous behaviour that the Judge had ordered the Court to be cleared.

Then, when order was restored the Judge said, 'Take him down.' Simms had fixed his hateful stare on Inspector Driscoll. As he was led away, he pointed at the policeman, his hand in the shape of a gun, first two fingers extended, thumb pointing upwards. Then, depressing his thumb twice, he pretended to shoot the inspector, his gesture seen clearly by almost everyone in the courtroom.

Three weeks later Inspector Driscoll arrested a petty thief and was assisting him into the police car when a motorcycle carrying two men drew up. One of them called Driscoll's name and, as he turned, the pillion passenger shot him twice in the chest. He was pronounced dead on arrival at the hospital.

There had followed an intensely dark period in Maureen Driscoll's life. Her family and that of her dead husband had been very supportive and she had put on a brave face, especially in front of her four-year-old son who was so like his father: but she grieved inside and for a long time believed that she would never learn to cope with such intense sorrow.

About six weeks after the murder of her husband she received a telephone call at home. The man was softly spoken with just a trace of an Irish brogue – or could it be Scottish? 'You don't know me Mrs. Driscoll. Frank and me went back a long way. He was a good copper, always fair and up front. You knew where you were with Frank. I respected him and I respect his memory. Simms had him murdered but there's no way the police can tie him to it. I have the right contacts in the right places. What I'm saying, Mrs. Driscoll is if you want justice done you've only to ring this number and say the word.'

'Who is this?' she had asked. 'Just what exactly are you driving at?'

'I think it's clear enough, Mrs. Driscoll. Simms is an evil bastard: drugs, theft, arson, pimping, fraud, extortion, and murder, you name it, and that Simms crew will be at the back of it. He is still running the family show even though he's inside, and you've got to think of yourself and your boy. Write down this number.'

'I don't think so,' she had replied coldly and replaced the telephone. Later that evening, she had found a square of white card on the front doormat with a telephone number written on it. She had thrown it into the bin. The following morning, she retrieved it and put it in her writing desk where it had remained untouched and, until now, forgotten.

She opened her desk and withdrew the card from where it had lain all those years. She studied the number. 'Not local,' she mused. There was no information other than the telephone number. She looked at it for long minutes then reached for the telephone.

'Just a moment,' said the soft voice. 'Ah Mrs Driscoll. It's been a long time. How are you?'

Surprised at being identified, so quickly, she replied, 'Rather worried actually.'

'Oh, I'm sorry to hear that. What can I do for you?'

'I'm not sure.'

'Something happened has it?'

'Well yes. It's my Terry,' she paused.

'Well?' said the sympathetic voice.

'He's being bullied at school. Everything seemed fine until a few weeks ago. He's been receiving awards for his hockey and he's going up for the junior county trials and what with one thing and another he's become a bit of a celebrity at school. I think that this is what has brought on the bullying. He came home last night in a terrible state. They'd actually hung him out of the train window. Then he was bashed up and his bag and stick were thrown from the train. They told him that if he told anyone next time they'd throw **him** out. He was in an awful state. It turns out that it's been going on for some time. He's in hospital for observation and treatment. They say that his injuries are not serious and that he's already well on the way to a complete recovery. That was a great relief to me but I'm worried because the ringleader of this gang of yobs is Justin Simms.'

'You've good reason to be worried. Will I sort it?'

'Look,' she said, 'I don't want to get involved in anything illegal.'

'I don't want to get into a discussion about legality and morality. You won't be involved. It's my opinion that you have no choice Mrs. Driscoll. The fact is Frank asked me to look out for you and the boy if ever you found yourselves threatened. He knew the dangers that he was facing by going up against Simms.'

'I'm not sure how to put this,' she went on, 'but if you're so certain about Simms' guilt, why didn't you do whatever it is you're hinting at, revenge for Frank I think, nine years ago?'

'This will sound strange, Mrs. Driscoll, but I want to know that you approve. That you agree that it's justice. Do you?'

'I don't know. I'm worried about my boy. I don't know what to say.'

'I said before that Frank and I went back a long way. He used to tell me how the job was so demanding, how colleague's marriages were breaking up because of their pressures of work. He used to say how lucky he was to be married to you and to have such a lovely little boy. He was a family man all right, and he was an honest and I mean this, an honest copper. I guess you're aware that much of what I do is outside the law. Frank was aware of it too and we both knew that if he ever got real evidence, he'd have had me banged up, friend or no. He was unorthodox, bit of a maverick – he hunted with the hounds, but he'd run with the hare when it suited his case. He didn't nail Simms by going by the book. He didn't find those eyewitnesses and persuade them to give evidence by going by the book. I've no idea how he managed to get people to testify against Simms, but he did. He beavered away to get justice. Simms and his cronies ambushed that young detective. All they needed to do was disable him for ten minutes, but Simms took a knife and stabbed him to death. He had a wife and a child too if you remember. It took him a long time, but Frank got him; sailed very close to the wind at times, ignored proper procedures, took risks that might have finished his career had things not gone his way, but he was never far outside the law. He turned down all my offers to sort it.'

'Isn't this risky for you? Talking like this on an open line? How do you know that I'm not taping all this?'

'I know because I know the woman you are,' replied the soft voice, 'and the line is quite secure. It cuts both ways you know. A secure line protects you as well as me. You and your boy won't be safe until the Simms have been dealt with. Make no mistake, they are all rotten – evil – stop at nothing. Even if you move away, they'll find you. It's my belief that Simms senior has had it in mind to take his revenge all the way ever since they locked him up and young Justin is a teddy bear compared to how he'll be when he comes of age. Don't be frightened. I'll see to it that you and Terry are protected. You just say the word and it will all be taken care of with no risk to you – nor to me.'

Indecision held her for a long minute.

'You still there?' asked the voice.

'Yes.'

'Well?'

'Do it,' she said, wiping the tears from her face as she put down the telephone.

★★★

On returning to the hospital she found that Terry, almost back to his old self, was waiting impatiently for her to take him home. Pleased to have him back safe and sound, she drove home and soon had him ensconced on the settee, complete with fluffed up cushions and the remote control for the television.

When asked what he would like for tea, he replied, 'What happened to lunch?'

'Well didn't they give you lunch?' she asked.

'It was awful Mum. Worse than school dinners.'

"So, you didn't eat it?'

'I had a bit, but I couldn't finish it. It was fish I think.'

'Don't exaggerate. "It was fish I think,"' she mocked him playfully. 'You're spoilt rotten my lad.'

'I'm really starving Mum,' he pleaded, with such pathos that she had to hide a smile. 'Bread and water do you?'

'I'd rather have eggs and bacon.'

'I see. Now you want breakfast in the middle of the afternoon,' she smiled down at him, pinched his cheek and said, 'I'm so happy you're better love. It's all been such a dreadful shock for you and for me for that matter.'

'It's marvellous to be back home Mum. I don't know why Justin does it. He's always been a bully but now he seems to pick on me all the time. Why's it always me?'

She decided not to tell him what lay behind Simms' recent behaviour.

Not yet, she thought, thinking back to those staring eyes in the school hall. I won't have him frightened.

★★★

CHAPTER THREE

Thursday night

Late night filmgoers, collars raised against the damp night air, hurried down the cinema steps and across The Square to the car park. Doors slammed; starters engaged and the stream of cars swept onto the one-way system; down past the old Town Hall, its once fine Corinthian façade disfigured by boarded up windows and weathered remnants of gaudy posters; on past the flaking stonework of the Corn Exchange; a red flare of brake lights as they entered the roundabout, accelerated into the curving lane marked 'All Routes' and then they were gone. Wisps of exhaust vapour hung layered in the orange glare of the streetlamps to mark their passing. The shining over-bright streets lay silent again. From their lofty perch, the security cameras monitored the urban emptiness.

The last bus drew away from the terminus and as it juddered onto the High Street its headlights picked out the pale faces of the youths gazing out from Tony's Espresso Bar. They had spent a dismal evening wandering aimlessly, suffering the familiar boredom but feeling uncomfortable with the presence of Justin Simms. He was aware of this atmosphere and, since the incident on the train the previous afternoon, was feeling less secure in his leadership. He sensed that things seemed to be unravelling. He wanted to belittle Ray in front of the others but could not be sure that he would come off best if it came to a showdown. Ray's willingness to disagree, to challenge his decisions had begun to unnerve him. He would just have to wait for the right opportunity to come along. From his seat, in the window he had noticed a young couple run up just too late to catch the bus.

As they stood together in their disappointment, Simms, recognising the girl, cried, 'Here we go,' and he led the way onto the street. They watched as the couple linked arms and began to walk away. 'That Naomi,' said Simms. 'I wouldn't mind having her again.'

'You never had her last time,' said Ray. 'Old Evans put a stop to that.'

Simms flushed angrily at being reminded of his humiliation when Mr. Evans had caught him in the girls' toilets. He had planned it so that they would trap Naomi, keep her in the toilets until everyone had gone home and then take turns to rape her and to guard the door. Mr. Evans, returning unexpectedly, and on seeing a guilty looking boy standing at the door to the girls' toilets, had sensed mischief, thrust the boy aside with one hand hitting the door open with the other. The suddenness of his entry startled the boys and he followed up with swift action.

'Do your bloody zip up boy!' he barked, almost felling Simms with a stinging slap to his cheek. 'Out. The lot of you,' he bellowed, pointing at the door.

The boys had scuttled away, avoiding his wrathful glare, tripping, and stumbling in their haste to leave the scene. Simms, a good head taller than the teacher, paused for a face-saving moment but, recognising danger in the man's stare, had run after the others.

Mr. Evans found a female colleague who comforted the weeping girl and they stayed with her until her mother came to collect her. Fortunately, he had burst through the door in time to prevent the rape, but he had seen them holding her down and pulling off her pants and he'd seen the distress in her young face.

There had been no legal action. The police had not been involved because Naomi's family had received a covert series of threats of violence that were quite terrifying in their graphic detail. Those boys named by Mr. Evans, who would never forget or forgive what he had witnessed that afternoon, were suspended from school for one week: a treatment they regarded as more of a reward than a punishment. Naomi, who was two years older, left school that summer and Mr. Evans took early retirement.

'I'm going home. It's too bloody cold to hang around here all night.' This from Ray again.

'It's early yet,' retorted Simms, seeing the chance to assert himself. 'Come on. We'll follow them, give them a fright.'

So it was that the gang allowed themselves to be led away from the bright town centre towards the darker streets through which Naomi and her companion had to walk to reach their homes.

The couple sauntered along chatting, happy in each other's company, stopping now and then to embrace and kiss, unaware that they were being watched. As the bright lights were left behind, the gang moved closer.

'We'll catch up by the children's playground,' muttered Simms. 'Come on, step it out.'

The couple turned the corner into Station Road and the gang took the opportunity to run quietly forward. As they turned the corner, Naomi, stooping to retrieve a glove, saw them, pulled at her companion's sleeve and they began to run.

The gang, wearing trainers, loped along easily, keeping pace with the couple as Naomi tried to run on high heels. She paused to slip them off and they made better speed, but the gang was catching up.

'That's not all that's coming off tonight Naomi,' yelled Simms.

Recognising his voice, she began to sob with fright. The couple ran into the only place that might have offered safety, the railway station, at least there were lights on; but it was deserted.

'This way,' cried the young man, taking her hand and running up the steps to cross the bridge, but the gang reacted quickly, a group of them breaking away to jump down onto the tracks, run across and climb onto the far platform.

The remainder, knowing that their intended victims were trapped, strolled along to the steps, and began to ascend. There was no escape. Simms and his group were approaching from behind and the others waited at the foot of the stairs in front; but they seemed to be arguing among themselves.

Suddenly Ray called, 'We're off Simms. It's too bloody cold.' And they were gone.

The couple ran down, even though they suspected a trick. The way ahead was clear but then two of the gang ran back, evidently deciding to stick with Simms. Naomi shrieked, snatched her hand away, jumped down onto the track and ran off between the gleaming rails into the darkness. Her companion clenched his fists, turned to face his pursuers, saw that it was completely hopeless, so he jumped down and dashed after her.

'Now we'll have some sport,' smiled Simms. 'Come on.' He jumped down to give chase. 'Come on,' he cried. But his followers stood still, watching him. 'Come on,' he shouted again, but they remained, still watching him. A pair of them climbed down just as the rest began to move away. 'Please your bloody selves then,' he called. 'Come on,' he said to the remaining two, as he began to run. 'Get a move on. We'll sort him out and then we'll have her drawers off.' Then, realising he was on his own, he looked back to see the last of his erstwhile companions climbing back up onto the platform.

'Bastards!' he shouted and continued running as best he could along the awkwardly spaced sleepers.

★★★

CHAPTER FOUR

'Have we heard anything at all from the Simms clan? It's nearly ten.' The speaker sat comfortably in his leather chair; large pale hands relaxed before him on the wide, polished surface of the desk. Both men facing him seemed reluctant to meet his gaze. His heavy gold cuff links gleamed intermittently in the light from the desk lamp as he drummed his fingers gently on the pristine blotter. He reached into a drawer and withdrew a large envelope.

'Know your enemy,' he said, removing a sheaf of photographs.

'The Simms run some ostensibly legitimate businesses which include new and used cars, turf accountancy, building and building supplies, laundrettes, travel agents and scrap metal. All of these of course provide ample opportunity for Arthur Simms's particular forms of creativity. Then of course there is their shadier side. In short, anything that goes on in their neck of the woods which involves drugs, corruption, graft of all kinds, pimping, extortion, arson, gang violence and murder, you can bet that the Simms are behind it.' He shuffled through the photographs, removing one and set it aside.

'That's Justin. You've already got one of him. Have a good look at these,' he went on, handing the first of the remaining photographs to the older of the two men one at a time.

This is Arthur Simms, head of the family. Look at the arrogance of the man, the broad face, high cheekbones, and hard eyes that say, "Cross me and I'll gut you like a rabbit". I see Holbein's portrait of Henry V111 in that face. Do you know it?' His companions shook their heads.

'If I squint slightly, I can superimpose one face upon the other. He's totally ruthless and expects to get what he wants when he wants it. If things don't go his way he flies into a rage and then anything can happen. He's serving life for murdering a policeman but still runs the family show from his cosy cell. He's got things organised how he likes them, so I'm told; a nasty bastard but nothing we can't deal with without breaking into a sweat.'

The older man studied the photograph, offered it to the younger man who shook his head, then put it on the desk without comment.

'This is the eldest son, James,' continued the man behind the desk. 'A disappointment to his father: very little brain and no guts. He's mainly involved with their motor trade; tries to be a hard man but it's not in his nature. He's unmarried, too comfortable at home I expect.'

The older man gave the likeness his attention for what seemed a long time. This face was altogether different from that of the father: round and pudgy. There was foppishness in the carefully styled dark hair and neatly trimmed moustache. Pale blue eyes stared through rimless glasses, a vain attempt to bring gravitas to an unremarkable face.

'He doesn't look as though he'd be much trouble,' remarked the older man, placing the photograph on the desk, 'Is that a rug?'

'It certainly is. He's extremely sensitive about his premature baldness. Evidently, he's known as "Humpty" amongst his staff, not to his face of course.'

The older man grinned as he took the third photograph and turned it the right way up. He was struck by its similarity to the first one.

'As you can see, the second son, Robin, is the image of his father. He has the same character too, the same propensity for violence, the same unpredictable fiery temper, and the same gift for alibi. He shows more foresight than his father, but he flies off the handle when things don't go his way. He's more of a planner than his father, and in that respect perhaps more dangerous. But again, nothing we can't handle. He runs the betting shops. He was married for a year or so, but he knocked her about, so she left, with nothing of course.'

The older man had nothing to say as he exchanged the photograph for the next one.

'This is Joshua,' said the man behind the desk. 'He and his twin are a couple of loose cannons as far as we can tell. They are their father's favourites, a fact that irks Robin no end.'

The older man looked at the handsome face and saw the same arrogance and strength as in the father.

'Well he looks a rough handful, and you say there's two of them? Twins?'

The man behind the desk pushed the next photograph towards him and was amused at the man's reaction.

'Wow! She's a peach.'

'Her name's Rebecca. She certainly is a beauty but don't let that influence you. Behind that lovely face lies a truly evil persona. She and Joshua run the travel agencies, but they seem to have a lot of free time, time for mischief of all kinds. There's talk of incest too, which is interesting don't you think?'

'What does Robin think of that then?'

'He's angry because neither parent seems concerned about it. The twins have been spoiled all their lives; allowed to do as they like. They caused such mayhem at their local school that their father was forced to send them away to boarding school. They lasted less than a month there and finished up being tutored at home. Not much fun for the tutors, I guess. Their mother's lost heart too. She lavished her affection on Justin, but he's grown up into a nasty piece of work as well. 'This is she,' he said, passing the last photograph. 'Her name's Alice.'

The older man looked at the likeness of a pretty blonde woman. She was smartly dressed and smiling at the camera, but the overall impression was one of sadness.

'She looks as though she's thinking about what might have been,' he said. 'She's not happy, is she?'

'You're right but that's not our concern. Now just how far have we got?' He drummed his fingers once again.

Prompted by this gesture of impatience, the older of the two cleared his throat and said, 'I rang again at nine like you said but their answer machine was on, so I left the same message. Maybe they was listening, but they never picked up.'

'So?'

'So, I've set things going. I've sent two guys down there and they're out looking for the Simms lad now.'

'They're reliable, are they? I can't overstress the importance of this business.'

'Yeah. Not the brightest, but very good at what they do.'

The lampshade cast a circle of light, illuminating three faces, one composed, the other two looking strained. The man behind the desk reached into a drawer and placed a shiny red apple on the pink blotter.

'And?' he prompted.

'They'll work him over to show them it's serious. It's like we said. Get in touch by eight or else.'

'Yeeeees.' The man behind the desk looked at his watch, adjusted his shirt cuffs just so beyond the sleeves of his expensively cut jacket then gave his attention to the apple. A small knife appeared in his hand and he drew it upwards bisecting the fruit into perfect halves, the sharpness of the shining blade evidenced by the fact that it divided the stalk perfectly as well.

'Word's come down,' he began, 'that the Simms are to be warned off a certain project of theirs and it's got to be done quickly. They've got a grudge on the go with the family of the policeman who was mainly responsible for putting Arthur Simms behind bars. It seems that the whole world knows that it was Simms Senior who arranged the murder of that policeman but there is no way that the force could tie him into it. Well the family of the dead policeman has a powerful friend who will put a stop to any plan they may have for further revenge. We are not dealing with a sophisticated professional outfit here; the Simms are nothing but a bunch of provincial bullyboys who've got where they are by violent means – they've got away with murder more than once.

'But I'll tell you this, if they don't play ball, then they'll find themselves on the receiving end of things. The friend I referred to has the resources at his disposal to shall we say chastise Simms and his family of thugs in ways they haven't even thought of. It would have been nice to keep them on-side but their failure to respond to our messages means that we must make this little gesture in order to make our point. It's a shame really, youngster like that. But business is business. They were warned after all. It's not as though they've got any choice anyway. They must know that. They're playing a dangerous game.' As he was speaking, he bisected the halves and the apple now lay in four equal parts, each retaining a quarter of the stalk. All this was done with impressive control and precision. The younger man had seen it all before but the older one was fascinated, staring in awe as the clever fingers manipulated the wicked little blade.

'I mean, if they were told about the danger to little brother if they didn't get in touch and then did nothing about it, well, it must be their own fault, eh?' He smiled at his own logic, suddenly plunged the knife into a section of apple and thrust it toward the older man. 'Go on. You'll enjoy it, keeps the doctor away.' He offered a second piece to the younger man who slid it from the blade and bit into it. The older man began to eat too.

'It'll take more than an apple to keep the doctor away from young Simms, eh.' The man behind the desk laughed again and his companions joined in. It seemed the wisest thing to do.

★★★

Barry and Sid had gone straight to the coffee bar, knowing that unless he had gone home early, that's where young Simms would most likely be found. They had gone in separately, sat at different tables and assessed Justin and his gang. Then Barry left and Sid followed five minutes later. They met at the bus terminus, sat on a bench from where they could watch the door of the coffee shop and waited.

'Poxy town this is,' grumbled Sid. 'Keeping tabs on bloody school kids. I bet there's more life on Mars.'

'Fancy a little green bint then do you?' asked Barry.

'Be a bit more exciting than sitting here looking at the bloody clock. We could be having a pint or three.'

They watched the last bus leave and saw the couple miss it and then saw their own quarry leaving the coffee shop. They then followed the followers.

They hung back and watched the action at the station and when he saw Naomi jump down onto the track Barry said, 'This way, quick,' and he ran back down Station Road.

There were several short roads to their right, each one ending in the chain link fence that prevented access to the railway. After running quickly past the first three of these, they turned into the fourth and ran between the cramped terraced houses with their dusty windows and neglected little gardens to where the pool of orange light from the last streetlamp lit a section of the cutting and the tracks below.

They watched the girl, running and stumbling in awkward haste. She had put her shoes back on and while they offered some protection from the sharp stones, they were not best suited to rapid progress. The boyfriend came into view and was making better headway until Simms overtook him and, after a brief struggle, knocked him down then continued after the girl.

Barry jerked his head to the left. 'This way,' and he led Sid along the fence until they came to a hole.

'Hey, Baz, how'd you know there's a hole in the fence?' said Sid.

'I used to live in the next road when I was a kid. There's been a hole in this bit of fence since I was about nine,' replied Barry. 'As soon as they fix it, the kids make another.' They clambered through and made their way down the grassy slope to the rail tracks.

'Watch out for the live rail there,' whispered Barry. 'We'll follow along the bank. He's so bloody keen to give her one we'll get close to him before he knows it.'

'What about her?' asked Sid.

'What about her?'

'We could give her one. One each eh?'

'No.'

'Why not?'

'One thing I've sussed since going in with Luke is do exactly what he says. Nothing more. Nothing less.'

'Come on, who's to know? How's he going to find out?'

'I can't tell you that. But it's not worth risking it. He's a complete bloody hooligan when blokes annoy him. Guns; knives; broken glass; it's all the same to him.'

'You're really scared of him Baz.'

'You got that part right. I've seen what he's done to blokes what annoyed him. She mustn't see our faces though.'

Ignoring the boyfriend as he groaned and began to stir, they made their way after Simms and the girl.

***

He could hear her stumbling progress ahead and knew he was gaining quickly. He then saw her in the light of the next street-lamp. He increased his speed, grinning as she tripped and went sprawling between the rails. He lunged forward intending to gather her up and carry her onto the side of the cutting. But, as it was, he barely had time to utter a grunt of surprise; one moment she was lying there on the filthy stones like a broken doll, the next she was rising to one knee wielding a hockey stick like an infantryman with a rifle and as he began to turn his head away, she drove it straight into his face. The end of the stick struck him with such force that his canine and several other top teeth were knocked clean out in a spray of blood and his nose was broken. He gave a great gasp of pain, dropped to his knees and then to all fours, blood running from his lacerated lips and gums. She dropped the stick and ran back the way she had come, her breath coming in huge sobs as she ran thankfully into the arms of her boyfriend, battered but on his feet and able to support her.

'We must make a move,' he said. 'It's too bloody dangerous here,' He put his finger on her lips saying, 'Tell me after. We're going before a train comes.'

Barry and Sid stood in the shadows and, keeping perfectly still, they watched the couple make their way back towards the station; the boy was almost carrying her. Then, quite unaware that they were being watched, they stole forward to look for Simms. They found him sitting at the edge of the track holding a handkerchief to his bloodied face.

'Hello Justin,' said Barry. Simms attempted to reply but what came out made no sense: the swelling lips and missing teeth made it impossible for him to utter intelligible speech. 'Tell your big brothers,' said Barry, leaning forward, 'that this is what happens when they don't do what they're told. Got that?'

As Simms, mystified by the message, tried to stand, Sid picked up a large stone from the track bed and struck him hard on the left temple. He collapsed with a groan and rolled forward, unconscious.

'Job done,' smiled Sid, hefting the stone in both hands before letting it fall at his feet.

They failed to hear the sharp intake of breath. Inside a disused rail-side shed, his pale face close to the grimy window, cowered the witness, fist pressed to his mouth, quaking in fear of discovery. He held his breath as he watched them carry the limp form up the bank and set it down with its back against the trunk of a small tree.

'I don't know if he can breathe through that nose,' said Sid.

'Well he'll just have to breathe through his mouth then won't he,' replied Barry. 'Don't worry about him. He's a nasty young bugger. Here you are the usual,' he continued, proffering a thin roll of notes.

'Well that's what I call easy money,' Sid chuckled. 'That face; right bloody mess. How could the bint have done him over like that?'

'Don't matter do it,' Barry answered. 'Let's go to mine. We'll watch a video and warm up with a couple of scotches.'

'Sounds good to me,' smiled Sid, 'Lead me to it.'

They climbed the steep bank, found the hole in the wire, and clambered through.

'Here, it's just dawned on me,' exclaimed Sid. 'How's he going to give them a message? He can't talk proper.'

'Not our problem," replied Barry, "Give him the message and a kicking," that's what Luke said. They'll know why. They've been told; it's a warning.'

'But he's in a right state, teeth knocked out and bleeding so heavy. You don't think Luke might reckon we was a bit OTT?'

Barry was not at all sure that Luke would be happy about the turn of events but what was done was done. He hoped that he could offer a satisfactory explanation if it came to it. After all, it was not his fault that someone else had clobbered Simms before they had got to him.

'Now,' he said, 'you coming or what?'

'Yeah,' grinned Sid. 'We'll get some chips.'

They ambled away into the darkness, collars up, hands thrust deep in pockets.

★★★

CHAPTER FIVE

Naomi and her boyfriend made their way back to the station with no further difficulties. His arms encircling her, they stood in the shadow of a protective wall, her sobbing under control at last. She seemed quite content to remain there, hidden in comparative safety.

Eventually she spoke. 'If only I'd taken the car, none of this would have happened. I don't know what to do Philip.'

'Do?'

'I can't stay here; not after this.'

'Oh, come on Naomi. You've done nothing wrong. He was chasing you. You can go to the police and have him charged with harassment or something.'

'You weren't there. You don't know what I did.'

'Tell me then.'

'I was trying to run as best as I could when my feet got caught up with something and I fell. And then everything seemed to go into slow motion. I was flat on my face wondering how a hockey stick came to be on the railway. How could it happen and why did it have to be there just as I was running past? I felt angry that it had trapped me – that it had put me at his mercy. His huge hands were reaching out and I thought it's all over now. This was all jumbling about in my mind as his grinning face came closer. One moment I was overwhelmed with fear, absolutely weak with it, the next; I was ramming the stick into his face with all my strength. It made an awful soft sound, and he gave a great moan and collapsed to his hands and knees. It was awful – all that blood.'

'There, there, you had to do it. Thank God you had the presence of mind. He's in the wrong over this, not you. I wish I'd been with you. You must have been terrified, but you were really brave. We'll go to the police and tell them exactly how it happened, and they can deal with him.'

'You don't understand. The police can't protect me. This is the Simms we're talking about. They're beyond the law. He'll be out for revenge for what I've done to him and I'm not staying here for him to find me. He tried to rape me at school; him and that gang of yobs he runs about with trapped me in the toilet and he would have done it if a teacher hadn't come charging in at the last minute.'

She began to cry again, and Philip felt saddened and helpless as the violent sobs shook her slight frame. He rubbed her back gently and did his best to soothe her. She raised her tear stained face to him and whispered between sobs, 'If I hadn't fallen over that hockey stick, he would have raped me. It's no good going to the police. He'll still get me one way or another. I've got to leave. It's the only way to protect myself from him.'

'You can't go off just like that. What about your folks? Your job? Everything? What about us?' Philip felt a rising sense of alarm as he realised how earnest she was. Even so she looked more like a little girl in need of her mummy and daddy than a young woman ready to go away and leave everything. 'I still think you're over reacting Naomi. You should give the police a chance. If you let those people drive you out, then you're allowing them to dictate how to live your life. Is that what you want? And there's something we haven't thought of. That bloke is so macho. He won't want the world to know that he was so totally disabled by a mere girl.'

'Do you honestly think I could rely on him not looking to get his own back because he's embarrassed? It's not that simple. I told you what they tried to do to me at school. You want to know why my mum and dad didn't go to the police? Why they nearly split up over it? I'll tell you why. They received threats through the post every day for over a month and then once a week, "Just a little reminder" they said. None of those threats were posted locally.

'They came from all different places and they said things like, keep your mouth shut because we know where your grandchildren go to school or, we know where your son-in-law plays squash or, how will he support his family if he suddenly goes blind? Or, if we send a finger or two, would you recognise them? They just kept coming, every one of them horribly frightening.

'Then one day we found a bag by the back door.' Naomi paused, unable to continue. 'They'd killed my cat,' she sobbed at last. 'They just cut off her head and her tail and left them in a plastic bag on the back step. Mum wanted to go to the police, but Dad wouldn't hear of it. They had such terrible rows I wanted to leave. It was just so awful. She called him gutless because he wasn't prepared to stand up to the Simms family, even though one of them had tried to rape his daughter. He said that she didn't know what she was asking – how would she feel if we went to the police and any of those threats against members of our family were carried out? It went on for weeks.

'So, don't talk to me about whether I want those people to dictate how I live my life. They've reached right into the heart of our home and it will never be the same again and I feel it's my fault because I must have said or done something to put the idea in Simms' mind. That's what everyone always says isn't it? She was asking for it?'

'You're much too hard on yourself. You know it wasn't like that. You're right though. I didn't understand what you've been through already. If you're really going,' he said quietly, 'I'd like to come with you. That bunch of yobs know me now.'

She managed a watery smile. 'You don't have to, but I'm so pleased you said that.'

'I mean it. If you're ready so am I. I want to be where you are.'

'I'm going home now. I'm going to clean up, pack a few things and leave a note for Mum and Dad. They are coming home tomorrow from visiting their friends in Devon.'

'I'll walk home with you,' said Philip, and they set off.

Her feet felt bruised and sore, but they managed a fairly brisk pace. They reached her front gate where they stood together.

She took his hand between hers but before she could voice her thoughts, he interrupted.

'Your hands Naomi, they're bleeding.'

'I cut them when I fell. It'll soon wash off.'

'You'll need to put some antiseptic on them. They could become infected.'

'I'll pick you up at the end of your road if you still want to come,' she said quietly, seeming quite unconcerned about her injuries.

'Course I do.'

'What'll you tell your folks?'

'I'll say I've just got to nip out for half an hour to give my holiday dates to Maurice. He's our fixture secretary and he's organising a cricket tour. We go on one most years.'

'They won't believe that. It's rubbish.'

'Yes, they will. I'll say he's going abroad, and he's already asked me for my dates, and I forgot and he's a bit cross.'

'It's nonsense.'

'It's almost true actually,' he admitted. 'It'll be just another of those embarrassing situations my memory seems to land me in most of the time. Mum'll just roll her eyes and say, "Honestly Philip," and Dad'll just shake his head in despair. Then they'll look at each other and she'll say, "What *are* we going to do with you Philip? Do you know what time it is?"'

'You look a mess.'

'I'll sort it.'

'Bring your passport if you can. You never know.'

'Make sure to put something on those hands for the same reason.'

★★★

Philip checked his watch again as he waited on the corner. He seemed to be checking it every minute, but the intervals felt very much longer. It was after midnight and decidedly chilly. He turned up his collar, looked up at the fine rain tumbling in the glow from the streetlamp and thought about his raincoat hanging on the hall stand at home. He had been almost exactly right about his parents' response to his story and getting away had been even easier than he had imagined.

A quick wash and change, shirts and underwear stuffed into a bag, passport and some cash thrust into his pocket he had called, 'Won't be long,' as he left by the front door. He was beginning to think Naomi had gone without him when he saw the approaching headlights at last and her blue Peugeot drew up next to him. She lowered her window.

'I'll understand if you don't want to do this.'

'I'm coming with you.'

'You're sure?'

'Absolutely.'

He opened the passenger door, threw his bag onto the back seat, and sat next to her. 'Get that heater going,' he said, rubbing his hands together. She smiled and they kissed. Then she let in the clutch and the little car drew away from the kerb, heading for the main road.

'You haven't said where we're going,' said Philip.

'I'm not sure what's best really. Let's just get far away for a start. I've got an idea, but we need to talk it through. How about if we crack on for a couple of hours or so and then stop somewhere for a sleep?'

'Suits me,' replied Philip, settling more comfortably into his seat.

Justin Simms remained propped against the tree, blood congealed on his face and shirt, his breath misting in the yellow light of the nearby streetlamp.

Sometime later a pale form moved furtively across the frosted grass and eventually addressed the seated figure.

'I say, are you all right? Would you like a hand?'

At the sound of the voice Simms raised his ruined face and tried to speak but his facial disfigurement and gurgling attempts at speech were so grotesque that the Good Samaritan lost his nerve and fled.

★★★

Philip and Naomi spent a chilly, uncomfortable night in a car park but managed, surprisingly, to sleep for a short while. On waking, they locked the heavily frosted car and went for a brisk walk to warm up and get the kinks out of their backs. Then they scraped the windows and drove until they found a café where they ate ravenously. Two full English breakfasts and four mugs of strong tea later, they were in a much-improved frame of mind.

'I must ring Mum,' said Philip. 'Dad will have gone to catch his train by now. I won't tell her what's gone on, just not to worry and I'll soon be in touch again.'

'Fat chance, Philip,' Naomi replied, 'she's a Mum. She's not going to stop worrying just on the strength of a vaguely worded phone call from you.'

'At least she'll know I haven't been kidnapped, although if I have, it seems quite promising so far!'

She kicked him under the table.

'Go on,' she smiled. 'Go and 'phone. When you come back, we'll go for a walk and think about what to do next.'

Philip returned to the table after a few minutes. 'Well I think I've reassured her, at least for the moment.'

'Shall we walk then?'

They strolled in the bright, cold morning air discussing their immediate future.

They decided that the best course of action would be to draw sufficient cash to see them through the next few days and move on so that if by any chance the transactions were traced, they would be long gone.

'We could have a couple of night's bed and breakfast to give us a breathing space,' suggested Naomi.

'One room or two?' asked Philip.

'Our money will last longer with one,' she replied, with a broad smile.

Philip laughed out loud. 'Just remember it was you who said that.'

'Someone has to be practical,' she said, failing to keep an entirely straight face.

'It's a good job I didn't tell my mum about this scheming woman who wants to take advantage of me,' laughed Philip.

He was impressed at the way she had pulled herself together. The terrible events of the previous evening and her floods of tears seemed to be forgotten. Here she was laughing and joking as if they were on holiday, not running from the Simms.

'I meant you could sleep on the floor,' she retorted. 'I've my reputation to think of after all. Perhaps you ought to sleep in the car if you're getting ideas like that.' She put out her tongue and Philip slapped his wrist and tried to look contrite. 'While we're on the subject of the car,' she continued, 'It's a dead give-away. We'll have to get rid of it.'

'How are you going to do that?' asked Philip. 'You need the vehicle documents for a start, not to mention loads of money.'

'I brought them with me and if we can trade down, get something older, an estate or a van say, it shouldn't cost too much.'

'I thought you liked your car.'

'I do but it's only a car.'

'Well that's your decision. I don't think it's necessary but go ahead if that's what you want. I think you're crediting the Simms with powers they just don't have. They're not the Mafia after all.'

'You're all too ready to underestimate what they are capable of. Let's not talk about them. You know I said I had an idea we needed to discuss? Well my Uncle Andrew has a farm on Anglesey. We could go there.'

'Well Anglesey is certainly off the beaten track. You don't think we'll stand out rather?'

'If we feel too obvious there then we can move on to somewhere else, but at least we'll have a breathing space; time to think.'

'What's he like, your Uncle Andrew?'

'He and my dad have fallen out, but he likes me. There's this old grandfather clock in the family and when my grandfather died, he left it to my dad. Uncle Andrew was upset because he said that Grandad had promised it to him, and that Dad should give it to him. Dad said that this would be going against their father's wishes and they had a huge row over it. They haven't spoken for years.'

'I don't feel very happy about turning up there if there's a family feud on the go.'

'He told me that even though he and Dad had had fallen out, I was his favourite niece and would always be welcome at his house.'

'Well you know him and if you feel he's okay, then I'm happy to go along, just as long as he's not likely to take a shotgun to me for having designs on his favourite niece.'

'Relax, he's lovely. I'm sure he'll let us stay. Do you want to give it a try?'

'You've talked me into it,' he grinned, giving her a squeeze.

'We need a suitcase; some toiletries and snacks, so let's go shopping. A second-hand case would do, in fact it would look better than a new one.'

They found one in reasonable condition in a dingy little second-hand shop, and then bought washbags, toothbrushes, and other toiletries at a chemists.

'One more stop for some snacks and petrol.' Naomi turned the car into a superstore's car park. Within twenty minutes they had completed their purchases and were seated in the coffee shop, each with a latte and a chocolate muffin in front of them and an AA road atlas between them.

'Chester looks a good bet to me,' Philip suggested. 'It's on en route to Anglesey and it's a pretty big place; we won't stand out there the way we might in a smaller town or village.'

'You're right. It's tempting to get off the beaten track but we're probably safer in a crowd,' she replied. 'We can suss out some used car dealers, see what sort of offers we might get.'

'So, Chester it is?'

'Chester it is.'

Naomi drove out of the car park, joined the traffic flow, and made her way to the A1, intending to head north and join the A606 to Nottingham via Melton Mowbray.

Philip watched her surreptitiously, wondering at her apparent assertiveness. Was she really as self-confident as she appeared, or was it just brittle self-deception? Whatever the truth of it, he knew he would support her in every way.

'You okay?'

'I suppose I am as happy as I can be,' she answered, running a hand through her dark curly hair, 'but a comfy bed and an en suite bathroom would make me ecstatic.'

★★★

CHAPTER SIX

Friday morning

Sergeant Ellis drove along his familiar route to work. Traffic was heavy as usual, so he had plenty of time to reflect on his departure from home that morning. He had been adjusting his tie in the hall mirror when his wife had put her arms round him, nibbled his ear, and said, 'Ooh, hurry back soon, my portly provincial policeman.' It should have been a most enjoyable moment but the word, 'portly' had hit him like a club.

She could have said cuddly or cuddlesome, he mused as he waited at yet another set of traffic lights.

He'd always been secretly proud of his impressive bulk and had developed a rather avuncular manner – the image of the stolid dependable, but canny policeman. It was something that went back to the days of his childhood. His best friend's father had been a policeman and young Ellis had been so impressed by this huge man who strode about the village with majestic tread, his black cape neatly folded over the handlebars of his enormous bicycle, that he decided at the age of six, that he was going to be a policeman when he grew up. Of course, all that cycling kept those old coppers trim I suppose, he thought.

He was aware nowadays, however, that when he looked down there was less to see of his shiny toecaps than there used to be. He had been surprised too on seeing his reflection in shop windows: he had developed quite a paunch. And he had to admit that simple everyday activities like tying his shoelaces made him rather breathless. But wasn't that normal? Wasn't it just middle age spread? Didn't everyone get it in the end? He thought about some of his leaner colleagues and was forced to acknowledge that, no, not everyone did get it in the end.

She didn't use that word unintentionally, he thought. Too clever for that. It's her way of letting me down lightly but at the same time telling me to do something about it. He would have to be more selective in his choice of menu. Did the canteen do meals for weight watchers? No more chips and pork pies. No more of those superb sugary cream doughnuts. No more huge slabs of cream layered chocolate gateaux. It was going to be hard. Physical exercise? he mused. No. Let's see how we get on first. Well, no more sugar in my tea, he thought. That's a fair start I'd say. He smiled. I'll give her bloody 'portly'.

★★★

He put down the telephone, returned his pen to his top pocket and turned to his colleague who had just come on duty.

'I hear they had Madam Simms in earlier. Evidently young Justin didn't go home last night so she came here looking for him in the cells.'

'That's daft,' said the constable. 'He's a minor. She knows we'd have to inform her if we had him here. Mind you, I suppose it's a good place to start looking for that young git.'

'She's always believed we've got it in for that young man, wouldn't believe he wasn't here, wanted to see for herself.'

'They didn't let her?'

'They thought about it, she was kicking up such a ruckus.'

'It's not the first time he's stayed out all night and I don't suppose it will be the last. He'll have been shacked up somewhere nice and warm.'

'That's what I thought but I didn't say that to her. It's hard to re-alise we're talking about a kid of what? Fifteen, sixteen? I was never so lucky at his age. I wouldn't have known what to do if I were. I'd have run a mile I reckon. Still, his Mummy thinks he's as pure as the driven snow. It's a pity he doesn't get caught at it really: but that's wishful thinking. No one with a grain of sense is going to risk getting on the wrong side of that family.

Now laddie,' rubbing his hands together, 'how about another mug of tea?'

'On my way Sarge. Still off the sugar?'

* * *

(Friday afternoon)

The blue and white tape fluttered in the chill breeze as the young constables attached it to twigs and branches and anywhere, they could, to form the perimeter of what had become the Scene of Crime. Children playing on the bank above the railway after school had found Justin Simms sitting where Barry and Sid had left him. Alarmed by the copious amounts of blood and the fact that they could not rouse him, they had run home and told their parents. The train services had been curtailed and the power turned off, while the Police organised a thorough search of the whole area.

Detective Inspector Harry Moss watched younger policemen as they did their best to erect the tent necessary to enclose the immediate area where the body had been found, as he waited patiently for the arrival of the Scene of Crime Officers and the pathologist.

The light's starting to go,' he thought. 'What a night this promises to be. He turned to meet the approaching constable who was pointing back to where a group of his colleagues were gathered down on the track. Moss joined him and together they made their way down to where the policemen waited. They were studying the bloodstains where Justin had first fallen when struck by Naomi.

'Right lads. Watch where you put your size twelves,' said Harry. 'Let's have a look.'

Being careful about where he put his own size nines, he examined the bloodstained ballast.

'Hmm. Lots of blood eh, and what about those?' he said, pointing to where the bloodied teeth lay amongst the dark ballast. He stood, stretching his back, and observed the splashes of dark blood which formed a trail to the foot of the bank. 'It looks as though he was attacked here between the rails and then made his way, or was carried, to the foot of the bank where he rested or was put down. We can deduce that much from the amount of gore,' he said, pointing to the larger pool of blood. 'If he got there under his own steam, he would have had to have his wits about him to be able to negotiate the live rail. If that's the case, then he must have climbed that steep bank, taken another rest against the tree, and passed out. It's possible he was carried up there, but he was a big chap. I think it would have taken more than one person to do it. Never woke up', he mused, 'Injuries or the cold?'

'Sir, over here.' Harry stepped over the rails and joined the officer who had called him.

'What about that Sir? Murder weapon?'

'Could be lad. Could be. Leave it lie for SOCO to assess.' He looked up, gauging the failing light. 'The floodlights will be set up by the time they arrive.'

★★★

Saturday morning. 09:00

Arthur Simms stood between two prison officers, his cold eyes holding the gaze of the prison governor. The latter, conscious of the tension in the air, and glad of the large desk between himself and Simms, cleared his throat and began.

'First of all, let me say how sorry I am to hear of your bereavement Simms, I know that your first wish is to be with your
family at this time. However, I have to refuse your application
for compassionate leave.' He held up a hand as Simms began to
protest. 'I'm sorry but your high-risk status and your uncooperative attitude make it impossible for me to grant this permission. To put it bluntly your past record is so bad that I have no
choice but to say no. As soon as we know the date of your son's
funeral you will of course be allowed to attend. I'm sorry that
I have to turn you down but there we are. That's the way it has
to be I'm afraid.'

Simms glowered down at the governor.

'It's just about what I expected,' he sneered. 'You sit there
like God Almighty while my wife is crying her heart out for
our boy and you just don't give a fuck. Keep your poxy sympathy – it's bullshit.'

The officers restraining him gathered themselves for the outburst of violence, which must surely follow, but Simms remained
calm. Nevertheless, the atmosphere was strained as they waited
for him to lose control – all the signs were there. Outside, the
extra officers waited ready to rush in once the sounds of mayhem began.

'This interview is over Simms,' said the governor. 'I'll inform
you of the arrangements for attending the funeral just as soon as
I know them myself.'

Simms sniffed derisively, never taking his malign stare off the
eyes of the man behind the desk. 'I know it may seem strange
to you Simms, but I run this prison,' said the governor, annoyed
with himself for allowing his feelings to show so obviously. 'Take
him out,' he ordered.

Suddenly Simms' face contorted with rage. He raised his eyes
and roared in anger as he thrust the escorting officers sideways,
put his foot against the edge of the desk and heaved it over towards the governor. The computer monitor and inkstand flew
through the air and the strident clangour of the alarm sounded as
the governor hit the button. The officers, both big men, leapt to

restrain him but he flung them about like dolls. Each was hand-cuffed to him, so he was able to simply swing them off their feet. He crashed his forehead into the nose of the first and blood spurted as the man went down, then, with his arm locked round the neck of the second man, he kicked the unconscious form against the door and held it there with his foot. All this happened with such bewildering speed that the officers outside, taken by surprise, were unable to force their way in.

The governor, badly shaken and looking very pale came out from behind the overturned desk and his deputy, equally affected, joined him as he faced Simms. The captive officer gasped in pain as Simms adjusted his grip to increase pressure on his throat.

'Let him go Simms,' ordered the governor. 'You'll only make it worse for yourself if you injure him. Look at what you've done already,' he continued, looking at the unconscious man. 'Just what do you hope to achieve?'

'Come nearer you wanker, and I'll soon show you what I can achieve,' smiled Simms. 'Come on. I'm wearing bracelets but I can still give it out, and your fucking mate. I can do for the pair of you: no bother.' The man on the floor tried to roll away from the door but cried out as Simms stamped his boot into his back. 'Don't get brave sonny,' he snapped. 'They don't pay you enough.'

The governor and deputy stood seemingly nonplussed as the alarm continued to sound its urgent clamour throughout the prison complex.

'No sign of the troops then,' Simms said, grinning at the discomfited pair. 'Now governor, you let me go home and I'll let this gentleman go. That's a fair deal isn't it?' he said, his voice heavy with sarcasm.

'You know very well that I won't bargain with you Simms. Let these men go, move away from the door and when you're back in your cell my report of this incident will recommend leniency because you have been badly upset by your bereavement.'

'Sounds to me like you're bargaining,' Simms gloated. 'How is your offer better than mine?'

He stiffened suddenly at the sound of breaking glass and looked towards the window. The men outside renewed their efforts to force the door and, as he strove to hold the man in place, a side door opened and suddenly the office was filled with men. Simms roared in anger and sank his teeth into the neck of his captive before half a dozen or so of the new arrivals swarmed over him. They bore him down and overcame him by sheer weight of numbers. Even so, several frantic minutes ensued while he resisted, biting, kicking, and using his enormous strength to such effect that he almost regained his feet. The staff fought hard to release their colleagues and to subdue the thrashing Simms. At last he was restrained securely and lay glaring up at his captors, his broad chest heaving from his exertions: spittle and blood dribbled from the corner of his mouth. The two injured guards were led away for treatment.

The prison governor looked down at Simms' contorted features.

'You know that you are your own worst enemy Simms,' he said flatly.

Simms strove against his restraints and glared back in defiance.

'Just remember I'm your worst enemy Mr. Governor,' he grated, in impotent fury.

The governor turned to his panting officers.

'Well done,' he said. 'You showed initiative and professionalism. I'm pleased with the way you men dealt with a nasty situation. Might I suggest that you cuff his hands behind his back and put restraints on his legs next time. We'll deal with the disapproval of the "Prisoners' Rights" brigade, as and when it arises.'

Simms was hauled to his feet and led away while some staff remained to right the governor's desk and put things back in order.

When they had returned to their duties, the governor turned to his deputy.

'You know all the years I've been in this post you'd think I'd know when to keep my mouth shut. He needled me just by giving that sniff and looking at me in that derisive way he has. He manipulated me and I gave him the excuse he was looking for to start his one-man riot.'

CHAPTER SEVEN

Saturday morning

The man behind the desk sat twisting the large signet ring on his little finger, his face a study in suppressed anger.

'Just what the hell went wrong Luke?' he demanded. 'You sat in that chair on Thursday night and assured me that your two lads were up to it. Christ, man how did they come to kill him? We get a bit of aggro blow up now and again, the razors come out, bones get broken, but the police don't really give a toss. They just freewheel a bit until it all settles down. But once a body turns up, they go up a gear. They start to investigate as though their bloody pensions depend on it. It's all so unnecessary.' He slammed his hands down on the desk in frustration. 'Well,' he demanded again. 'What went wrong?'

'I came straight here when you phoned,' replied Luke. 'This is the first I've heard. I ought to hear their side of it.'

'Yes, do that,' said the man. 'I don't need to tell you, the um, the organisation has become extremely nervous over this. They want it sorted. Quick. So, you need to get on with it for all our sakes.'

'I'll get on to it now,' said Luke, rising from his chair. The younger man, remaining seated, studied his well-polished toecaps.

'Put it right Luke,' said the man behind the desk. 'The people I referred to don't take kindly to this sort of thing. The purpose of that little job your blokes fouled up was to bring the Simms to heel. Now this has happened they're going to come out fighting. We can handle it of course, but something that was simplicity itself is threatening to become complex and bloody expensive just because you've fallen down on the job. Now the buck stops with you. Do you understand me?'

'I'll fix it tonight. There's no need to worry. They don't even know about you. There's no way it can come back on you.'

'They know you, you idiot.' The man's voice was becoming shrill with anger. 'They know you and you know me, and I don't like that one little bit. Make it soon Luke; very soon indeed. You have to take them right out of the picture. It's you or them. Is that clear enough for you? Now get out and get this right. I'm telling you for your own good.'

Luke unlocked his car and slid behind the wheel. He was rattled by this turn of events and puzzled as to how his employer had got his information about young Simms' demise so quickly. His first thought was to get out of the country, but he knew that they would trace him wherever he went. The organisation, as he had called it, was known to be extremely thorough and patient in such matters.

***

Later on, Saturday

Luke sat in the corner of the bar where he could watch both entrances. Barry appeared at last, ordered himself a pint at the bar and sat at the table next to Luke's. He looked nervous, having been summoned to the pub in such a brusque manner.

'Just what did you and that bloody cretinous mate of yours get up to on Thursday night,' hissed Luke, keeping his voice down.

'We just did what you said.'

'Is that right?'

'Yes.'

'Well he's dead, Barry.'

'Oh my God.' Barry looked stunned, as though he had been punched in the stomach.

'Don't blaspheme Barry. It serves no purpose. You were to give him a bit of a kicking that's all not bloody kill him.'

'He was alive when we left him Luke. Sid whacked him with a big stone. He fell down and we carried him up off the railway and propped him against a tree, more of a bush really. And that's where we left him. Thing is though, he was chasing after a bit of tottie and her boyfriend and they must've somehow surprised him. We saw her and her bloke go back towards the station. Then when we caught up with young Simms he was in a right state, teeth knocked out and his lips all split. He couldn't talk proper with it; blood all over the place.'

'But you still clobbered him?'

'Well yeah. You said it had to be done as a warning to his folks like.'

'Yes, well I didn't expect someone else to get in on the act. You're sure he was alive when you left him?'

'Yeah. He was unconscious but he was breathing okay.'

'Well he ain't now and I can tell you the shit has hit the fan and we're in big trouble, really serious trouble Barry. You say it was Sid who whacked him?'

'Yeah. He was sitting there looking sorry for himself, blood all over the place, when Sid fetched him one with a big chunk of ballast from the track. He went out like a light.'

'Right Barry. Watch my lips. You and me are now in the bad books of some very nasty people because the job went wrong. I mean really nasty people. People who take a dim view of mistakes – especially when the mistake upsets their plans. They don't like it. They deal with it by making sure that the guys who make mistakes don't ever do it again. They kill 'em Barry. Our best bet to get ourselves back in favour is to make sure that Sid can't put us in the frame.'

'He wouldn't. He's a prick but he wouldn't do that Luke.'

'Rest assured that he will if they get to question him Barry. They have certain inducements – they can be very persuasive – I've seen them do it. There is only one way to make sure they can't get at him.'

'You mean what I think you mean?'

'What else? Can I leave it up to you?'

'Yeah. How soon?'

'Soonest, okay?'

'How can I contact you?'

'I'll ring you tonight.'

'Tonight? Christ, we are in a hurry.'

'Can do?'

'Can do. Got to, by the look of it.'

'You never said a truer word mate. Don't mess up. Get this right and we're in the clear, okay?'

Barry finished his drink, lit a cigarette, and got up to leave. He looked back as he opened the door. Luke was looking thoughtful.

Never seen old Luke rattled before, he thought. Must be big trouble all right.

★★★

Detective Inspector Harry Moss keyed in the numbers, listened for a few moments then replaced the receiver. He turned to face his junior colleagues.

'Answer machine; missed him. I was hoping to catch him to see if we're any further forward. We don't yet have the official cause of death, but at the scene he was sure it couldn't be the facial trauma. Said he'd seen worse on the rugger pitch. '"You'd be amazed how easily one can dislodge a few teeth with a well-aimed elbow or knee." You know how he affects to revel in blood and broken bones.' Harry continued, his imitation of the pathologist's rumbling tones bringing smiles to his colleagues' faces. 'He thought the blow to the temple was the most likely cause of death. A forceful blow with a blunt instrument caused the contusion by the left eye, probably caused a blood clot that resulted in pressure on the brain. His line of thought is borne out by the fact that death was by no means instantaneous – some hour or two later, so he believes. Now he's gone home we'll have to wait 'til morning. Last time we brought him in on a Sunday he was most uncooperative; like a bloody bear with a sore head – the rest of us all pussyfooting round him. Never mind. Let's go over what little we have so far.'

Detective Sergeant Hazel Blissett opened her notebook and began to read.

'At the scene we collected a schoolbag with schoolbooks inside, a hockey stick and, at your suggestion Sir, certain of the large stones that lay around where the victim appeared to have rested before climbing the bank. All these items are with Forensics at present.'

'Thanks Hazel,' said Harry. 'Now Danny?'

Detective Constable Danny Prior cleared his throat.

'Not much from the children Sir. They saw the victim, got the wind up, and ran home to mum. Mum called us out. The door to door hasn't been very helpful either. A couple of the residents in Station Road heard a bit of a disturbance going on at the station, but no one saw anything.'

'So,' said Harry. 'There we are for the present. Still it's early days. We'll perhaps know more when we hear from Doctor Harris and the Lab. I've got a nasty feeling about this one you know. The fact that the victim was a Simms is what worries me. It could mean that we've got some kind of turf war in the offing. I can't see anyone local tangling with that particular family. We could be hearing from the Met before too many days go by.' He looked at Hazel and Danny and smiled. 'Sorry. Just thinking aloud. Go on. Off you go. There is nothing more to be done here just now. I'll try Doctor Harris again before I head off. He'll tell me what I want to know – anything's preferable to coming in on a Sunday. It's just a matter of catching him at home.'

★★★

CHAPTER EIGHT

Saturday

Philip leant forward to inhale the rich aroma of coffee as he depressed the plunger of the cafetiere; all around, the gentle clatter of cutlery and low murmur as fellow guests enjoyed the excellent breakfast.

'It's funny the way people lower their voices in hotel dining rooms,' he remarked.

Naomi finished her bacon and put her napkin to her lips. 'You're doing it yourself,' she replied in a theatrical whisper.

'So are you. That's what happens. Everyone seems to do it. Good coffee eh? What do you think they're all talking about?'

He regarded the other diners conversing in subdued voices. They merged well into the genteel, old-fashioned dining room with its heavy oak furniture and traditional décor. They were all middle-aged or older and he had begun, in his fanciful way, to match them to various professions when Naomi nudged him.

'I think that most of them are talking about us.'

'What makes you say that?'

'The way they stared at you when we came in.'

Philip moved his hand under cover of the tablecloth and checked that his zip was properly fastened. Naomi, noticing his movement, snorted with laughter, a reaction that earned her several interested stares from the surrounding tables.

'Honestly, you blokes and your zips,' she whispered, shaking her head, and dabbing her eyes with her napkin. 'What you did then: typical man.'

Philip grinned at her and said, 'That's reassuring. Now what makes you say that we're the main topic of conversation?'

'It's obvious. We're the only ones in here with a pulse; we were the last down to breakfast and the bags under your eyes show that you had a disturbed night.'

'You also had a disturbed night as I recall, and there are no bags under your eyes.' 'Really? And they say it's a man's world,' she smiled.

They were quiet as the waitress, who looked about fifteen, refilled their cups. They finished their toast in silence and sat sipping their coffee, both wanting to prolong this precious interlude.

'Time to move on?' Philip asked eventually.

'Yes, I suppose,' she sighed. 'I could get used to this.' She continued, looking round at the former grandeur, now rather showing its age, but still impressively ornate.

'Well we could have a look at Nottingham if you like. I've never been here before. Have you?'

'No. There's a castle isn't there? We could have a look at it. Let's go to the castle and then push on about lunchtime.'

'Suits me. I'll go up and get the case, and then we'll settle up.'

'I'll come up. I want to go to the loo.'

They checked out of the hotel having spent rather more than they had intended and agreed that their next overnight stop would have to be very much cheaper.

'It was lovely though,' Naomi sighed, as they stepped out into the bright, nippy morning and linked arms to walk to the castle.

Nottingham Castle proved to be a disappointment, as it turned out not to be a castle at all.

'I was expecting battlements and a drawbridge and a portcullis and chutes for pouring hot tar and gungy substances down on the attackers' heads and all that castle stuff,' said Philip as they regarded what was really just a rather large house. What a swiz. We went into a pub once called The Nottingham Castle and to look at their sign you'd think the real castle was a proper job, not like this at all. I mean it's not very Robin Hood is it?'

'Come on,' urged Naomi. 'It's probably great once you're inside; warmer too, I hope.

It was indeed. They found the museum interesting and enjoyed the art gallery but found themselves hurrying through everything. 'I think it's because we're so anxious to move on,' said Naomi. 'Let's have a cup of coffee and go. We're not in the right mood for sightseeing.' They saw from a display that the castle was at another location but decided not to visit.

'Maybe another time,' said Naomi. 'Let's push on. I'm cold.'

'You're right,' Philip agreed. 'We could have a lunchtime stop somewhere, then I'd like to phone home. I told Mum I'd ring on Saturday when Dad's home.'

★★★

Saturday

Detective Sergeant Hazel Blissett and Detective Constable Danny Prior stood at the front door of 8 Rosebery Drive.

'Wouldn't mind a pad round here,' remarked Danny.

'Not on your wages Danny boy,' replied Hazel, ringing the ornate, brass bell. They listened as the strident chime died away. 'It's all a bit grand compared to the Gibbs' semi' isn't it?' she continued, looking round at the impressive, detached properties, each one standing in its own grounds. 'I'm not being unkind,' she hastened to add. 'I thought the Gibbs' place was lovely, but this is what I would call gracious living.'

'But would you swap it for your comfy flat?' Danny asked with a grin.

'You are daft Constable,' she replied, giving him a sideways look. 'It does look as though young Naomi might be going up in the world though doesn't it?'

'No one in I reckon.' Danny was reaching for the bell push when the door opened and

a tall woman holding a pair of gardening gloves and wearing an apron stood looking down at them.

'I'm so sorry to keep you waiting. I'm having a tidy up day in the garden. Can I help you?'

'Good morning. Mrs. Watkins?' Hazel asked.

'Yes, that's right. I'm Mrs. Watkins.'

Both police officers held out their warrant cards for inspection as Hazel continued, 'I'm DS Blissett and this is DC Prior. We'd like to talk to Philip Watkins if it's convenient.'

'I'm afraid he's not here. Is it important?'

'Yes, it is, very. May we come in?'

Mrs. Watkins' composure faltered for a second, but she stood aside saying, 'Certainly,' as she gestured towards the sitting room door.

Hazel, followed by Danny, paused in the doorway, momentarily arrested by the light airy ambience of the room. Her rapt gaze took in the classical white marble fireplace, shining brass firedogs and scuttle; the step up to the spacious bay window where family photographs and an old-fashioned Bakelite telephone stood ranged atop the black lacquered grand piano. Matching sets of fine leather-bound books in glass fronted bookcases gleamed along one wall and the richly textured soft furnishings suggested elegance and homeliness, all at once. Every hard surface glowed from diligent polishing, vividly patterned rugs lay just so upon the pale oak parquet floor, the air redolent of a subtle fragrance of wax polish.

Is that lavender? wondered Hazel as she stepped into the room. It's lovely, she thought. A beautiful showpiece, yet lived in.

Mr. Watkins comfortably ensconced in his leather armchair looked up from his newspaper, as he became aware of their presence. He folded the paper as he stood and cast a quizzical look towards his wife.

Now there's a cosseted male, Hazel thought. She drops everything to answer the front door while he remains in his sanctum reading the paper: I suppose the boy's the same. She felt a degree of contempt for Mr. Watkins but on looking at Mrs. Watkins she realised that the woman wouldn't have it any other way.

'It's the police dear,' explained Mrs. Watkins. 'They want to talk to Philip.'

'So, do we,' he replied, shaking hands with each of the officers. 'Do sit down.'

'Do you mind if my colleague takes notes?' asked Hazel.

'Not at all. You carry on,' he replied expansively.

'As I said,' Mrs. Watkins continued,' Philip isn't here. He went to the cinema on Thursday evening; came home rather late and then went out again to see his friend Maurice. He didn't come home that night but he 'phoned on Friday morning at about nine to say he was fine and would ring again on Saturday. It's the first time he's done anything like this, so we're rather puzzled about what he's up to. I must say we're a bit worried. He's such a vague boy sometimes.'

'We need to interview him about his movements on Thursday evening,' Hazel began. 'It's a serious matter. A boy has been found dead in suspicious circumstances. He died in the early hours of Friday morning having been assaulted some hours before.'

'You can't believe Philip is involved surely,' cried Mrs. Watkins in disbelief.

'There was a disturbance at the railway station on Thursday night,' Hazel continued. 'A gang of local youths chased a young couple into the station. The couple must have been desperate to get away because they jumped down from the platform and ran off along the city-bound track.'

'They jumped down onto the tracks?' said Mr. Watkins incredulously.

'What about the live rail?' cried his wife. 'It's lethal.' She shuddered involuntarily.

'It most certainly is, seven hundred and fifty volts,' Hazel went on. 'That shows just how desperate they must have been. The gang lost interest at that point but their leader, Justin Simms, was last seen chasing them along the track on his own. We have interviewed the youths concerned and they all confirm that this is what happened. They told us that Simms was intent on having sex with the girl with or without her consent. He had tried it once before evidently, while she was still at school.'

'Brute!' interjected Mrs. Watkins.

'Anyway, as far as we can tell that was the last time Simms was seen alive. As the young couple seem to have been the only other people at the scene, it is imperative that we speak with them.'

'Is he one of the infamous Simms's?' asked Mr. Watkins.

Hazel nodded. 'Was,' she corrected. 'Did Philip know him?'

'I'm pretty sure we'd know about it if he did. I've never heard Philip mention him.'

'I don't see why you need to speak to Philip,' said Mrs. Watkins.

'The girl is called Naomi Gibbs,' Hazel began.

'Naomi!' Mrs. Watkins interrupted. 'Philip goes out with her. She's a lovely girl.

'Now do you see why we're here?' asked Hazel. 'We have a witness who claims she saw someone answering Philip's description get into a blue Peugeot car late on Thursday night. Naomi Gibbs owns such a car.'

Mrs. Watkins sat white faced with a hand to her mouth. Her husband reached across and took her other hand in his. Both stared at Hazel, dreading what she might say next. Detective Constable Prior turned a page of his notebook.

'The statements we have all indicate that Philip or Naomi, or both of them, had motive and opportunity to assault the victim and inflict the injuries that contributed to his death some time later. The fact that Philip and Naomi appear to have run away does not help their case. It might be that they acted in self-defence; it might even be that a third party was involved. We have identified the weapons used to attack the victim and now have the results of forensic tests carried out on them. I'm told these tests have yielded a significant amount of information – sufficient I believe to indicate that Simms was the victim of more than one attack. You see how important it is that we find these two quickly. You say you're expecting Philip to phone today?'

Mrs. Watkins, her lips compressed, nodded.

'Well my advice to you is tell him to get to a police station as soon as he can and explain who they are. The sooner they co-operate the better it will be for them. We've spoken with Naomi's parents. They have confirmed the rape attempt at the school, and they've explained why no complaint was made to us at the time. Naomi left a note, but it gives no indication of where they might be. You'll do as I suggest?'

'Oh yes. Certainly,' replied Mr. Watkins. 'You can count on it. If Philip has anything to do with this dreadful business, we want to know about it. I can't believe he'd ... do this awful thing.'

'Well the sooner we hear their side of it, the better,' said Hazel. 'We're off now,' she continued, offering her card. 'Other people to see. You'll ring me then?'

'We most certainly will Sergeant,' Mr. Watkins replied.

Hazel looked across at Danny as she fastened her seatbelt.

'There's a worried couple.'

'They've plenty to worry about, haven't they? I wouldn't want to be in their shoes.'

Danny looked back at the house and saw Mrs. Watkins standing in the bay window.

'She's on the phone now,' he said.

'I guess she's ringing Naomi Gibbs' parents,' Hazel mused. 'That's the first thing I'd do.'

Saturday

A second interview was taking place in an alley behind the High Street, but it had nothing to do with law and order.

Joshua and Rebecca Simms stood side by side blocking the entrance to the alley.

'Now then Ray,' Rebecca began, her deep blue eyes riveted upon those of the boy. 'You tell us all about Thursday night and we let you go. Simple enough.'

'Piss off,' snapped Ray. I don't have to tell you anything.'

'Do as she says son,' Joshua sidled closer.

'Bollocks! You can't keep me here. He leant his bicycle, an expensive lightweight model, against the wall, saying, 'Don't start something you can't finish Simms.'

Joshua moved forward; blue eyes fixed upon Ray. The boy was taller and considerably heavier, but it was Joshua who had the speed and the right moves. A few moments later a bewildered Ray was down on one knee, badly winded, with blood pouring from a split eyebrow.

'Now tell us what happened on Thursday night before he does you some serious damage,' said Rebecca, her voice low and menacing.

Ray peered at the twins with his undamaged eye. He was confused by the ease with which Joshua had knocked him down. It was a new experience, as never before had he been beaten in a fight. He had been overwhelmed by the flurry of bruising blows and he knew that whatever it was that had split open his eyebrow, it was not a fist. He remained silent but fearful: he experienced self-doubt for the first time in his life. There was no doubt in his mind though that these two were prepared to hurt him badly in order to get what they wanted, and that he would be unable to stop them.

'Now listen you prick,' Rebecca continued. 'I had to take mother to identify Justin. She hasn't stopped crying since. She keeps going on about his poor face. They won't release his body so we can't make any funeral arrangements and it's breaking her heart. You were there, just tell us what went on.' She stepped forward and thrust her long scarlet nails towards his face. 'Speak up maggot or I'll blind your other eye.'

Joshua placed a hand on her shoulder. 'Give him a minute Becks.'

His voice was calm, but Ray could feel the underlying threat in it. He remembered the Simms twins from school. They were four or five years older so he had never suffered at their hands, but he could recall what they had done to some of the bigger boys: and girls too. He looked at Rebecca's sharp nails and at Joshua's grim expression, and knew he had no choice.

'We was all in Tony's,' he began. 'There was this couple missed the last bus. Justin said, "let's follow them … give them a fright like." We went along with it, but we weren't keen. He was too fired up. We chased them. They ran into the train station and we followed. We had them trapped on the bridge, but I didn't like the way it was all turning out. It was obvious he meant to shag her, so I said I was off because it was too cold to hang about.'

'Go on,' commanded Rebecca, her eyes never leaving Ray's.

'Well I left and some of the lads came away too.'

'You left him!' She exclaimed in disbelief.

'He still had half a dozen or so mates with him when I took off. He wasn't on his own. Actually, a couple of guys ran back to him as well. I went home and that's all I saw.'

'It's not all you know though, is it.' Joshua slapped his open palm with a heavy steel key.

'In the end they all left him. Some caught up with me and they said the girl and her bloke had run off up the track and Justin had gone after them on his own.'

'Who was it who told you this?' Ray paused but he lacked the courage to lie to these two.

'It was Bernie, Sam and Kevin.'

'They saw it all?'

'Yes. That's what they said.'

'Who was the girl and the boyfriend?'

'I didn't know the boyfriend.'

'Don't get bloody smart,' snapped Rebecca, moving forward in a threatening manner. 'Who's the girl then?'

'Naomi Gibbs,' Ray answered, feeling wretched and anxious to avoid further punishment; ashamed of how easily these two had cowed him.

'Now tell us about the train.'

'We got hold of young Driscoll and hung him out the window. It got real scary for a while there. I honestly thought Justin wanted to kill him. He seemed to go a bit mad.' The twins exchanged a glance as though Ray had confirmed something for them.

Rebecca snapped her fingers under his nose and laughed derisively as he flinched.

'We're going, wimp,' she sneered. 'You say one word about this, and we'll gut you. You'll just have to tell Mummy you fell off your bike.'

Joshua put his foot against the front spindle and kicked hard, buckling the alloy rim, and bending the front forks beyond repair.

'Nice bike that,' he grinned. 'Now we're off to see Bernie, Sam and Kevin, and if their version doesn't tally with yours then it'll be more than your bike that'll need mending.'

★★★

CHAPTER NINE

Saturday

Back in the car, Philip and Naomi consulted the atlas again and selected their route to Chester. 'We can go A52 to Derby and continue to Ashbourne, say twenty-five miles or so, then stop for lunch,' suggested Naomi.

'What about going down onto the A50 on the other side of Derby?' said Philip. 'It looks as though going south of Stoke-on-Trent might be easier than going north. There doesn't seem to be a ring road. After that we go onto the M6 to junction 16, then onto the A500 to Nantwich then the A51 to Chester. What do you think?'

'You haven't forgotten about changing the car?' asked Naomi. 'We could look for a dealer in Stoke.'

'Right if you're still sure you want to do that; we can do it from the south. There's Newcastle-under-Lyme as well. Sure, to be a good few motor dealers in that lot. We can still go down onto the M6 afterwards and follow the route I said.'

'Then it looks like Uttoxeter for lunch,' said Naomi.

They soon found the Derby Road and had an uneventful drive to Uttoxeter, where they found a café that did not t look too expensive. Half an hour later, Philip, having enjoyed roast beef and two veg', decided to look for a telephone. Naomi ordered a second cup of tea, having decided that sitting in the steamy warmth of the café was preferable to standing in a telephone kiosk, with the door half open.

★★★

'Mum, it's me,' he said as he heard his mother recite the familiar number.

'Where are you?' she demanded. 'Oh Philip, what have you done? You've no idea what it's done to us. We don't know what to think. All your lies about Maurice and …' she broke off, weeping.

'Mum? Mum! What is it? What's the matter? What's happened?'

'I'll tell you what's happened,' said his father. 'I just hope and pray you don't know all ready. A young lad has been found dead and the police seem to think you're implicated in some way. They were here asking questions this morning. We couldn't tell them where you were. You can imagine how we felt. God knows what you are supposed to have done lad, but the best thing you can do now is get yourself to the nearest police station. They are looking for you. It'll look better if you give yourself up. They're looking for Naomi as well, and you were seen getting into a car late on Thursday night. Your mother is frantic with worry. We don't know what to think. They've spoken to Naomi's parents as well.'

'Dad I'm sorry I lied to you. Believe me, I had good reason, but I don't know anything about anyone being killed. I am with Naomi. She ran away because she had no choice. I came with her because I love her. I just couldn't let her go off on her own. It all blew up so quickly. A gang of yobs chased us, and we ran for it. The leader of this gang tried to rape Naomi before, and she is understandably terrified of him. He's called Justin Simms. He tried to rape her at school.'

'That's the name of the dead boy Philip. The police asked if you knew him. I said I thought not, as I'd never heard you mention him.'

Philip stared at the telephone – shocked into silence.

'Are you still there Philip?' his father called.

'I've got to go Dad. I'll call again soon. I promise you I've done nothing to be ashamed of – neither has Naomi. Please tell Mum that. I'll call soon. Bye.'

He replaced the receiver and stood thinking about what to do.

★★★

73

Detective Inspector Moss reached up and gave the knocker a sharp double rap. The door opened and there stood Maureen Driscoll smiling at him.

'Now Harry,' she said, 'that was a real policeman's knock. Won't you come in?'

Harry smiled, 'I hope it's a convenient time to call.'

'It certainly is,' she replied. 'I'll put the kettle on, and we'll have a nice cup of tea.'

As she closed the front door, Harry's thoughts went straight to the day of Frank Driscoll's funeral. It all seemed so recent. Maureen still looked just the same. But then he saw Terry coming out of the sitting room and was amazed to see how much he had grown.

'Terry,' he cried. 'You're taller than I am. How are you getting on these days?'

'I'm fine thanks,' the boy replied. 'It's nice to see you Mr. Moss.'

They followed Maureen into the kitchen where she busied herself preparing the tea.

Harry pulled out a chair and sat at the table. Terry sat facing him.

'I ought to explain the reason for my visit,' Harry began.

'Not social then?' Maureen replied.

'Not entirely. I don't know if you've heard about the Simms boy?'

'Justin?' asked Terry.

'The very same,' replied Harry. 'I'm afraid he's dead.'

Maureen gasped with shock and sat down heavily. 'What do you mean?'

'He was attacked on Thursday night and badly knocked about. The Path' Report indicates that he died a couple of hours later.'

Maureen dropped into a chair; all thoughts of tea forgotten.

'Maureen. You're as white as a sheet. You look as though you need a drink,' cried Harry, looking worried.

'Mum?' said Terry, concerned at his mother's distress.

'I'm all right dear, just a bit dizzy. Thanks,' she said, as Harry poured the tea and slid the mug across the table. 'Just give me a moment.'

'It looks to me as though a brandy might be in order,' Harry suggested. 'This hasn't had time to draw properly.'

'Tea's fine,' she smiled, 'just as long as it's hot.'

'Shall I go on then?' Harry asked.

She nodded.

'Well all this unpleasantness happened on the railway line of all places.' He went on to outline the events of Thursday night which had culminated in the death of Justin Simms. 'My reason for calling today,' he continued, 'is because we found your school-bag on the line Terry, and your hockey stick. I gather, from talking to his mates, that young Simms threw them from the train.

The sound of the front doorknocker interrupted them before Terry could reply. Maureen got up to answer it and was soon back with a smile to say that two of Terry's friends wanted him to come out.

'Go on, do you good Son,' she said. 'They've ridden over specially. I can tell Harry about the bag and the stick. Put your coat on it's turning cold.'

As the youthful voices receded and the front door closed behind them, she turned to Harry saying, 'That young swine Simms and his yobboes held Terry out of the train window on Tuesday and then they threw his bag and stick out as a warning. They said if he told anyone they'd throw him out next time. You should have seen the state he arrived home in. Luckily old Matty Cobbett helped him to get home from the station. They kept him in hospital overnight. Thankfully, his injuries turned out not to be serious.'

'You reported all this?' Harry asked.

'I went to the school, but the head said it was a matter for the transport police. I was so, preoccupied I gave him a flea in his ear and left.'

'I heard you made a surprise entry at school assembly. You made quite an impression you know. Well it's a bit of poetic justice Maureen. I shouldn't be telling you this but I'm sure you'll keep it to yourself. Someone used Terry's stick to knock out most of young Simms' front teeth and break his nose. Very painful I imagine, but that's not what killed him. He suffered another attack in which he sustained the serious head injury from which he died. We've talked to his pals and they said the last they saw of him was running along the track in pursuit of the young couple. Several of them said that Simms' behaviour had been rather odd lately, especially in the way he'd been picking on your Terry. They were upset over the incident on the train; ashamed is the better word. Your remarks brought that home to them.'

'What happened to the young couple?' Maureen asked.

'They've dropped out of sight for the moment. That's an odd business too. Evidently Simms had already tried to have his way with the young woman before she left school.'

'Well I wouldn't have wished him dead, but I can't say I feel any sympathy for that young man or his family. Frank told me one or two blood curdling facts about Arthur Simms and the two eldest boys.'

'Not boys any more Maureen. Frank certainly did his best there: took a hardened killer off the streets. But what a dreadful price you've had to pay.'

'I still go to Mass Harry, but it's not a matter of Faith in The Almighty. I go because we always went together, and I feel as if he's still with me. When I'm in that church, I imagine that if I turn to look, he'll be sitting there on the other side of Terry, and that we'll all walk home together, the way we used to.' She was close to tears.

Harry reached across the table and placed his hand on hers.

'You know the file will never be closed Maureen.'

'What's the use Harry? Frank's gone. If you were to find incontrovertible evidence tomorrow linking Arthur Simms to Frank's murder, what would it achieve? a closed file? That bloody swine is already serving life. I could take no satisfaction in a conviction because I know already that he had my Frank murdered; shot down in the street. Put me outside his cell with a gun in my hand and I'd put him down for the mad cur that he is.'

'I'm sure you would,' said Harry gravely, nodding his head. 'I'm sure you would.'

'Some years ago, Harry, I listened to a radio programme about bereavement and I heard a psychologist say that in his opinion, desire for revenge and desire for justice can be virtually indistinguishable and both are normal reactions when grieving. He said that the desire for revenge could be just as necessary to the grieving process as any other human emotion. I know I felt a whole lot better about myself when I heard him say that. Until that moment, everything I felt towards that bloody man had been so at odds with my upbringing. I want him dead. I want his life as payment for Frank's and if that's not Christian, at least it's the truth.'

'Well they do say it's a dish best served cold Maureen.'

'I wholeheartedly agree Harry: absolutely stone cold.'

'Well I really must go. It's nice to see you again. You know those of us who knew Frank often talk about him. He had true devotion to duty. He was an example to us all and we miss him too.'

'Thanks Harry. Terry is so like him you know; gentle on the outside but with an inner determination to do things his way: too impetuous for his own good sometimes. Don't leave it so long next time Harry. We're always pleased to see you.'

She had been on the verge of telling him about her telephone conversations with the Irishman but thought better of it.

She watched him climb into his car and wave as he drove away then went straight to her bureau. She picked out the white card and rather shakily keyed the telephone number.

'The number you have dialled has not been recognised. Please check and try again.' She stared at the card in disbelief. Aware of her nervousness, she painstakingly keyed the number digit by digit only to hear the same well-modulated voice deliver the same message once more. She checked the card against the telephone display – the numbers matched. She hung up. She thought back to the last time she had rung the number and her last words – 'Do it.' Had she condemned the Simms boy to death? Is that all that was required to end a life? Two two-letter words? She'd had Arthur Simms in mind at the time. He was the one they had been talking about after all, not a schoolboy.

'I can't undo those words,' she said aloud. 'Be honest with yourself Maureen, you wouldn't give a damn if the whole bloody lot of them were put in a sack and dropped off Beachy Head tomorrow.'

★★★

CHAPTER TEN

Harry Moss was having thoughts of his own about Justin Simms' pursuit of Terry. Statements taken separately from Justin's mates all agreed that the spate of bullying had begun recently and, in only a short time had escalated to the near extreme violence of the train incident. It was clear that as far as the gang members were concerned, their erstwhile leader had overstepped the mark there. Their statements indicated that they had all, several of them independently, decided that they wanted no more to do with him before they had heard of Justin's death.

It's as if he found out quite recently that Frank was Terry's father, Harry mused, as he drove back to the police station. 'Terry's sporting successes certainly attract a great deal of attention in the town; maybe that's what sparked off Justin's interest? The lad's often featured in the local paper. Maybe he heard his family talking and put two and two together? Maybe Arthur Simms feels that all these Driscoll achievements are rubbing his nose in it and has decided that now is the time to take his revenge a step further by making use of Justin in this way? Are Maureen and Terry in danger or am I letting my imagination run away with me? Is all this just too fantastic? Is it anything more than feuding among schoolboys? But then he thought of the malevolence of Arthur Simms and was reminded that the man was capable of any wickedness.

Which way is he going to jump now that Justin's dead? he wondered. Then there's the question of who was it that dealt the fatal blow? Could someone local have settled a score? Have the many nefarious activities of "Simms & Co" proved sufficiently profitable to attract the interest of outsiders planning to muscle in, to oust the Simms? It's quite possible that someone in the prison could pick up on things and feed information to a major player, in return for a favour. These questions occupied his mind for the entire journey and, had he been asked to do so, Harry would have found it difficult to remember which route he had driven.

One thing was clear though, they were going to have to keep a close watch over Maureen and Terry. If the Simms were planning to attack these two it would be necessary to catch them in the act; to intervene at the correct moment. Experience had shown that they were past masters of the alibi.

★★★

Saturday

The moment he re-entered the café, Naomi's heart sank. Philip was so very pale. Something awful must have happened. She remained in her seat while he collected two more cups of tea and as he joined her, asked, 'Philip. What's happened?'

'I don't know how to tell you,' he replied. 'My parents are in a right panic, yours must be as well.' He looked into her eyes and held her hands across the table. 'Naomi. I'm so sorry.' She saw the tears welling in his eyes and became thoroughly alarmed.

'What is it? What's happened? Tell me!'

'Justin Simms is dead.'

Everyone in the café heard her sharp intake of breath. Several heads turned towards her, and the proprietor, a large man with the battered features of a boxer, eyed Philip with suspicion. Philip squeezed her hands as she sat, unable to find a word to say.

After a long time, she whispered, 'I'm in serious trouble now Philip. I didn't mean to kill him.'

'I don't see how you could have. You said there was a lot of blood, but people don't die from a dig in the mouth. I can't see how what you did could be fatal – not unless he was a haemophiliac. The very worst-case scenario is that he died as the result of what you did to him. Wait a minute,' he added, cursing his own clumsiness as she began to cry, 'That didn't come out the way I meant it to. You acted in self-defence. We all know that. Please don't be so upset. I can't bear it. He wasn't worth one of your tears. We know what he intended to do if you hadn't stopped him.'

'What are we going to do Philip? What are we going to do?' said Naomi, twisting and untwisting her wet handkerchief, her voice taut with anxiety. She shook his sleeve in her agitation. 'Tell me what to do.'

'Well, let's think what options we have?' said Philip.

'We could go to Ireland,' Naomi replied.

'Think about it,' said Philip. 'The police are looking for us, so I don't think Ireland is a good idea. They'll be watching. Our Passports would give us away immediately. Anyway, what would we do if by some stroke of luck, we managed it? Do you know anyone over there?'

Naomi shook her head.

'We can go on to your uncle,' Philip continued, 'go to the nearest police station or head for home and hope to get there without being arrested. We could phone our folks to say we're coming – that would show good intent on our part if we're picked up on the way. Our parents would back our story. I don't think it would be fair on your uncle to involve him in this, and I would rather surrender to our local police than the police up here.'

Naomi stood up, dabbing at her eyes with a tissue. Philip took her arm and they walked towards the door. The sour faced proprietor, still giving Philip hostile looks, called out, 'You all right lass?' Naomi nodded, gave him a tearful smile, and held on to Philip.

'We've just had some bad news,' said Philip.

The man came around from behind the counter, a look of concern on his rugged face. Naomi's tears had genuinely moved this lumbering giant of a man. He smiled and placed a huge hand on her shoulder.

'You take care now lass. Things are never as bad as they seem. You make sure you look after her lad,' he added, giving Philip a friendly smile.

Philip nodded his thanks as the man pulled the door open.

Clang! The strident chime rang loudly through the café as the door closed behind them.

'Seconds out,' chortled the proprietor, raising clenched fists and licking his thumbs as he always did, easing his bulk back behind the counter.

The regular customers made no response. He had uttered this catch phrase so often that it had lost all novelty entirely and become unremarkable.

★★★

'If we don't go back it'll look as though I'm guilty,' said Naomi. 'If we do, then I'm right back where the Simms can get me. They're sure to believe I killed him; especially as I ran away. Everyone's going to say I did it. You were right. Taking off was a big mistake. I should have stayed. I must phone Mum and Dad.'

They walked back to the telephone kiosk but after three fruitless attempts to get through, Naomi replaced the receiver saying she would try again later on the way home. Their plan was to drive for about an hour and then telephone Philip's parents to say they were on their way. Mr. Watkins would then pass this news onto the police.

★★★

It was an uneventful journey, passed mostly in silence. They each had plenty to occupy their thoughts. Eventually Naomi drew into a lay-by where there were two telephone boxes side by side.

'Ever thought about a mobile?' asked Philip.

'Yes. I'm the only one in our house who hasn't got one.'

'Dad has a pathological hatred for them. Sometimes he comes off the train in a fuming rage because someone's been holding long conversations on their mobile. When he's really mad, he gives us chapter and verse including his own comments to the culprit, like,' and here Philip gave a very passable impression of his father's plummy voice, '"Madam. I'm sure we've heard quite enough about the intimate nature of your operation. It might be better if you continued your conversation elsewhere." I think he lays it on a bit thick, but even if only half of it's true I'm amazed at what people do talk about in public. My Aunt Margery was given a mobile the Christmas before last, but she'll only use it in a phone box because she says she feels silly holding it to her ear in the middle of the pavement.'

'Well I'm expecting one for my birthday. It won't be much use if I'm in prison though will it?' Tears welled up in Naomi's eyes as she leaned towards Philip.

'It won't come to that love,' he said, taking her in his arms. 'I'm sure they'll see that you had no choice but to do as you did. Mind you, if we'd had one on Thursday night maybe none of it would have happened. They might have backed off if they'd seen us phoning for help.' They just sat for several minutes and then she broke away.

'Come on. Let's get on with it. Can I phone home first?'

'Sure,' Philip replied.

Naomi's mother answered the call and, after expressing her relief that they were en-route for home and her opinion of Justin Simms' behaviour, listened to Naomi's account of all that had gone on and what they intended to do next.

'Just come home safe my love,' she said. 'We're all waiting for you.'

'Bye Mum. See you soon. Love to everyone,' said Naomi and hung up.

Philip then rang his father.

'Hi Dad. We're just south of Nottingham and should be home between seven and eight. Naomi will drop me at home, and I'll go to the police station with you and Mum if that's okay.'

'Certainly, Son. I'll phone Detective Sergeant Blissett and give her some idea of when to expect us.'

'Naomi will go with her mum and dad at much the same time.'

'Right. I'll pass that on too. Now, safe journey and try not to worry. I'm sure it can all be sorted out. See you soon.'

'Bye Dad. I'm sorry about all this.'

'From what I've gathered Son, you couldn't have done much else. Take care now.'

★★★

Inspector Browning picked up the telephone and listened to the call.

'I'm afraid D.S. Blissett's not in the station just now sir. Can I give her a message?' He listened carefully, repeating one or two points to make sure he'd got it right and then assured Mr. Watkins that he would pass on the information post-haste. Before he did so, however, he rang another number saying, 'That young couple you're interested in are on their way home. They've just 'phoned in from near Nottingham and expect to get here about seven thirty. I guess they'll come Cambridge way along the A14. Once they get to Stowmarket though they'll have quite a few options.'

★★★

Joshua replaced the telephone and looked across the table at his twin.

'That was our tame copper. He's just taken a message for a colleague and heard that Naomi Gibbs and Philip Watkins have phoned home. They're on their way back, coming from Nottingham way. That's why we weren't able to find them, they legged it. They reckon to be here round half past seven; looks as if they're going to talk to the Old Bill.'

Becky looked at her watch. 'We could go out that way and welcome them home,' she suggested, smiling. 'They'll probably come Cambridge way on the A14.'

'That's a very long shot Becks. We'd have to strike real lucky to spot them in the dark.'

'Let's do it Josh. It's worth a go, isn't it? I want to get my hands on that little bitch.'

'Well let's say we got lucky and found them. What then? Stop their car? Get them out of it and into ours without drawing attention to ourselves? It's all pretty iffy, and if we got that far, what then?'

'We take them out to Kingsfield and make them tell us what happened to poor Justin.'

'Becky, I know you're keen to get at them. I want to know as much as you do. But it's too late now. It's too dark. Anyway, the Old Bill knows roughly what time to expect them, so they'll be missed if they don't turn up. The best thing we can do is wait 'til they've made their statements then we'll lean on our little mole and find out what they've said. Then we can watch for a chance to pick them up. It would make sense to get them one at a time. Kingsfield's a great idea; no-one goes there these days.'

'I guess you're right,' said Becky, disappointedly. 'We don't want to cock it all up by being too hasty. There's this thing with Driscoll's widow and the boy too. Dad is keen to get it done quickly. You remember our last visit? Remember what Dad said to Robin? "Do it for me son. Quick as you can eh." That's what they were talking about. It all seemed to be happening too, but something's gone wrong there. Robin and James are definitely having problems.'

She looked at the door and leaned towards him, 'And we're not going to add to them,' she whispered. 'Robin's not included us in his plans, so we won't include him in ours. We'll sort out Naomi and the boyfriend ourselves; no need for big brothers to know; not yet.'

'Robin will go bloody mad if he finds out,' replied Joshua.

'How can they find out? It's only us two that know. They're not likely to go out to Kingsfield, are they?'

'What if he had answered the phone just now instead of me, and taken that message from Browning? That would have tipped him off and he'd have gone raving mad. You know he would. I say we tell him what we've got in mind.'

'What for? Why's everyone so scared of bloody Robin.'

'You saying you're not?' challenged Joshua. 'James is. You only have to watch him when Robin has a rant. He's terrified of him.'

'We're all wary of him except Mum and Dad, but we won't give him any reason to go mad, will we?'

'I hope not,' muttered Joshua. 'I really hope not. I've got really bad feelings about this Becks.'

'Don't be so bloody soft,' she laughed. 'It's the right way to do it – believe me.'

***

Saturday. 19:30

Naomi brought the car to a stop outside Philip's house and leant back in her seat looking pale and tense.

'Well it won't be long now,' she said, attempting to smile. 'I'm really worried Philip.'

'I know you are,' he replied, 'but I'm sure it's the right thing to do. It's the only thing to do. I'll go in now and we'll meet up later at the police station I guess.' He opened his door, leant across to kiss her cheek and said, 'Cheer up. It'll soon be sorted, see you soon.'

She nodded, too choked to speak, and watched him gather his belongings from the back seat. As he stood back and slammed the door she let in the clutch and moved off.

Philip watched her out of sight then ran up the steps to the front door and let himself in.

'Mum, Dad,' he called. 'I'm home.'

Mrs. Watkins, closely followed by her husband, rushed into the hall, and embraced Philip.

'Thank heavens you're home Philip. We've been frantic.'

Philip's father, being less demonstrative, held out his hand.

'Welcome home old son. Detective Sergeant Blissett rang back to say that you and Naomi can make your statements at home if you prefer to.'

'Let's go to the police station. I've told Naomi I'd see her there.' A tightness in Philip's voice betrayed his anxiety. 'She's very worried about all this you know.'

'Give her a ring. See what she wants to do.'

'She's so anxious, Dad. You're probably right; she'd be more at ease in her own home. She's terrified of being sent to prison.'

'Why?' Mrs. Watkins' voice became strident. 'What on earth has she done?'

'She's done no more than defend herself from a would-be rapist Mother. She was in danger and took action to protect herself. I'll tell you more about it once we've got these statements out of the way.'

Philip rang Naomi's number and she told him she'd decided to make her statement at home.

'I'm not surprised. You were so worried about going to the police station. You'll find it much less of a trauma with your family round you.'

'I'm still unhappy Philip. I just can't stop thinking about what could happen if things go against me; if it turns out that it was me who caused his death.'

'I'm sure that won't happen. I'll phone as soon as I've finished. Or shall I come round?'

'Phone me.'

'Okay, I love you Naomi. Try not to worry.' Philip looked pensive as he hung up.

***

CHAPTER ELEVEN

Mrs. Gibbs answered the doorbell and admitted Hazel Blissett and Danny Prior. Without speaking she led them through to the living room where they found Naomi, white faced, perched on the edge of the sofa. Her red rimmed eyes testimony to the fact that she had been crying a great deal.

'I'd prefer to stay but I suppose you want me to leave you to it,' said Naomi's mother.'

'That would be best Mrs Gibbs,' replied Hazel.

Hazel sat down next to Naomi while Danny settled himself into the facing armchair.

'Now Naomi, we know you've had a hell of a time these last few days. Running off like that wasn't helpful but we do understand why you did it. I wouldn't mind running off with that Philip myself,' she added, attempting to bring a smile to Naomi's face. The girl's taut features relaxed a little at this, and she allowed herself the briefest of watery smiles. 'Now Naomi,' Hazel continued softly, 'remember we are here to take your statement of what happened on Thursday night. Try and relax and give yourself time to think. D.C. Prior will take down all you say and when you're finished, and, if you agree that it is a true representation of what you've told us, I'll ask you to sign it to that effect: happy with that?'

'I thought you'd use a tape recorder.'

'It'll have to appear on paper in the end so we may as well get straight to it. It's normal practice. So, start when you're ready and do take your time.'

Naomi nodded, clearing her throat, and putting her hands in her lap. She began to describe the events of that Thursday night starting at the point where she and Philip had missed the last bus.

Her voice was under control as she recounted all that had gone on and she began to relax, encouraged by Hazel's supportive manner. It was as she started to tell of how she had tripped and fallen that she began to falter.

'I thought, it's all over now. He was so close. I could hear him laughing and then I put my hand on the hockey stick. I've tried to explain this part to Philip. First of all, I felt let down, betrayed, as if everything was conspiring to put me in his power … Oh, I can't explain, I can't go on with this.'

She sat shaking her head from side to side, tears streaming down her cheeks and sobbing in her distress.

'Come on love, you're doing really well.' Hazel took out a handkerchief and dried Naomi's tears. 'Give yourself a minute or two. It'll be all right. You'll be fine.'

Danny caught up with his writing then sat poised to go on.

'He was going to rape me,' she began at last, her voice husky, as if she had a cold. 'I had to stop him if I could. I wasn't going to just roll over.'

She stopped suddenly.

'I can't believe I said that,' she cried, as she realised her unfortunate choice of phrase. She stammered as she tried to regain her composure but then broke down completely. Hazel put her arm around her and gave her the handkerchief.

'That's right. Let it all go.' She held the sobbing girl in her arms, rocking her gently and patting her back as a mother comforts her child. After what seemed an awfully long time, during which Danny found it necessary to blow his nose, Naomi stopped crying and sat up. She took a deep shuddering breath.

'All right now?' Hazel was close to tears herself.

Naomi dabbed at her swollen eyes and blew her nose.

'I can go on now. I can't have any tears left. All this has turned me into a right cry-baby.' She managed a smile and took another deep shuddering breath.

'I think you're being very brave.' Hazel patted her shoulder. 'Carry on if you feel you can.'

Naomi nodded at Danny to say that she was ready to continue.

'I picked up the stick and turned to face him. I'd scraped my hands and the handle was sticky with blood. As he lunged for me, I rammed the stick in his face with all my strength. Ugh,' she shuddered, 'I can still feel the jolt of it and hear the gasping sounds he made. I knew that once I'd decided to do it, I'd got to really go for it: hard as I could: half measures would only make him angry. One moment he was reaching for me, the next, he was down groaning and spitting blood. It was awful, so much blood. I dropped the stick and ran back towards the station. Then I met Philip.'

'What did he do?'

'He said we had to get away from there; said it was too danger- ous; said a train might come. I was so weak and trembly he had to support me. He lifted me over the electric rail, and we went back along the bank to the station. He almost had to carry me. I was so shaky, I suppose it was shock, and my feet and hands were so painful.'

'You didn't go back to Simms?'

'Philip insisted that we must get away from there as quick- ly as we could.'

'Leaving the injured Simms on the railway where he was in danger of being hit by a train?'

'Philip didn't know what I'd done.'

'He didn't know Simms was injured and in danger?'

'No.'

'But you did Naomi.'

'I didn't even consider it. That never crossed my mind. I just wanted to be far away from him. You know what he'd tried before.'

'Would you tell us why you and Philip left town like that?'

'I told Philip that I would have to leave because Justin would be looking to get even with me. He tried to talk me out of it; tried to get me to go to you but I said no. The Simms family has already got at us in a big way. Mum and Dad say they've told you all about that. Anyway, Philip said he'd come with me and away we went. I was too frightened to stay here. I didn't think you could protect me from them. I still don't, come to that. They are wicked people and they always seem to do just what they want.'

Hazel put her hand in her pocket and produced a card.

'We just don't have the manpower to provide twenty-four-hour protection, but we'll do our best to keep an eye on things. If you feel threatened, ring this number. Now Danny?'

The police officers exchanged places, Danny settled next to Naomi and they read through the statement, together stopping occasionally for one or the other to clarify a point. Eventually Danny sat back, flexing his fingers.

'That look okay to you?' He flattened out the paper and handed it over. Naomi frowned, concentrating on her last read through.

'Fine. That's just how it was.' Taking Danny's pen, she signed in the space he indicated and sat back, relieved to have it finished.

'There – we're all done.' Hazel stood and was smoothing down her skirt when Mrs. Gibbs appeared with tea and biscuits. She smiled as Danny, anticipating her request, drew the low table nearer for her to set down the tray. Mr. Gibbs joined them. He sat next to Naomi and put his arm round her. She leant against him, her head on his shoulder.

'What happens now?' he asked, as his wife helped the officers to tea and offered biscuits.

'We continue our investigation. There are still loose ends to tie in. The boy was injured in two incidents. Once with the hockey stick when chasing Naomi and again when he was struck on the temple.' Hazel paused to sip her tea.

'Is Naomi in trouble? That's what we want to know.'

'Well her statement tallies with the others we've taken. There is no doubt that Simms was chasing her with evil intent. This is corroborated in statements given by his companions, several of whom heard him say what he was going to do to Naomi when he caught her: that is sexual intercourse with or without her consent. The blood on the hockey stick, if it's Naomi's blood, will support her claim that she struck the blow in the way she has described; self defence; last resort. The stone that caused the more serious and ultimately fatal blow bears traces from the boy's temple but no blood to match that on the hockey stick. It looks as though a blood test will confirm Naomi's account of things. We must of course take a statement from Philip Watkins and see how it fits with what we have so far. What would make life a lot easier is an eyewitness but given the location and time of night I don't imagine one of those is going to turn up. As it is, it seems the only person who might have seen who struck that blow is dead.'

'You seem to be implying that young Philip might have done it?' Mr. Gibbs looked serious as he put this to Hazel.

'As I said just now, we need to see how his statement ties in.'

'You can't believe Philip did it!' Naomi was on her feet glaring furiously at Hazel.

'It's not a question of what we believe Naomi.' Hazel's voice was calm, and she chose her words with care. 'Who or what gets ruled out or ruled in depends on the evidence we can gather, circumstantial or otherwise. We have to bear in mind that you and Philip have had the best part of two days in which to, shall we say, tailor your story. Please understand that I am not saying you've done so. I'm saying that it will be apparent to all who come into contact with this case that you've had that opportunity. It's my job to show, if I can, whether or not that is what happened. For what it's worth I don't believe for one moment that Philip would do such a thing, neither do I believe that you would stand by him if he did, but if you quote me on that I'll say that you misunderstood me.'

'I wish this bloody business was over and done with. I can't stand it anymore!' Naomi fled the room, slamming the door behind her.

'Stay there Brian. I'll go to her.' Mrs. Gibbs put down her cup and hurried after her daughter.

'I'm so sorry Mr. Gibbs. I do understand that Naomi has been under extreme pressure, but this is after all a murder enquiry: a most serious matter. We're doing our best to reconstruct the events of Thursday night and we must consider each piece of evidence with utmost care. If we're going to present conclusions, we must be seen to have been rigorous in our enquiries. Please don't think we are heartless. We have to be impartial and we have a job to do. Please accept my apologies for upsetting Naomi. I certainly didn't come here this evening to do that. After seeing how deeply this has affected her, I feel that she needs counselling. It can be arranged through Victim Support. Perhaps you'd like to talk it over as a family. Let me know what you decide.'

'Thank you, Sergeant. I'm quite sure that you didn't mean to upset Naomi and we fully appreciate the fact that you have a difficult job to do. We believe that you will get at the rights and wrongs of this business. As you say Naomi's been under a lot of stress. Bearing that in mind I shan't apologise for her outburst. I don't suppose it will be her last. She's been through a lot of grief at the hands of that bloody family; we all have.'

'Thank you, Mr. Gibbs. My heart goes out to her. I only hope that once this is all sorted, she'll be able to put it all behind her. I'm sure that you and Mrs. Gibbs will give her every support. You'll let me know about the counselling?'

'You can be sure of that Sergeant. I'll see you out.'

***

Later that evening Philip rang to see how Naomi had fared with the police. Her mother told him that she had become upset and had gone to bed.

'Have you given them your statement Philip?' Mrs. Gibbs sounded concerned.

'Yes. They came to me after they left you. They didn't mention anything about Naomi being upset. Is she okay? What was it that upset her?'

'How did you get on with them?'

'Seemed to go all right I suppose. They wanted to know what I'd seen of course but, as I explained, he'd knocked me down and by the time I was back on my feet Naomi was running back towards me. She told me afterwards about how she'd whacked him, but I didn't see a thing; wish I had; at least then I could have backed up her story.'

'How were they with that?'

'Fine, as far as I could tell. I certainly got the feeling that there's nothing for us to worry about.'

'Well that sounds more encouraging. I'll tell her when she wakes up. Maybe it'll set her mind at rest.'

'You didn't say what it was that upset her?'

'I think she felt that she might have got you into trouble. She's not thinking straight which is hardly surprising after all that's happened to her. I'm sure she'll tell you all about it tomorrow.'

'Right. I'll say good night then Mrs. Gibbs; see you tomorrow?'

'Yes of course. Good night Philip,' she replaced the receiver.

'I don't know,' she said to no one in particular, 'he seems happy enough, but I wonder if he's got hold of the right end of the stick.'

'You know Philip.' Her husband had entered the room and grasped immediately the meaning behind her words. 'That young man is the only person I've ever met whose cup is never less than half full.'

He moved across the room and placed an arm round his wife's shoulders.

'You know I wish we'd never moved up here. We'd have been saved a mountain of grief if we had stayed put. We were doing all right in Kent.'

She stood back and looked directly into his eyes.

'You can't take that tack Brian. We were living from one Final Demand to the next if you remember. At the time, it was a perfect move. It was a promotion, a big salary increase just when we needed it; John in his third year at university, Lucy about to start and Naomi finishing junior school. It seemed Heaven sent; you remember. We weren't to know that all this was going to blow up. Don't you dare let Naomi hear you talking like that, she feels guilty enough as it is.'

'She's no need. She's done nothing wrong.'

'Of course, she hasn't but she still feels as if it is somehow her fault. She told me so earlier when she ran upstairs. I do feel that policewoman could have been a bit more sensitive.'

'She's got her job to do. I thought she was pretty sympathetic once she'd laid it on the line.'

'Well we weren't there during the interview, who knows what she said then. Our little girl is so upset it's breaking my heart.'

***

Saturday. 22:30

'I want to know what's in their statements, and I want to know soon.' Joshua paused to listen for a moment then said, 'Don't put obstacles in my way Browning. We snap our fingers, and you jump – just like always. Or perhaps you want to terminate our little agreement?' He listened again with a smirk on his face. 'I thought not. How is the good Mrs. Browning these days? You do as you're told, and it remains our secret eh.' He laughed as he dropped the telephone into its cradle.

★★★

Inspector Browning sat with his elbows on the desk and his face in his hands. It had gone on for so long but, as always, he could not find the courage to end it. His marriage and his career would be finished. He loved his wife and he longed to tell her all about his past indiscretion, but he could not face the thought that she probably wouldn't forgive him. He knew she would take their son and leave him.

He'd become friendly with Arthur Simms when he'd moved to the town some ten years ago. He had been rather flattered by that first invitation to a round of golf and had become involved socially before a colleague had warned him that he was mixing with a well-known villain. Even so he had accepted an invitation to a party and could not see how he could get out of it without causing offence. His wife was in the local hospital having their child and Simms knew that he was on his own for a few days. He had suggested that he come along and have a little fling because once the baby came home it would be all nappies and sleepless nights. It had all seemed so harmless.

He remembered going to Simms' house and being made welcome by all the family. They had looked after him, made sure his champagne glass was always topped up and that he had plenty to eat.

'You must soak up the alcohol son; can't have you getting legless eh? Not with you being a policeman.'

Bitterly, he recalled Simms' beaming face and his own stupidity in allowing the convivial atmosphere to overcome his good judgement.

The next part of the evening was less clear. He remembered going on to the casino and feeling embarrassed at the large sums of money that Simms had kept pressing on him, refusing to take no for an answer.

He remembered being in a lift and in a hotel room with gilt numbers on the door and, to his shame, the two scantily clad girls who had removed his clothes and then their own before pleasuring him through the night in ways he had only read about.

He had woken alone in that room with a fearsome hangover and as he dressed, he had made up his mind that it had to stop. He had been bloody stupid, but it was time to tell Simms that the friendship could not continue that it was inappropriate.

He remembered being welcomed into the house again and making a terrible hash of trying to extricate himself without giving offence. That was when they had sat him down, given him a drink and showed him the video.

Simms manner towards him had then become cool and business like.

'You do us the odd favour now and again son. That's all. What if your missus or your bosses were to see that disgusting film of what you got up to with those two naughty little scrubbers? Can't you just see the headlines? Policeman in threesome sex romp while wife gives birth in hospital. You'd be famous lad, famous as a divorced ex-copper. Now here's a little something to be going on with. There'll be lots more. You can count on it.' He had pushed a fat envelope towards him, and they had watched for a long minute, waiting for him to pick it up.

He had no choice but to pick it up. Well there had been the choice between long term misery or instant ruin. He had chosen misery.

The familiar waves of self-disgust engulfed him as he squirmed in abject despair and, not for the first time, contemplated suicide. It was the coward's way. But then he was a coward, wasn't he?

★★★

CHAPTER TWELVE

'You're a fucking good mate to me Baz.' Sid's speech was slurred, and he was trying extremely hard, but not very successfully, to focus on his friend. He reached out, grasped Barry's sleeve, and shook it to make sure he had his attention. 'I mean, we're such a fucking good team. You turn up with a job and we just go and do it – no sweat. Bloody perfection: that's what it is, bloody perfection. Then we come back here, and we always have a noggin or two of the Irish and a bloody good laugh eh. Bloody marvellous Baz. You're such a fucking good mate.' He downed yet another large whiskey as Barry, still sipping his first, waited patiently.

'You haven't got much to say for yourself. You okay Baz?' Sid peered drunkenly at his companion. He swayed in his chair and then he tried to screw his features into an expression of concern for his friend, but his facial muscles seemed to have turned to rubber and were now beyond his control. The result was comic.

Barry spluttered, trying to suppress his laughter. 'I'm fine mate, just a bit sleepy. Come on don't just sit there like a bloody gargoyle. Drink up. Your glass is empty.'

'I don't mind if I do,' Sid giggled. 'Gargoyle,' he chuckled as he tried to pour himself another. 'Oh shit! Look at that,' he exclaimed as he fumbled, and the spilt whiskey soaked into his trousers and ran down his leg onto the carpet. Barry reached forward, took the bottle, and upended it over Sid's tumbler.

'Cor, that's a fucking big one Baz, ain't you having any more?'

'I'm okay Sid. I've another bottle in the car; don't worry yourself.'

'You're a fucking good mate Baz,' mumbled Sid as he tried to clink his glass with Barry's. 'Here's to the best mate a bloke could wish for,' he slurred, missing Barry's glass altogether and lurching half out of his chair. He stared up at Barry. 'I'm so pissed I can't stand up,' he chortled. He slid the rest of the way to the floor and sat blinking, trying to gather his fuddled wits. 'I need to piss Baz. Give us a hand.'

'Come on then just lean on me.' He got Sid onto his feet, supported him to the bathroom and steadied him while Sid fumbled ineffectively with his fly.

'I can't do it mate,' Sid mumbled, a note of panic in his voice. 'Quick. You've got to help me. Quick Baz. I'm going to piss myself.'

'I reckon you'd better drop your trousers and sit on the loo mate; state you're in you're going to piss everywhere.'

'Yeah well I've still got to get my zip undone. Why ain't you helping? I'm having an accident here.'

Barry reached down reluctantly and partially drew down Sid's zip.

'Thanks mate. I just said you're a fucking good mate, didn't I? We aim to please,' Sid giggled. 'You get it? We aim to please.' This set him off into a fit of nasal sniggering as he tottered on rubbery legs trying to undo his belt. He managed this eventually, thanks to Barry's support, and flopped onto the lavatory seat.

'I'll wait in the lounge mate. Give us a shout if you want anything.'

Barry waited outside the bathroom door listening as Sid pee'd into the bowl.

'Yeah Baz,' called Sid. 'You have another drink mate. I'll be out in a minute.'

'I reckon you will at that,' muttered Barry. 'Out like a bloody light.'

'Christ, I'm going like a bloody horse in here,' mumbled Sid. He began to sing, 'horsey, horsey don't you stop,' he then lapsed into a sequence of snorting giggles which were gradually diminishing until a resounding baritone fart started him off again. 'Hey Baz, what about that then?' he managed to shout between bouts of wheezing laughter. 'My mum always said I was musical.' This last outburst of coarse laughter dwindled gradually into a series of soft whinnies and finally petered out.

Silence.

Barry waited until he heard Sid snoring then he stepped into the bathroom and studied the sleeping form. He shook him gently, then with more vigour. There was no response from Sid as he slumped to the floor.

'You won't call me Baz again, you drunken little sod,' muttered Barry as he drew on a pair of latex gloves.

He turned on both bath taps and began to strip the clothing from Sid's recumbent form. When Sid was naked, he picked him up and lowered him into the warm water. There was no reaction from Sid. Barry then produced a large bottle of white tablets and a cutthroat razor.

'Come on mate,' he said, sitting on the side of the bath and tilting Sid's head.

'Swallow these. They'll make you feel better. That's it; good boy; here's another, that's the way.'

He continued coaxing and encouraging in this way, pausing to give a little water from time to time, until the bottle was half empty: Sid swallowing, making soft little sounds of acquiescence.

Barry placed the bottle on the floor and drew a deep breath.

Taking the open razor in his right hand, he reached across and grasped Sid's left and held it, palm upwards, just under the water.

He placed the sharp edge against Sid's wrist, held his breath, but before he could go on, he began to shake. He was no stranger to violence, and he did not like Sid, but he wanted to throw down the razor and run away. He willed his hands to stop shaking. 'Come on,' he muttered to himself. 'Get a bloody grip; it's a piece of piss – done it before – no sweat.'

'Baz?'

Barry almost dropped the razor with shock. Sid's brown eyes were wide open, staring. For a moment he looked quizzically at Barry then his eyelids drooped, and his head flopped to one side. This galvanised Barry and he found the will to dig the sharp blade in and draw it across sharply. Even though he was prepared for it, the powerful surge of blood shocked him with its force and quantity. He pushed the pumping wrist back under as the bath water began to turn a rapidly darkening red.

As the flow of blood began to diminish, Barry placed the handle of the razor in Sid's right hand and closed the fingers round it. They relaxed immediately and allowed the razor to disappear to the bottom of the bath. Barry was gagging with the rank smell and staring in fascination at the blood-spattered walls. That first powerful gush had hit the tiles with such force that blood was splashed far and wide across the bathroom, much of it on himself. It tracked slowly down between the tiles like angular congealing veins forming sticky puddles on the edge of the bath before continuing down into the crimson water. Barry shuddered. There was a rumbling release of air, he saw the bubbles rising between Sid's legs and turned away in disgust as the stink of it filled the small room.

'Still talking through your arse Sid,' he muttered as he hurried for the door, 'and having the last bloody word as usual. Still, that really was the last word this time.'

He returned to the living room and picked up the empty whiskey bottle. He left the glasses where they were. If ever he was questioned about it, he would say that he had called round to try and cheer up his mate who had been a bit down lately. We had a few drinks and a laugh and then I went home: simple enough. He placed the bottle on the floor by the bath, together with the smaller one containing the remainder of the tablets, let himself out of the flat and walked across the road to his old Ford Orion.

As he drove away, his hands began to tremble, and he found it difficult to concentrate on driving the car. There was the feeling that he had overlooked something important nagging at the back of his mind. He promised himself a stiff drink when he got home. 'Got to get rid of these clothes and have a shower,' he said aloud. He shivered with the cold and turned the heater on full blast. He felt no remorse for the passing of his garrulous partner in crime.

He failed to notice the car that drew out of the cul-de-sac and followed at a distance.

★★★

'I want you to go up there and make your way to 24 Grove Walk. She's expecting you.'

'You did say I was to take care of Luke, Mr. Edmonds.'

'That's all in hand Billy. Now Mrs. Driscoll and her boy reside at 21 Grove Walk so by posting someone at 24 we can keep tabs on them; make sure they're okay.'

'You said she, Mr. Edmonds?'

'Yes, Miranda, wife of Huw Jenkins; useful bloke. He's inside at present, doing someone a favour as it happens. He's actually doing someone else's bird: taking the rap, as the Americans say. Suffice to say he's being very well paid for his trouble. He'll finish before too long and go home to a nice little nest egg: set up for life really. What's really important to us just now though is his address: a rather nice coincidence: perfect spot from which to observe any comings and goings that might pose a threat to our friends the Driscoll's. I bet they don't know that their near neighbour is a jailbird.

Now you get yourself up there P.D.Q. It's all arranged, Dan and the others will meet you. They will be staying close by. Take your weapon. If the Simms make a move, they'll be tooled up, so we have to be ready for that: meet fire with firepower, so to speak. You won't be the only one carrying.'

'Right, I'll get to it then. I can be under way in half an hour.'

'Good lad; quick as you can eh.'

'Yes Mr. Edmonds.'

★★★

Billy was quite stunned when the front door opened and the attractive, dark haired woman stood there regarding him, a seductive smile on her face as she quite openly appraised him. He reached out to shake hands and introduce himself when she took his hand in hers and drew him inside, pushing the door to with her foot.

'Come in lovely boy,' she murmured in a husky Welsh voice, and kissed him on the mouth.

Billy was at once her slave.

They left a trail of clothing on the stairs as they made their way to her bedroom and had made love twice before she asked his name.

'My name is Megan but it's so bloody plebby. I prefer Miranda. It's more exotic, you know, mysterious, don't you think?'

Billy agreed wholeheartedly as she rolled on top of him again.

★★★

Barry reversed into his drive at last, yanked on the handbrake and, after some fumbling with his keys, pushed the front door open and made straight for the drinks cabinet. He poured a generous measure, knocked half of it back at once, grateful for the warming spirit as it smoothed his ragged nerves. He drank the remainder more slowly, relaxing as the old brandy warmed him with its magic.

'Never had a bad go like that before; must be getting old I reckon. Still it's all squared off now and we're in the clear.' He smiled to himself as he poured another large brandy and settled back in his armchair, congratulating himself on a job well done and sipping at his drink. He felt comfortably at ease: content.

★★★

The ringing telephone woke him. It was Luke.
    'All right Barry?'
    'Fine mate, fine, all taken care of, no bother.'
    'No loose ends?'
    'No; all tied up nicely.'

'Christ Barry, you're a cool sod. I don't know how you do it. Anyway, let's have a celebratory drink. You've done bloody well there.'

'Another time mate. I'm really clapped out – cream crackered.'

'Come on you miserable bugger. You getting past it or what?'

'No, really mate. I'm pretty pissed as it is. I need to get to bed. I'll be fine tomorrow. We could have a drink then.'

'Go to bed then you bloody wet blanket; well done; see you soon.'

'Yeah. Cheers mate.'

The desire to pee had become urgent during this conversation so he hurried upstairs on wobbly legs intending to use the bathroom and then turn in. Once he arrived at the toilet, he decided to sit down to pee rather than try to stand in his drunken state.

'Just like old Sidney,' he smiled to himself as he sat down. His eyes closed and his head fell forward. He recovered with a start. 'Can't go to sleep on the loo,' he muttered, 'got to have a shower.' He was preparing to rise when he saw it. 'Christ no!' There on the back of the door, where it had hung for years, was his razor strop. He had meant to take it with him to Sid's flat. He cursed his stupidity. 'Nice one Barry,' he said aloud. 'You stupid bloody sod!'

He pictured the scene when Sid's body was discovered. All the circumstances would point nicely to suicide but then some smart-arse copper would say, 'If that's his razor, where's he sharpen it?'

So what? Sid could have got hold of a cutthroat in any one of a dozen or so second-hand shops in the locality. He could have had it for years. For all anyone knows it could have belonged to his grandad. All of this seemed woefully weak to Barry because he knew that he had slipped up. His self-confidence was shaken.

'Who are you trying to convince?' he asked himself. 'Been enough balls-ups lately. The proper place for that strop is on the back of Sid's bathroom door.'

What to do now? He would have to go back. It was the only thing to do.

He had no keys to Sid's first floor flat, but he was fairly sure the rim lock would pose no real problem. If the front door was a no-go Sid's bedroom window was always open a crack, so he had no real worries about getting back in. It should be simple enough to climb onto the coal bunker and then onto the roof of the outside toilet. The trouble was he was rather the worse for wear – likely to fall off the roof and create a right ruckus. He clattered about the house in his panic to get ready. At least there was no wife to complain about his racket. She had left him years ago. He un-hooked the strop and unscrewed the hook from the bathroom door, intending to refix it in Sid's bathroom.

His biggest fear was that of being stopped by the police and breathalysed – he knew that he was well above the limit. Driving was going to be difficult because his co-ordination was all over the place. He brewed a pint of strong coffee and drank it down. It was the best he could do. He checked to make sure that he had his penknife, it had a gimlet to start the hook, and he stepped out into the cold early morning. His hands were trembling again.

A car door closed with a soft clunk somewhere nearby, but the sound failed to impinge on Barry's troubled thoughts. He opened his car door, threw the strop onto the passenger seat, and had started to get in when he was seized suddenly from behind. His arms were pinioned, and he was handcuffed in a trice. There was no police caution though – there was no sound at all. As he strained against the cuffs, he discovered they were soft around his wrists – some kind of padding but he was held securely. His captor drew him backwards away from the car, forced him face down onto the unkempt lawn and held him there in an iron grip.

'Who are you? What do you want?' he asked, thoroughly frightened and ashamed of the tremor in his voice, as his silent attacker straddled him, forcing his face into the turf. There was no reply. He then felt the stinging pain as the needle went into his neck. This lent him strength but struggle as he might, there was nothing he could do – a gloved hand was clamped over his mouth, smothering his cries for help.

'Luke!'

This moment of lucidity was his last as he felt himself slip away and over the edge, tumbling down into the darkening pit of unconsciousness.

Once the injection had taken effect, Luke left him and gathered up the keys from where they had fallen. He raised the up and over garage door and, with some difficulty, he heaved Barry into a fireman's lift, carried him to the car and placed him in the driving seat, then, switching on the ignition, he was gratified to see that the petrol tank was over three quarters full. Reaching in over Barry's inert form he released the handbrake and strained hard to push the car into the garage. Stopping a few moments to check for twitching curtains or nocturnal passers by and to regain his breath, he unlocked the front door and was soon back with a pile of blankets. These he rolled neatly and placed on the floor parallel with the threshold but far enough inside to allow him to close the door when the time came. He produced several lengths of cord, which he looped under the rolled blankets and arranged so that they were evenly spaced across the width of the garage and both ends of each lay together outside about a yard beyond the threshold. He drew the door down partially as slowly and as quietly as possible. He checked all his preparations, adjusting where necessary.

Barry had fallen across the front seats, so Luke sat him up behind the wheel, removed the handcuffs, placed the syringe in his right hand and pressed the thumb against the plunger. The syringe dropped into Barry's lap as he fell sideways again. Luke lowered all four car windows and checked that the single window in the rear wall of the garage was shut firmly: there was no side door. He started the engine, stepped outside, then drew the door down the rest of the way until it clicked shut. He withdrew the lengths of cord from under the door, being careful to pull them evenly until the rolled blankets were all snug against the bottom of the door. Then he pulled gently on one end of each and withdrew them singly. Anyone trying to enter the garage would have to pull the door open and it would look as though Barry had pushed the blankets against the door from the inside. He stood listening. It was all quiet. He put his ear to the garage door and could hear the rumbling of the engine.

'Shouldn't take too long,' he murmured.

He checked his watch and decided it was not too late to pay his girlfriend a surprise visit.

★★★

CHAPTER THIRTEEN

Sunday morning

Mr. Edmonds sighed as he put down his knife and fork, dabbed at his lips with a napkin and picked up the telephone.

'Yes?' His displeasure on being disturbed at his Sunday breakfast came through loud and clear. It made his caller apprehensive.

'It's me Mr. Edmonds. Sorry to disturb you but you did say to ring if there were any developments.'

'Developments?' The level of rancour expressed in this single word did nothing to set Billy at his ease.

'The Filth have turned up at the Driscoll house.'

'And?' Resentment lingered but seemed to be diminishing.

'Well they've put a surveillance team in the house opposite, one's a woman, a white van just down the road which I guess is full of coppers and a bloke round the back. Do you want me to hang around now they're on the job?'

'You're at number 24?'

'Yes, came up last night as you said.'

'Scanner?'

'Loud and clear.'

Have you been outside since they arrived? Could they have seen you?

'No.'

'Right. Stay out of sight and watch what goes on. Where are Dan and the others?'

'Close by. A phone call will bring them in no time.'

'Out of sight?'

'Yes.'

'Tooled up?'

'Four of us altogether.'

'Do they know about the police presence?'

'No. I rang you straight away.'

'The thought occurs to me that the police might have heard a whisper that the Simms have got something going down and that they mean to pick them up when they make their move. The white van couldn't be the Simms could it?'

'That's a thought. I just assumed it was part of the police operation.'

'Bear it in mind Billy. We have received an answer from the Simms at last, but it was not um… helpful. It was very short, and I suppose one has to say that it amounts to a declaration of war. We expected something like this when their boy died of course. It's stiffened their resolve.'

'Well that was Luke's balls up, wasn't it?'

'He was picked up at his girlfriend's place last night and that's all been dealt with Billy; all done and dusted.'

'He's gone away then?'

'His personal possessions have gone from the flat and his car's gone, so I guess he must have Billy.'

'Any idea where?'

'It's not been decided what to do with him yet. His girlfriend was sent on ahead.'

'I see. They won't be coming back then?'

'I think we can say they're gone for good Billy.'

'I was looking forward to doing him Mr. Edmonds. He was an arrogant sod.'

'I know you were Billy but you're doing something far more useful. It won't go unnoticed, or unrewarded. Word's come down that they're pretty impressed with you. Now apprise your blokes of the situation there. They are to remain out of sight but ready to move quickly if required. You must all keep your wits about you. I don't have to remind you how important this is. Be vigilant Billy. In fact, call one of ours in to share the watch with you. We don't know how long this will take and you can't stay awake the whole time. The Simms might have a trick up their sleeve; we don't want to be caught napping. We can't assume that just because the police have come into the picture, that the Driscoll's are safe. It wouldn't be the first time a stake out has backfired.

In fact, this close police attention is a bloody nuisance: an un-welcome complication. If it were just the Simms, we could take them down very easily.'

'Yes Mr. Edmonds.'

'A word of warning Billy; no hanky panky with Miranda. She's very fond of a bit on the side but if Huw were to find out he'd do you permanent damage, no question. Now I have some favours to call in. Keep in touch.'

Billy replaced the receiver and winked at his temporary landlady.

'He says I'm to stay here Miranda and call one of the guys in to share the watch with me: that okay with you?'

'What do you think?' She stood up allowing her dressing gown to fall open and moved to take his hand.

'Choose someone tasty and I can work you in shifts,' she laughed.

She led him back upstairs to his chair in the bay window and sat him down. Then she straddled him and lowered herself onto his lap.

'There.' She put a hand behind his neck and kissed him hard on the mouth. 'You can keep me amused and do your watching at the same time eh. You've only to look over my shoulder see.'

'If I don't go blind first. I've had too much excitement al-ready. Anyway, I can't see past you. You're a big girl Miranda.'

'Don't give up on me Billy. Life is so dreary here on my own. I get so bloody randy.' Smiling broadly, she raised her arms above her head and gyrated her hips.

'Ooh … wicked. I don't know if I'm up to this, too much red wine. When's your man up for parole?' Billy leant back, en-joying the moment.

'Next September so we don't need to rush at it.'

Billy laughed out loud. 'You're a bloody comic you are.'

She took his hands and placed them on her breasts.

'I hear he's the jealous type,' smiled Billy. 'What if he finds out?'

'How would he? He's banged up bloody miles away. Anyway, he can't expect a lusty girl like me to live here like a bloody nun, can he? You can bet your life he's not going short.'

'He's inside for fuck's sake.'

'That won't stop him getting his end away.'

'What? You mean …?'

'Come on Billy. Don't be so bloody naïve. All those hairy blokes locked up together, it's hormone bloody city. He'll have some blue-eyed boy there with his trousers down.'

'So old Huw's not above putting his key in the back door?'

'You better believe it. Old Huw goes for any keyhole that takes his fancy.'

'Doesn't that worry you?'

'Worry me? Why should it worry me? He can look after himself if someone gets jealous. He's a tough cookie.'

'That's not what I mean. I'm talking about AIDS Miranda.'

'We always took precautions. It was a bloody shock when I first found out, but I've tested negative and as you know I don't do unprotected sex so don't worry. I know he's a toe rag. When he comes home, I'll just have to try hard to make him go straight if you follow my meaning.'

'Well they'd better build him up a bit before you get your hands on him. How come you fancy such a little bloke anyway?'

'He's not little all over Billy. He might surprise you.'

'I'd rather he surprised you.'

She giggled and murmured, 'Come on my lover,' as she felt his swelling response to her slow sensual surges. She reached into her dressing gown pocket, brought out a condom and removed the packaging. Billy groaned ecstatically as her practised fingers unrolled the latex sheath onto his erect penis.

'Did you do that with one hand?' he whispered in astonishment.

'You have to pay attention Billy Boy,' she chuckled, pulling him closer.

He made no reply, apart from involuntary gasps of pleasure, being lost in the intense delights of his quickening excitement.

'Oh,' she whispered. 'I love you young blokes. A cup of tea and a bit of toast and you're all ready to go again.'

★★★

'Good morning Matty. To what do we owe this privilege?' Sergeant Ellis, standing with hands turned outwards against the edge; of the counter and his stomach held in, studied the unkempt visitor.

'Good morning to you Sergeant. I er ... I need to speak to someone.'

'Anyone in particular Matty?'

'I'm not too sure Sergeant. I'm not at all used to this sort of thing you know.'

'What sort of thing's that then?'

'Well it's just that I happened to see something unpleasant the other night and it's preying on my mind rather: truth is it has rather upset me. I thought I might discuss it with one of your chaps: get their thoughts on it you know.'

'It's a police matter, is it?'

'Well yes, I think so Sergeant. But, as I say, I don't know the form in these things.'

'Would you like to tell me about it? Perhaps I can set your mind at rest Matty.'

'Well please don't be offended Sergeant but I thought, you know, someone more ... er ... someone more senior perhaps?'

'Sounds serious Matty,' Sergeant Ellis' eyes twinkled at Matty's embarrassment. 'How about if you tell me what you saw, and I'll tell you if someone more senior might find it of interest.'

Matty, suspecting a leg-pull, paused to give Sergeant Ellis a searching look before deciding to go ahead. Sergeant Ellis barely managed to keep a straight face.

'It was on Thursday night. I was down on the railway bank. There's this hut by the track where I sometimes spend the night you know when I can't face the walk home.'

'Go on.' The twinkle and the bantering tone were gone. Matty had the Sergeant's full attention.

'I saw a pretty young woman running along the track: most odd.' Matty shook his head. 'Two chaps were coming up behind.

The big one knocked the other one down and continued the chase. She fell and he almost had her when damn me, she bashed him with, of all things, a bloody hockey stick. Down he went like the proverbial ton of bricks and off she ran; perhaps I should say hobbled; she was obviously finding the going painful.'

'Hold on Matty. You've got something important there. You're absolutely right. This is definitely a matter for someone more senior.'

He beckoned to a constable, 'Show this gentleman to Interview Room One and see what you can do about a mug of tea and some biscuits. You go along with the Constable Matty and I'll arrange for someone to come and talk to you: someone more senior eh.' He gave Matty a conspiratorial wink. He was about to ring through to CID when the constable returned with Matty who was looking rather shaken.

'He won't go in Sarge; says he's frightened.'

'I'd rather not Sergeant. It's such a very stark room; makes one extremely nervous; claustrophobic's the only word for it.'

Matty became agitated. He took objects from his pockets, examined them closely and returned them as if he had mislaid something special. He looked everywhere except at the two policemen.

'I think perhaps I ought to go. This is not turning out the way I thought it would at all. You want me to go in there. Why? I've done nothing wrong: nothing at all. It's all so distressing; my nerves won't stand it. I can't go through it all again. I must go outside.'

Matty's face was pale; beads of sweat had formed on his brow: his face took on a waxy look.

'Now, now Matty,' Sergeant Ellis placed a gentle hand on the old tramp's shoulder.

'Just take a few deep breaths old son. That's it, calm yourself. We know you've done nothing wrong. You're not in any kind of trouble Matty; in fact, we're grateful to you for coming in with your information. It looks as though it might be especially important. Now how about if the constable takes you along to the canteen? It's not how we usually do things, but I think we have to treat this as a special case. Have a nice cup of tea and a bite to eat and I'll arrange for an officer to take your statement. How would that suit you?'

'Canteen eh.' Matty brightened up. His colour began to improve almost immediately. 'Yes. That would suit me very nicely. Would they do me some bacon and eggs d'you think? Fried bread? A grilled tomato or two?'

'Now constable, you've heard the gentleman's order. See what you can do.'

Sergeant Ellis was pleased with himself at having won Matty round so easily.

'The canteen Sarge? You sure?' The constable looked aghast.

'It'll be okay son. Let me worry about it.'

The constable, looking peeved, led the now smiling Matty away towards the canteen as Sergeant Ellis picked up the telephone. He explained what had happened and was gratified to hear Hazel Blissett's shriek of, 'Yes!' when he told her what Matty claimed to have seen.

'You've put him in the canteen you say Bert? I don't think that'll go down too well with the troops.'

'I had to do something quick Hazel. He was for the off: no messing. As soon as he saw the inside of the Interview Room, he turned the colour of putty and got ready to leave. I thought it best to hang on to him in view of what he'd told me.'

'You were right. I'll go down there and persuade him to come to my office; tell him it's more private; better suited for taking such an important statement.'

'He'll want to bring his eggs and bacon Hazel; you ready for that?'

'I can cope Bert, thanks.'

He hung up, wondering if she would be able to cope with Matty's distinctive body odours.

★★★

Fifteen minutes later Harry Moss strode in through the main door wearing a wide smile.

'Morning Bert. Looks as though we might have an eyewitness then. Hazel tells me that he claims to have seen both attacks on the Simms boy.'

'I knew he'd seen the girl Sir. He started to tell me all about it. That's when I got on to Hazel.'

'Well done you. It could button things up nicely. We've been a bit stymied to tell the truth. Let's hope this moves us forward eh,' He said, leaning forward and lowering his voice. 'Might give Chief Superintendent Jessop something to smile about eh?'

Sergeant Ellis shrugged his shoulders keeping his expression blank but closing one eye.

'I'm too close to my pension to make mutinous noises about the governor,' he whispered.

Harry clapped him on the shoulder, turned away and was off up the stairs two at a time in his haste to get to the CID suite.

'You'll need to keep your coat on Sir,' the Sergeant called after him.

'Oh. Why's that?' Inspector Moss paused on the staircase looking puzzled.

'Because if I know Hazel, she'll have all the windows open by now.'

'Why on earth would she do that? It's November Sergeant. Hazel hates the cold.'

Receiving no reply, he shook his head and resumed his athletic ascent of the stairway.

Sergeant Ellis smiled to himself as he lowered his gaze to the Sunday newspaper.

★★★

Philip called on Naomi after lunch and, as the day was clear and bright, they decided on a brisk walk. Her mood improved considerably when he told her about the police visit to his house.

'They seemed very laid back you know. I'm sure they're not gunning for you. They just need to find out what happened. I wish I'd seen the action – I'd be able to confirm your statement.' He squeezed her hand.

'I got the impression they were gunning for you last night, but I was overwrought. I shouted at her and stormed out in a right strop. I was so bloody angry.' Naomi's troubled expression returned.

'Never mind. It's Sunday. Let's relax and go for a coffee. We can't change anything by going on about it.'

They waited for a gap in the traffic and crossed the road.

'I'm afraid it'll have to be Tony's. Everywhere else is closed.'

'That's fine with me. It's good coffee actually.' She pulled his arm. 'You're such a snob Watkins. Tony's is okay.'

'It's certainly popular. Let's hope we can find a table.'

★★★

They sat drinking their coffee and Philip was forced to concede that it was rather good. He was impressed, having expected some sort of bland milky concoction with a pretentious name. He looked surprised when Naomi announced that she had decided to go back to work the following day.

'We must both go back. It'll take our minds off this awful business – at least for some of the time.' She reached for his hand, smiling. 'What do you think?'

'You're right. I was coming round to the idea myself, but I wasn't sure that you'd feel up to it just yet.'

'I'll be fine. They're a good lot in the office. They won't pester me if I say I don't want to talk about it. How about you?'

'There's only the three of us. We don't talk that much. They love football – hate cricket: I'm the opposite.'

'You never said. It sounds pretty grim.'

'No. It's okay really. We tolerate each other's little foibles. The work can be pretty demanding though. I'll have a hefty back-log I expect. Who'd be a trainee accountant? I don't think I can face a lifetime in accountancy.'

'You'll have to tell them where you've been.'

'Yes. There's a thought. I might get the sack: happy release. Only joking,' he grinned as he saw the dismay on her face. 'Come on. Cheer up. What would you like for Christmas?'

'Oh don't. I haven't even thought about Christmas yet. I wish that Christmas were all we had to worry about though. Wouldn't that be a relief,' she added with a smile.

They held hands across the table.

★★★

CHAPTER FOURTEEN

Monday evening

Naomi left the office and descended the stairs at the end of a busy day back at work. There had been no difficult moments, no references to her absence and she had enjoyed being back among her colleagues with plenty to occupy her mind. She was smiling as she pushed through the double doors out to the car park. Philip had 'phoned that morning to see how she was and to wish her a happy day, back in the office. The security lights snapped on, illuminating the parking area as she walked towards her car. She was miles away thinking about Philip and how much she had come to love him. He was a bit old fashioned with his cricket and three-piece suits and he came across as a bit of a snob sometimes, but she had come to realise how dependable he was and how he made her feel safe. She had even got as far as wondering if she might become Mrs. Watkins one day when, just as she thumbed her remote control to unlock the car, a young woman carrying a clipboard stepped out in front of her.

'God, you gave me a scare jumping out like that.'

'I am sorry.' The young woman looked so contrite that Naomi regretted her brusque reaction. 'I wonder if you would spare me a few minutes to complete a consumer survey?'

'I've had a bit of a long day actually, so if you don't mind, I'll pass.'

She studied the woman, saw she was attractive with long dark hair, wore an expensive long woollen coat and carried a soft tan leather handbag on a shoulder strap.

'Have you got permission to do your interviews here?' she asked.

'No, I haven't but it's been a bit of a washout today. I thought this might be worth a try. If I don't complete any questionnaires, I don't get paid.' She looked cold and dispirited.

'I'm sorry but I am rather tired. My boss will be out soon, and he'll probably take a dim view of your being here.'

'Okay I'll move on. I'm sorry I made you jump.' She gave a rueful smile. 'I need to get to a Post Office before they close. Is there one nearby?'

Naomi walked forward until they could see round the corner and pointed to the far end of the car park.

'You see where that red brick building juts out? Well just beyond it there's an alley leading to the High Street. Turn left at the end and the Post Office is just along on the left.'

'Thanks for your help. I'm sorry I troubled you.'

'It's okay. I hope you have better luck in the High Street.'

As the young woman walked away, Naomi noted that her shoes looked expensive too.

She walked back to her car, opened the door, and swung herself into the driving seat. Suddenly, as she was about to insert her ignition key, a powerful hand gripped her just above the knee with such force that she cried out in shock and the pain, as the fingers tightened their grasp almost causing her to pass out.

'Please. Please. You're hurting me,' she managed to gasp. 'What do you want?' She almost fainted again as the grip on her knee intensified.

'Rule number one,' said her tormentor. 'No questions.'

He relaxed his grip slightly and she tried to gather her wits as the pain began to diminish. He'd obviously entered the car while the young woman had diverted her attention. How could she have been so stupid? She'd been so determined to keep her guard up.

'Close your door.'

She managed to let her bag slip to the ground unnoticed as she pulled the door to.

'Seatbelt.'

She drew the seatbelt across and as she looked down to clip it in place she shuddered and suppressed a gasp of horror as she saw the long gleaming blade laid across his lap.

'Start the car.'

The interior light went out as she inserted her key and twisted it. The engine fired first time, as always, and settled into a busy tick-over.

'In a moment I'll tell you to drive off. You'll follow my directions. Don't try any heroics or I'll kill you where you sit. Understand?'

He increased the pressure on her knee until she gasped, 'Yes. Yes! I understand! I understand!'

'I'll keep my hand there the whole time: hurts, doesn't it?'

'Yes,' she replied through clenched teeth.

'Drive out and turn left – not too fast – not too slow.' His grip relaxed, and she experienced a wave of relief as the crushing pain receded.

As they approached the exit the bright security lights went out and in the sudden darkness the frightening realisation struck her that she was disappearing effectively. Her abductor could kill her and dispose of her body and her loved ones would not have the slightest idea what had happened to her. She would just cease to be. She felt weak inside at the proximity of that long-bladed knife.

If only she had waited and walked down with Mr Fellowes.

★★★

Philip walked into the car park and looked around for Naomi's car. Failing to find it in its usual space, he walked round the staff parking area but soon realised it was not there. He finished the short search back where he had begun and was about to leave, thinking she had gone home early, when the security lights snapped on to reveal her boss in the act of locking the door.

'Hello Philip. You've just missed her.'

'Good evening Mr. Fellowes. How was she today?'

'I think she was okay. She seemed perfectly happy. Actually I'd 'phoned round the staff and asked them not to enquire about her unpleasant experience in case she became upset. I'm sure no one mentioned it. They're a good lot.'

'Thanks. That was thoughtful of you.'

'She's a lovely girl Philip; lights up the whole office with her personality. We've got to look after her. What a wretched business eh. Let's hope it soon gets sorted out and she can put it all behind her. Trouble is that family is well known for taking the law, as they see it, into their own hands. They were clients of mine years ago and I have to say I was mightily relieved when young Jackson offered them a better deal and they left me. Even so there was a great deal of unpleasantness over a refund. I paid up in the end. You wouldn't believe the threats they made against my family and myself. The police didn't want to know of course.'

'I hadn't even heard of them until all this blew up,' said Philip, 'but I'm hearing plenty now – they're like the Mafia it seems to me, too clever for the police. Do you think there's bribery at work there?'

'Oh, I wouldn't know about that sort of thing Philip. You may have hit the nail on the head of course but it's not an accusation I would care to make. I must get on. Nice talking to you and let's hope Naomi is soon back to her old self. Can I drop you somewhere?'

'No. Thanks all the same. I'll enjoy the walk. Good night Mr. Fellowes.'

Mr Fellowes gave a friendly wave as his Volvo rolled towards the exit. Philip set off at a brisk walk. He would have his meal, catch up with some of his work and then ring Naomi to ask her about her day.

★★★

She had attempted to drive through the town without lights in order to draw the attention of passers-by, but her passenger soon noticed and gave her knee a warning squeeze.

'Don't annoy me Naomi,' he threatened. You'll be sorry if I get rough.'

He directed her out onto the A12, and she drove on in silence. If her handbag was found, she thought, it would at least let people know that something was wrong, but it wouldn't tell them where she had been taken.

'Take the second exit,' he said as they approached a roundabout.

She slowed to let a car and a van pass in front and then entered the roundabout. Suddenly there was a squealing of tyres and a long blast on a horn as a third vehicle, a green Mondeo, fishtailed across the road in front of them.

'Christ Almighty! You stupid bloody tart,' shouted her captor punching her hard on shoulder.

The driver slowed and raised his middle finger, mouthing a silent threat, and then sped away.

'I didn't see him,' said Naomi. 'He was going too fast. I'm sorry.' At least someone knows where I am, she thought; just so long as he remembers.

'Keep your bloody wits about you. I won't tell you again.'

After a few minutes they came to a second roundabout.

'First exit,' he said. 'No more stunts or I'll draw blood this time.'

She drove on for about two miles in silence.

'Next left,' said her abductor.

The lane they turned into was narrow and bordered by high hedges. The headlights revealed a poorly maintained surface and Naomi was forced to slow down. After a few miles, the road markings petered out and clumps of grass appeared growing in the centre of the road. She was aware by now of a pair of following headlights.

'Just round this next bend you'll see a big entrance,' said her abductor. 'Turn in and follow the driveway round. I'll tell you when to stop.'

The gateway had once been a magnificent Corinthian structure with tall iron gates, but now they stood open and one column had begun to lean away from its partners so that the massive pediment tilted dangerously and looked ready to fall onto the drive and block the entrance.

Naomi turned in as instructed and saw the car behind come through after her. She followed the long winding drive, through a tunnel of overhanging foliage and bare branches, which seemed to go on forever, until at last her captor ordered her to pull up. She gazed nervously into the darkness where the lights of the cars showed a shadowy jungle, a confusion of rampant shrubbery and self-seeded trees on both sides of the drive where it had grown unchecked for decades. The drive itself was mostly clear of vegetation, but she could see small stumps thrusting up through the gravel here and there, where young plants had been cut down.

She jumped as her door opened suddenly. It was the young woman from the car park, but she was no longer smiling.

'Yours, I think,' she said bleakly, tossing Naomi's bag into her lap. 'I can't imagine what good you thought it would do you leaving it there like that. Perhaps you thought they'd come looking for you with a bloodhound eh? Well there's no chance of anyone coming out here so you can forget it, it won't happen. You can scream your bloody head off, and you will,' she said as an ugly expression crossed her face, 'but there's no one but us to hear. You're not the first guest we've entertained out here.'

She stood back as her fellow abductor pulled Naomi from the car, dragged her coat off and tied her elbows together behind her back.

'That's it,' he laughed, throwing the coat onto the back seat. 'Shoulders well back. Look at those tits. Lovely.'

She turned away from him as he reached to feel her breasts.

'Don't do that.'

She tried to speak with firmness but was unable to control the tremor, which betrayed her fear.

She watched as he reversed her car into the dark cavern beneath the enormous overhanging rhododendrons until it was completely hidden.

He went to the second car, returned carrying a powerful torch and pushed her on in front as they made their way along the uneven overgrown path, eventually arriving at a two-storey wooden building with an outside stairway. He reached under the bottom step and withdrew a key. She was led up the steps to the door where they waited while he first unlocked the heavy padlock and then produced a second larger key, which he inserted in the keyhole in the door. Once inside with the door closed, they lit several candles.

They pushed Naomi over to the wall and the man put his hands under her jumper.

'You're really very sexy with your tits sticking out like that; gets me going you know.'

The woman pushed him aside and untied Naomi's elbows.

'We're in a hurry Josh, leave her,' she muttered crossly.

She produced a longer length of rope one end of which she threw over a beam and, having bound Naomi's wrists and pulled her arms above her head, secured it to a ring on the wall.

He stepped behind Naomi and, reaching round under her raised arms, began to fondle her breasts again and to nuzzle her neck.

'Mmmm, you smell nice. I've got something here for you Naomi,' he murmured, and she could feel his hardness thrusting against her thigh. 'You've got me all excited you know. I can't help it. Let's just go ahead and do it now eh, get all this heavy lust out of the way. I'm really good at it, have you moaning with desire and begging for more in no time. What do you say?'

'No! Get away from me!' she shouted and managed to turn and face him and backed away as far as she could. She met his lascivious stare, her face a mask of contempt.

'You must remember,' he hissed, stepping closer, 'you're in no position to talk back. I don't want to see that defiant look in your eye.'

Without warning, he slapped her face so hard that she was knocked off her feet. She hung by her arms, dazed by the force of the blow as he reached out and gripped her chin, twisting her face upward so that she was forced to look into his eyes. He slid his other hand under her skirt and up to her crotch, forced it between her legs and squeezed hard.

'Just remember you snooty cow,' he sneered, 'I'm having lots of this tomorrow.'

She twisted away from him and lashed out with a foot. Her heel caught him under the jaw so hard that he felt a crunching in the bones of his neck as he staggered backward and crashed into the wall, his features rippling like jelly with the force of the impact.

'You bloody little bitch,' he bellowed, recovering quickly, and advancing on her as she hung helplessly from the rope. 'I'll wring your scrawny fucking neck, you little cow.'

Fortunately, the woman stepped in and wrapped her arms around him.

'Stop it Josh!' she cried. 'You know as well as I do the law will be straight round to ours once she's missed. We've got to be there before they arrive. Calm down for God's sake or you're going to wreck everything. She'll still be here tomorrow; then we can take our time with her.'

He was breathing heavily, his features flushed and distorted with rage and it looked as though he might throw the woman aside and carry out his threat. She shook him gently.

'Come on Josh. Stop thinking with your dick. You know we've got to go.'

'Yeah,' he said eventually. 'It's okay, Becks I've got a grip now. You just wait until tomorrow Miss Snooty,' he continued. 'Rough sex eh: every young girl's dream. You'll love it. We might even bring that nancy boyfriend of yours so he can watch while I'm giving you one.'

'Don't you call him names, you pathetic bully,' Naomi retorted furiously. 'He's a man. You just get off on beating up people who can't defend themselves: can't fight back.'

'You're asking for another slap you silly cow,' he laughed, squeezing Naomi's bottom as he walked by into the adjoining loft returning with an old bucket, which he placed close to her.

'That's for you to piss in your ladyship,' he grinned. 'I should hold your breath though; it stinks to high heaven. Oh dear. You can't pull your panties down. Shall I take them off for you? Make you more comfortable?' He rubbed his hands together and put his head on one side in the manner of an obsequious shop assistant.

'Why are you doing this to me?' asked Naomi, close to tears.

Rebecca thrust her face close to Naomi's and said quietly, 'You're going to pay for what you did to our Justin. I had to take mother to identify his body. She hasn't stopped crying since. She keeps going on about the state of his poor face. You can't deny you did it, we know what you told the police in your statement.'

'He was going to rape me. Can't you understand that? He'd tried to do it before. I had to stop him. I was frightened.'

'Why didn't you just let him get on with it? You might have enjoyed it. Mind you I would have thought Justin preferred someone with a bit more flesh on her bones.'

'Well you should know if anyone does,' her brother interjected with a snort of amusement as he squeezed Naomi's bottom again. 'If you like Naomi, you and your poncy boyfriend can watch while I give old Becks one as well. We're a very close family.'

'Oh, do shut up Josh,' snapped Rebecca, flushing, and glaring at him.

'I had to stop him,' cried Naomi, ignoring their byplay. 'I had to.'

'So, you smashed his face up?'

Naomi was aware suddenly that the woman was working herself into a rage and was preparing to strike her. Wisely, she hung her head and said nothing.

'Your sort make me want to puke!' Rebecca was spitting in anger. 'You bloody little tart. You're the worst kind of tease. You strut about on your high heels, waggling your tight little arse and sticking your tits out, making all the big boys horny. But you can't hack it when they make a move.'

Naomi remained head down, avoiding eye contact. She was seriously afraid of what this ranting woman might do to her if provoked.

'That's not true,' she mumbled at last and tensed, prepared to be knocked down a second time.

'Leave it, Becks,' said Joshua. 'You're right. We need to get home before the law shows up. There'll be plenty of time tomorrow.'

'Yes, we need to get a move on,' she replied, loosening the rope, allowing Naomi to lower her aching arms. She pushed her to the floor saying, 'We'll be back, cow. You've got the whole night to think about that.'

'Give us her mobile, Becks,' said Joshua. Rebecca rummaged through Naomi's bag but found no 'phone.

'I don't have a 'phone,' muttered Naomi.

'Give me yours then,' he said to his sister. Rebecca handed it over.

'Now listen Naomi,' he went on. 'I'm going to leave the 'phone over here on the floor and when we drive through the gate in the morning, I'm going to ring it. When you hear it ring four times, you'll know that you'll only have to wait a few short minutes before I'll be through that door and all over you like a rash; Prince Charming eh; come all that way just to give you a good seeing to. There's a lovely thought to sustain you through the long, lonely night. I know I'm looking forward to tomorrow. I can't wait. Ooh it's just like Christmas and you're my big present under the tree. And I'm yours,' he whispered, nuzzling her neck and cupping her breast in his hand.

He produced a greasy paper bag of food scraps and scattered them across the floor.

'Just so you won't be lonely,' he grinned. 'I should think you'll have lots of visitors now: friendly little furry jobs. Good night.'

They blew out the candles and she heard them open the door.

'We'll be nice and early,' said Rebecca, 'you can count on it.' She ran down the stairs and soon returned with two large bottles of water which she placed close to Naomi. 'There,' she said, loosening the caps. 'Mustn't get dehydrated must we.'

Naomi almost cried out, 'Please don't leave me,' as she heard the key turning in the lock and their footsteps receding as they descended the stairs. There was no doubt that they were a terrifying duo and that their sudden mood swings had put her in fear of her life, but the thought of spending the night alone in this awful place unnerved her completely. Her state of panic was becoming extreme until she forced herself to realise that she must overcome it: she must remain calm, she told herself. The impenetrable darkness and thoughts of what it might conceal was her worst fear.

She thought about how her father used to reassure her when she was a little girl by telling her that the dark is only there to help you go to sleep. Her mother would tell her everything's just the same when it's dark; it's just that you can't see it. They played the pointing game where they would switch the light back on so that she could look around and see where her toys were placed. Then the light would be switched off and she would say the name of a toy and point to its whereabouts in the room where she thought it was. When the light was switched on again, she was always right. She longed with all her heart to feel her father's arms around her and hear her mother's gentle voice, singing her off to sleep.

Outside, her abductors paused while Josh returned the keys to their hiding place. Then they hurried away along the path.

'What did you want to go and say that about us knowing what's in her statement, Becks? That could fuck up everything if she tells the Old Bill. It could put them on to Browning and that would be the end of our inside contact. Robin would go abso-bloody-lutely ballistic. I daren't think what Dad's reaction would be.'

'You know as well as I do Josh Simms, once we bring them out here, they don't tell anyone anything,' his sister replied, grabbing his arm suddenly, making him turn to face her. 'They don't even see anyone else to talk to do they. She won't tell the Old Bill or anyone else because she'll be fucking dead. If you haven't got the guts for it, I have. I'll do it and then we'll drop her in the well and no one'll be any the wiser.'

'I've got the guts for it, don't you worry about that,' Josh retorted angrily. 'How many have you killed so far Becks? I make it four. This one will make five. What are you going to do about the boyfriend? Is he in line to be number six?'

'He didn't do anything according to what they told the police. He claims to have missed the action,' answered Rebecca.

'You believe it?'

'Let's wait and see what we get out of her. She'll be glad to tell us what really happened when she sees what I'm going to do.'

'What have you got in mind then?'

'I'm going to start with her teeth. She'll know how Justin felt then.'

'Yeah, well I'm going to shaft her first, before you start knocking her about. I never knew you were so fond of Justin, Becks. You never got on that well – not like you and me.'

'He was family Josh. You let one get away with it and there's no telling what it could lead to? Anyway, we're twins, that's special.' She moved closer to him, held his chin, and kissed him gently on the lips. Josh turned his head gently from side to side, in an effort to ease his aching neck.

'I've got my own little score to settle up there. I'm going to have a right stiff neck in the morning.'

'Not just your neck if I know you,' laughed his sister.

Naomi heard their car turn on the gravel and drive away at speed. She blew on her hands and clenched and unclenched her fists trying to keep the circulation going in her fingers. Slipping off her shoes she rubbed her icy feet together in a vain attempt to warm them. She drew some consolation from the shocked expression of pain she had seen on Josh's face when her kick connected with his jaw and he'd crashed back into the wall: a small triumph – but at what cost?

She found she was able to sit against the wall and if she bent her knees up, she could rest her arms on them. This soon became uncomfortable, but her choice of positions was limited, and the floor was hard.

Her tightly bound wrists were hurting; her bruised face had started to ache, and the foul-smelling bucket was making her nauseous.

She thought about Philip and about her parents. They would be frantic by now, but they couldn't help her – no one could. This was her worst fear come true. She was a prisoner in the back of beyond and no one knew where she was. Thoughts of Joshua forcing himself on her made her unimaginably despondent because there was nothing that she could do to prevent it from happening. It seemed as though her fate, to be raped by a member of the Simms family, was pre-ordained and that there was no escape from it. As frightened as she was of Joshua though, it was Rebecca who seemed to pose the more serious threat. She had an ominous air of purpose about her, it was clear that she had already decided on a course of action, and Naomi feared that it was going to have most unpleasant consequences for herself.

It might even be that even Joshua's unwelcome attentions could be the least of these. She wondered whether his macho behaviour was a pose to impress on Rebecca that he could be every bit as nasty as she was. She felt though that Rebecca was the truly dangerous one. Joshua seemed to be trying to keep up somehow; but he had left her in no doubt about his intentions towards herself and the cruelty behind his ideas of leaving the mobile phone and scattering food over the floor to add to her terrors showed that he was quite capable of dreaming up his own evil schemes.

It appeared that when either of these mercurial characters was seized by a sudden fit of rage, the other was able to exert a calming influence and bring them back to a state of comparative normality. Naomi believed that before too long, she might well find out what happened when they both went crazy together.

God help me when that happens, she thought. Rebecca's words: "You can scream your bloody head off, and you will, but there's only us to hear." And "You're not the first guest we've entertained out here," came back to her.

She's not going to let me get away from here alive; she realised with sudden, shocking fear

She felt so cold, so alone, so utterly without hope. Her eyes filled with tears as she stared into the impenetrable darkness and did her best to ignore each little scurrying sound and tried hard not to think about what creatures might be dragging their tails across that dusty floor.

In an effort to chafe some life into her cold hands she twisted her wrists forward and back against the turns of rope and succeeded in loosening them a little. She knew that in doing so she had tightened the knots but as these were where she couldn't reach them anyway it didn't matter. Undoing the knots was not an option and, although she had rubbed her skin sore, she soon began to feel pins and needles as the feeling returned to her fingers.

★★★

Philip put the last set of papers into his briefcase, drained his coffee cup and reached for the telephone.

'We thought she was with you Philip,' said Naomi's mother in response to his request to speak to Naomi.

'I haven't seen her since yesterday Mrs. Gibbs. I popped round to Fellowes' after work, but I missed her. She'd already gone. I thought she must be tired and wanting to get home.'

He heard Mrs Gibbs call her to her husband, 'She's not with Philip. He hasn't seen her since yesterday.'

Mr Gibbs took the phone, 'Philip?'

'I haven't seen her today. She'd gone by the time I got round to Fellowes after work.'

'That's not like her Philip; not like her at all. I'm calling the police.'

★★★

Naomi's ordeal – Mon night to Tue morn

Hours later Naomi stirred, opened her eyes, and, after a moment of confusion, the awful nature of her predicament returned with a stomach-churning jolt, as she recalled where she was and the terrors of the day to come. In her depressed state of mind, she was reminded about something she had once read about a huge black bird sitting on someone's shoulder representing total despair, or had it been death? Whichever, she felt the presence of the black bird or something like it. Maybe it had been a black dog? It was quite amazing that she had slept at all, given her perilous situation and degree of physical discomfort. As she sat shivering and flexing her fingers, she became aware of what had woken her, she was conscious of a growing need to urinate. Slipping her shoes on and clambering to her feet with a groan of exasperation, cursing her bladder for its weakness, she decided to explore her surroundings as far as was possible, given total darkness and the limitation imposed by the amount of slack on the rope: anything to distract her mind from the need to pee. Using that disgusting bucket was completely out of the question.

She remembered there was a corner to her left, so she shuffled towards it, feeling the wall, and counting the upright studs as she went. Just as she reached the full extent of the rope her fingers encountered rough sacking, a makeshift curtain. Pulling hard on the dusty layers, she felt the fastenings give way and was able at last to draw them aside to find it was early daylight outside, her watch showed 07:40. The glass was gone from the window and a chill draught blew into the loft, causing her eyes to water. Cold as it was, she found this breath of air from outside invigorating and felt the first stirrings of hope. She yanked hard again and again until the sacking gave way, parting from its fastenings one by one until it dropped to the floor in a dusty heap.

She found herself looking across a wide expanse of long scrubby grass and unkempt bushes at the back of a once magnificent house. She could see leggy shrubs and small trees growing inside the walls and ivy climbing inside and out, covering large areas with its dark green foliage. There was a sign attached to the wall and even though much of the red lettering was peeling and faded, she could still read: KEEP OUT DANGER OF FALLING MASONRY. Part of the roof and all of one wing had gone and a tall wooden pole had been placed to support the main ridge, where it projected over the space once occupied by the missing wing. Most of the walls were intact and the tall, stone mullioned windows, even without their lead and glass, spoke of a one-time grandeur. The brickwork of the main chimneys reared up into the pale morning light, each terminated by beautifully constructed barley twists crowned with intricately patterned oversailing brickwork. Green algae covered the walls on the shaded side and stunted buddleia bushes, denuded by the season, clinging to the old house like the bones of roosting birds completed the picture of total abandonment.

Naomi thought that the house might have been built in Tudor times because the warm red colour and size of the bricks reminded her of a building she had once seen in Greenwich while on a school trip. One of the teachers had told her that it was Elizabethan. She remained at the window for a long time, captivated by this magical presence, until her distended bladder signalled that prompt action was now required.

The early light showed her that the flooring below the window was partially rotten and there was a small hole near her feet. She kicked down hard on the crumbling floorboards and managed to enlarge it considerably.

'That'll do,' she said aloud, and grasping her skirt with numb fingers she pulled one side then the other until she had it gathered round her waist. Then she slipped her thumbs into the waistband of her tights and by dint of wriggling and high stepping managed to ease them down, at first using her fingers as far as she could reach, then, with more teetering contortions, pushing with her toes until she was able to kick them off and push them to one side. 'At last,' she gasped with feeling.

During this far from dignified procedure, she found it impossible not to laugh. It had after all a comical aspect. She was glad that no one could see her as she performed like a manic gymnast cum contortionist. Tears ran down her cheeks as her laughter became nervous, then turned to involuntary hysteria. There was nothing she could do to prevent these uncontrolled outbursts: it was so horribly surreal that she began to fear she might be going mad.

'Come on Gibbs,' she shouted at last, 'it's not bloody funny!' Gradually she brought herself under control then feeling calm at last, she squatted over the hole in the floor, pulled the crotch of her pants to one side, and sighed in sheer bliss, able to relieve herself at last.

'Well done you,' she said, allowing herself a brief smile as she jiggled vigorously in an effort to dislodge the last drips. 'And no splashes.'

It was now 08:10 and her fears were renewed at the memory of Rebecca's parting shot about coming back nice and early. What had she meant by early?

★★★

Unbeknown to Naomi, two events had occurred. The first of these was that the police had begun to search and were doing all they could to find her. The second was to have a more immediate effect on her situation, because it meant that Joshua and Rebecca would not return that day.

★★★

When they arrived home on the Monday evening, they had found Robin in a particularly foul temper waiting in the hall. He had become concerned about their mother's unhappiness as she grieved for Justin and, after trying unsuccessfully to comfort her himself and finding James to be worse than useless, he had been trying all day to contact them. He was in a filthy temper and harangued them at length about their selfishness and their lack of responsibility and told them that they were to spend time with their mother instead of swanning around wasting their time like a pair of teenage nitwits. His voice quivered with emotion as he went on to say that things were going to change.

'The Coroner's Office has said that they are releasing Justin's body, so we've a funeral to arrange and you two are going to play your part. It's time to grow up and once young Justin's laid to rest and things begin to settle down; notice that I've not used the phrase – get back to normal; you two will start to show some commitment to the family's affairs. You will put in a full day's work every day and I expect to see a significant improvement in your business performance. I'll be keeping an eye on the books. You've been getting away with murder up until now.' Joshua avoided Rebecca's eye at this. 'When I talk about family affairs, I'm referring to the travel agencies, the legit' stuff. You do your dealing and other stuff on your own time. If you don't pull your weight in future, I'll cut you both loose and don't think I can't do it; and don't go grizzling to Dad because he's as fed up with your immature behaviour as the rest of us are.'

They doubted this but were not about to cross swords with Robin in his present mood.

As he turned to go, he added, 'You will not leave this house tomorrow without my say so.'

They were shocked by the degree of Robin's vehemence and stood mute as he ranted; his face darkened, and his voice made ragged by a rage that was frightening in its intensity. Clearly, they would not be going out to Kingsfield Park the following day.

Tuesday morning found them both feeling miserable but still shaken by their older brother's resolve to bring them into line.

Joshua assuaged his frustration to some extent by ringing Rebecca's mobile from time to time and imagining her distress as she thought of his imminent arrival to ravish her. This brought him little satisfaction though. His neck was so painful he could hardly turn his head and he had a pounding headache. He felt wretched. The slightest movement sent pulses of agony booming up the back of his neck into his head. He had turned to Rebecca for sympathy but so angry was she at being baulked in her desire to return to Kingsfield Park, that she treated him as though it was entirely his fault. He nursed his personal agony and dwelt on the ways he would thoroughly humiliate Naomi.

Even in this personal plotting though, he experienced some feelings of regret for what would happen to her once Rebecca got to work. He knew that nothing was too wicked for his sister to consider once she had begun to "punish" her victims for their sins, real or imaginary.

After killing her first victim, a homeless girl who had harangued Rebecca for the way she had kicked out at her as she sat begging in the town centre, Rebecca had undergone an alarming change of personality. They had abducted the girl and taken her to the loft in Kingsfield Park where they stripped off her clothing, suspended her by her wrists and slapped her around while they drank from a bottle of red wine. They were well down their second bottle when Rebecca began to burn the girl's legs and breasts with cigarettes, in order to make her apologise for shouting at her and calling her a stuck-up slag.

As the girl cried out in pain, Rebecca told her sneeringly that if she would apologise, kneel, and beg for mercy, they would release her and let her go. Her response had been to shout, 'Fuck off bitch,' and to spit in Rebecca's face.

Befuddled by alcohol, he had watched with some amusement as his sister wound her long fingers round the girl's neck, placed her thumbs together and squeezed. Amusement changed first to disbelief then to horror as the girl's tongue protruded from her mouth and her head flopped, while Rebecca continued to shake her violently. Rebecca's eyes were shining with a fervour Joshua had never seen and such was her exultation in the act that Joshua was, for the first time in his life, alarmed for his sister's mental state.

Still panting and excited by her exertions, she had kissed him passionately and there, on the floor under the sightless eyes of the dead girl, undone his clothing and they had indulged in a frantic sexual encounter.

Afterwards, she had rejoiced in telling him about the fantastic rush that she had experienced as she had felt the girl die in her hands.

'She was a tough one you know. Her eyes were on me the whole time and I could feel the hate coming off her. She was glaring at me as though I was dirt. And then it changed. Suddenly she knew I meant it. She knew I was taking her life and just for a moment I felt the fear in her. It was fantastic. God, it felt so good as I squeezed the life out of that dirty little bitch; snuffed her out like that!' She snapped her fingers to emphasise her point.

She justified her action by claiming that such unwashed itinerants were worthless and would be missed by nobody. She certainly seemed to believe that she had done nothing wrong and had obviously enjoyed this new excitement; had found the whole experience fulfilling in a way that was beyond his understanding. Joshua found it extremely disturbing. Until then, he had felt himself to be the dominant twin, particularly when it came to sex; but there had been a shift of roles. She had led the way and he had found the urgency of her desire for sexual gratification and her strength and vigour in achieving it, alarming, not to say bruising. She had displayed a hitherto unsuspected streak of malignancy that had set them apart. He couldn't understand her compulsion to kill, and she couldn't understand why he showed no desire to follow her example.

Recently, they had carried out a second abduction, leaving their victim, another homeless girl, seriously mutilated. He had looked on as Rebecca had strangled her with the same air of concentration, followed by the same intense sexual desire and now two bodies lay at the bottom of the well. It was then he knew for certain that she was using drugs, something they'd vowed never to do. When he confronted her, she had laughed at him, told him to grow up, be a man, said he didn't know what he was missing. He had tried to reason with her and pointed out the danger they were now in if the girls were missed and their bodies should be discovered.

'Those vagrants stick together you know and if the police start asking around, they'll soon find out that you've had arguments with them. Then where will we be? Where will you be if Robin finds out you're sampling the merchandise? He'll go bloody mad. You know he will.'

But there was no stopping Rebecca. He felt totally ineffectual, another new experience. She told him that if he didn't like it, she would do it on her own. She didn't need him anymore.

There had been two others since then, a boy and then a girl. He had supplied the brawn necessary to subdue them and get them to the loft but had taken no further part himself. He could only guess at what had happened to them. Rebecca went out there alone sometimes. She was unable to lift the cover off the well by herself, so he had no idea where their bodies were. He suspected that she had killed them somewhere in the cellars under the house, but he was reluctant to go back down there after his never to be forgotten first and only visit.

They had come across the entrance as children while sheltering from the rain, and had ventured down the uneven steps, eager to see where they would lead. With no light, they could only go a few paces before they found themselves in total darkness and Rebecca had suggested that they stand still until their eyes became accustomed to the dark. After a few minutes, she had seized his hand, crying, 'Come on,' and had begun to move forward when an indistinct form suddenly collided with them and dashed past. Rebecca screamed as she fell back, and he experienced a moment of intense terror before they'd heard the footfalls hurrying away up the worn steps. They ran outside once they had recovered their wits but saw no one.

'That's the last time I go down there,' he'd vowed, leaning weakly against the wall, relieved beyond measure to be out in daylight again. She'd laughed at him and called him a big girl's blouse, but it was a promise he'd made to himself that he had no intention of breaking, ever. Even now, as a grown man, he had only to hark back to that incident to relive the prickly moment when that sudden shock had run through him like the penetration of a cold blade. It was not something he could forget and the idea of going down into that darkness, perhaps to find the bodies of Rebecca's victims, was something he did not wish to contemplate.

The truth was he had become frightened of and for his sister. Seeing her in the grip of her lust to kill and of her desire for sex immediately afterwards, unnerved him. He had tried to tell her that she was degrading herself, but she had laughed at him, telling him he was unable to understand. He had taken to locking his bedroom door at night, an action that amused her. She tried the handle every night, smiling to find the door locked.

He saw that her claim to be taking revenge on Naomi for what she had done to Justin was nothing more than an excuse for her morbid satisfaction. The truth was that circumstances had provided his sadistic sister with another victim.

★★★

Believing that her captors would return soon, Naomi made her way back to the window in the hope of finding some broken glass with which she might be able to cut through the rope. She had woken thirsty in the night and with some difficulty had managed to open one of the water bottles and take a long satisfying drink. She felt a little better and felt quite bucked at what seemed a brilliant idea. But there was no glass left in the window frames. She examined the frames within her reach and saw that all the glass had been broken off flush with the frames and probably thrown out of the window. This was a big disappointment. When she had bought her car, her father had given her a small magnetic box for her spare ignition key and shown her how to attach it under the wheel arch. It must still be there. She had been so sure she would find triangles of glass sticking up ready for her to saw through her bonds and escape through the window.

It was while she was coming to terms with the fact that her brilliant idea had come to nothing that she remembered the scraps of food Joshua had scattered on the floor. She shuddered with revulsion, remembering all the night-time scurrying and scratching when she saw that every last fragment was gone. Suddenly the phone rang four times. She began to cry with the hopelessness of it all.

★★★

CHAPTER FIFTEEN

'It's a D.S. Wickens from North Kent Area, he's asked to speak to someone in CID Sarge.'

'I don't believe it,' Hazel muttered to herself. 'Put him on.' She sighed and leant back from the never-ending stack of forms. She'd had an extremely busy Monday, culminating in the disappearance of Naomi Gibbs and the ensuing flap that had resulted. Today promised more of the same, and still the outstanding mass of paperwork remained undiminished.

'Morning D.S. Wickens, D.S. Blissett here. What can we do for you?'

'Good morning to you Sergeant. Please call me Ron.'

'Okay. Ron. I'm Hazel.'

'Fine. Lovely name that; you got the eyes to go with it?'

'They'd turn you to stone Sergeant. Now, how can we help?'

'Well we've had a bit of a rum do down here; couple of apparent suicides which now appear to have been murders.'

'So where do we come in Ron?'

'The two deceased guys, Barry McBride and Sidney Hammond were buddies. They did, quote, jobs, unquote, together, but out of town; word has it they did a bit of rough stuff for a big London operation; debt collection, stuff like that.'

'They had previous then?'

'Yes, they'd both done time for G.B.H. That was probably how they met up. We had the usual suspects in for a chat and it seems they had just recently been busy up your way. McBride kept his cards pretty close to his chest, but Hammond used to let things slip when he'd had a few; bit of a toper by all accounts. He'd been shooting his mouth off about a little job up Essex way: near Ipswich actually, so you can see geography wasn't his strong point.'

'Oh, I see. You'd like to know if we've come across their little job?'

'Well it did seem worth the asking Hazel.'

'Hmm. We do have a case on the go as it happens. An eye-witness turned up on Sunday having seen an assault involving two men last Thursday night. They left their victim by the railway and he died, so we are now seriously looking for them. They could be the two you're interested in. What's happened to them?'

'Well it's a bit of a story, are you okay for a few minutes?'

'Yes of course. I'm extremely interested.'

'First thing was a call from the Ambulance Service. A local jobbing builder had a roof repair to do in Salisbury Road; a couple of slates slipped down. He turns up this morning to fix them but finds he's left his job sheet back at the yard and there was no one there to answer the 'phone. He decides to do the job and sort out the paperwork later; no problem there. He takes a wander round the back alleys, looking for the slipped slates but locates three properties with the same problem. It's a pretty run-down area; nice old places but a lot of them have been let go. Two of them were in when he knocked and as neither of them had sent for a builder, he reckoned it was a fair bet that it had to be the third who had called. He got his ladder, a big wooden job, humped it round to the back of the house in question and was just rearing it up when a bloody great ginger cat lets out a howl and charges out from behind an old tumble drier, straight between his feet. He does a bit of a dance, loses control of the ladder and it goes through the upstairs window.'

'You're not winding me up here are you Ron?' Hazel was finding it hard not to laugh, 'because it's beginning to sound like that thing about the barrel of bricks.'

'No, I'm not. You'll find it less comical in a minute. According to the paramedics, he said he was having a bad day at that point; bit of an understatement I'd say. He sorted out the ladder and up he went to measure for a new pane of glass. That's when he sees the late Sidney in a bath full of blood with the room all splattered, like an abattoir. He very nearly lost his grip and fell, because his immediate thought was that the broken glass had fallen in and killed the guy. He manages to get down in one piece and make a three nines call on his mobile. The ambulance crew called us. The poor bugger was looking pretty poorly by then, so they took him in for observation.'

'God. That's awful. Is he okay?'

'Don't know yet. We haven't heard. We got all this from the medics. They couldn't stop him talking. There's more.'

'Go on then.'

'While all this is going on, we get an anonymous telephone call to go to a residence in Carstairs Avenue on the other side of town. The caller had tried the garage door and found a car inside with the engine running, and the garage thick with exhaust fumes. My guess is he was an opportunistic thief trying his luck. Anyway, that's where we found the lately departed Barry McBride, lying in the car, shot full of heroin, self-administered it seems, and well boozed. The odd thing is that Hammond's wrist was slashed with a cut-throat razor – it was in the bath – and we found a razor strop on the front passenger seat of McBride's car.

'Another oddity is that one David Lucas aka Luke, an associate of the two dead men, has done a runner. His flat has been cleaned out – all his belongings and his car are gone and so is his girl friend. She's not the sort you'd expect to run around with a villain like him; a hard-working girl; partner in a beauty salon in the town centre; funny old business eh? Looks like a bad on bad crime wave – two bodies so far – watch this space. I'd like your witness to have a look at the pic's of Hammond and McBride. Did he get a good look at them? D'you think he'd be able to ID them from a picture?'

'Well it was night-time of course, but they were fairly near to a streetlamp so it's certainly worth a try Ron.'

'Okay, what's your email address?'

★★★

Hazel's colleagues were doing everything they could to find out what had happened to Naomi and to console her frantic parents. Fellowes' car park was marked off with blue and white tape, and the Police had been looking for anything that might give them a clue to what had happened to her. Their painstaking search had yielded nothing helpful.

Her parents, looking gaunt, expecting the worst, sat in the company of a young female police officer, waiting for the telephone to ring. Across town, Philip, and his parents, looking and feeling much the same, sat waiting too.

The Police were also looking out for a sighting of Matty. Hazel felt that the sooner he came in to look at the pictures the better.

★★★

CHAPTER SIXTEEN

Tuesday morning

James Simms' Jaguar prowled slowly up through the levels of the multi-storey car park as he searched for a vacant space. Every bay was occupied, and he could see no one who looked as though they might be getting ready to leave. It had been like this since the Council had cut the number of on-street parking spaces so drastically that it had become virtually impossible to find one empty.

'So, we all chug round in here playing musical bloody chairs,' he fumed.

He checked the clock in his dashboard and saw that he would probably be late for his appointment. At least, the excuse that one was unable to park would be received with some sympathy. It had become a universal experience. He was going to talk with his bank manager about plans to expand the car sales business, plush new showrooms for the main agencies and a major revamp of the used car premises: bigger turnover, bigger profits, more cars – the irony escaped him.

At last the powerful car grumbled out onto the last level, the roof, where the rain was still falling steadily.

'Last chance,' he muttered, and was preparing to start down again when a car moved out suddenly. James touched his accelerator and cruised expertly into the rather narrow bay. He watched the long queue of cars circle the roof area and enter the downward spiral to continue their frustrating search. He shook his head in a gesture of despair, as he turned up his collar and strode through the rain to buy his ticket.

Minutes later, after pressing the lift call buttons to no effect, he resigned himself to the fact that he would have to walk down several flights of stairs; stairs open to the November wind and rain. Doing up the buttons on his smart overcoat, he stepped out onto the top landing. The outside wall was just under shoulder height, so while it allowed him a view of the adjacent buildings it did little to shelter his upper body from the elements.

He was about to begin his descent when he heard footsteps and female voices coming up and even though the stairs were wide enough to allow one ample room to pass, he retreated to the corner of the landing and smiled as two young women thanked him and hurried inside. He could hear more ascending footsteps and so remained in the corner. Two men appeared, deep in conversation, and passed in through the door seemingly unaware of his presence. A third man, his shiny head absolutely devoid of hair, appeared at the bottom of the flight and had begun to walk up when suddenly James was seized, raised up high and strong hands held him in a sitting position on the wall. The first two men had turned and lifted him whilst he was watching the third. It happened in a trice and now he found himself balanced on top of the wall, a drop of perhaps sixty feet behind him. The third man stared up into his eyes and spoke in a hoarse Londoner's voice: a voice accustomed to command obedience.

'Turn round and look behind you Simms.'

James sat still, too frightened to move.

'I want you to look down and see how high it is Simms.'

He nodded at his accomplices and James cried out in fear as they leaned him out into space. They held him there whimpering for an age then, on the man's signal, they brought him back to an upright position.

'Now turn your fucking head and look down.'

James did as he was told this time and was unable to stifle a tremulous whimper as he saw how far it was to the ground.

'Now Simms, James, isn't it? My two associates here are going to hang you over the side while you listen carefully to what I have to say. If you make me happy, they'll bring you back in out of the rain but if I get annoyed, they'll drop you like a fucking stone.'

He nodded at his accomplices, 'Over and out!' and James shrieked in terror as they lifted him bodily, pushed his legs beyond the parapet and, holding his wrists, suspended him above the awful drop. The man reached over and seized James by the hair. There was a great guffaw from one of the others as James' hairpiece came away in his hand. He looked at it in disgust before allowing it to fall to the ground.

'They said you wore a wig. I forgot. I expect you paid a lot of money for a job like that. I wouldn't be seen dead in one myself, still neither will you now will you.'

All three sniggered at the joke.

James was gabbling in terror.

'Please. Please. Pull me up. Pull me up. I'll do anything. I'll give you money. Pull me up please.'

'Stop your bloody grizzling and listen to me James. You might have noticed that all the buildings around have no windows looking onto the car park. Who wants to look at an ugly old car park eh? Then; no one walks along this side because the stairs lead out through the front. If we let, go of you now not a soul would see you fly. The impact would shove your knees up through your shoulders – not a pretty sight. We've disabled the lift and we've got a guy directing people to the other stairs, so no one's going to see what's going on up here.'

James was by now almost insensible with terror. He had lost control of his bladder and bowels and was uttering a continuous high-pitched keening sound.

'Now listen up good James. See what we have here is a conflict of interests. Your people want to harm a certain lady and her son, and my people want your people to lay off. Clear? If your people don't do it our way, there will cease to be any of your people. Clear? We want you and the rest of your folks to know that your refusal to parlee voo is really pissing us off big time. We're sorry about your young brother. That was a mistake, but it wouldn't have happened if you done what we said. Anyway, I heard he was a nasty little shit. Now this is it plain and simple. Do not in any way ever harm Mrs. Driscoll or her son Terry. If you ignore this advice, you'll all be taken out P.D.Q., You got that? The whole Simms family will be history – vanished without a trace. Just an unpleasant memory.'

He stood back and signalled his accomplices to bring James back in. They dumped the shivering, dribbling James in the corner and stood back.

'Look at me Simms,' the third man commanded. 'Did you hear what I just told you?'

James nodded frantically, still uttering his shrill babble like a child in the grip of a nightmare, tears coursing down his pale cheeks.

'Repeat it then.'

James lay nodding and whining seemingly bereft of the power of speech.

'Repeat it Simms or we'll drop you for real.'

He twisted James' ears and shook him.

'One word from me Simms and they'll chuck you over if you don't repeat the fucking message now!'

At last he was able to stammer out a close approximation to the message. It was enough to show that he had understood that Maureen and Terry Driscoll had powerful friends and that mother and son were not to be harmed.

'You're to go straight home Jimmy and tell that family of yours what's just happened to you and why. There's a number on your answer machine. We shall be waiting for a call to say you've seen the error of your ways – an apology for fucking us about would be nice too but we're reasonable people – we won't rub your noses in it eh. Just remember we can find you again very easily if you make it necessary. London's only forty minutes away and that's about how long you'll stay alive if you don't do as we say. Watch my lips. Leave … them … alone. Clear? You'd better get this right Jim.'

He put his face close to James.'

'If the call doesn't come soon, Jimmy, or if the message is not what we want to hear, we shall reduce your family by one member. Tell Robin that. Make sure he understands.'

Pulling a white lawn handkerchief from his breast pocket, he threw it down at the still blubbering James.

'Wipe that snot off your face for Christ's sake, you're making me feel ill.'

He jerked his head to indicate to his accomplices that they were leaving.

'What about the lift?' asked one.

'Leave it,' he replied, and they were gone.

James remained crouched in the corner at the top of the stairs, soaked by the November rain and his own urine in a state of shock, his heart racing. People averted their eyes, mistaking him for one of the sad drunks who wandered the town begging and making noisy, belligerent demands of passers-by.

Eventually, he was able to unclench his fists, get to his feet and make his way down to the toilets. He was relieved to find the gents' empty but the sight of his reflection in the mirrors above the wash basins pulled him up short. He stared in disbelief at the enfeebled, bald headed figure staring back at him, and he began to cry again at the memory of what they had done to him.

He pulled off lengths of paper towelling, cleaned himself up as best he could and went in search of his hairpiece. He was relieved to find it still lying in the wet grass where it had fallen. He picked it up gratefully, shook out most of the water, reshaping it with care. He replaced it on his head and immediately felt a little better. He kept his eyes down though until he was back inside. He could not bring himself to look up at the spot where he had been so terrorised and humiliated. He had no thoughts of revenge, only fear and a desire never ever to see that terrifying trio again.

He climbed the stairs back up to his car, the lift still seemed to be out of order, and he was surprised to find that his parking ticket was unexpired. It seemed so long ago that he had paid for it and walked out into the rain and that heart-stopping ordeal. The

soft closing of the door, the subtle interlocking of finely engi-
neered components, failed for the first time to elicit his pleasur-
able pride of ownership. He could shut himself in, in his leather-bound, veneered security but he could not shut them out.
The engine fired and the sleek machine rolled forward. Robin
would know what to do.

★★★

The mobile phone rang twice more that morning and once in
the afternoon. Each time she waited in terror to hear her tormentors' footsteps on the stairs and see the door crash open. She
waited longer than the five or so minutes she thought it would
take for them to arrive, her fear mounting, convinced that they
were playing cat and mouse with her. But nothing happened.
After the third ring Naomi began to give serious consideration to
the notion that the intimidation might have been no more than
empty threats designed to terrorise her when all along, the twins
meant to leave her to die of starvation. Could it be?

As the long day progressed, she sipped from the second bottle and
longed for something to eat. She had taken nothing since a cup
of coffee and a couple of biscuits the previous afternoon and as
the time passed, she began to feel lightheaded and feverish. The
numbing cold hurt her bones. She dragged the pile of sacking
nearer and wrapped herself in it, in an effort to keep warm and
managed to doze for short periods, but each time she woke she
felt worse. She was sure she had a temperature, and she was conscious of an increasingly sore throat. The miserable day dragged
on until at last the daylight began to fade.

★★★

Hazel Blissett flopped into her chair with a sigh, the exasperated
exhalation of someone with two many unfinished tasks on the go;
a juggler who, with too many balls in the air, knows control is

at full stretch and dreads the sound of balls bouncing all around. She asked for an outside line, keyed in the number, and sat with eyes closed, drumming her fingers to the distant double beat of the ringing tone.

At last she heard, '… Police, a hasty switchboard operator who had the gift of speaking just before opening the line, thus depriving the caller of her first word.

'This is D.S. Blissett would you put me through to C.I.D. D.S. Wickens is expecting my call.'

Again, another interminable wait for the connection. Then a woman's voice,

'Just a moment please. I think he's still in the station.'

Hazel sensed the resignation in the woman's voice – identified with the unspoken, I'm far too busy to be fielding other folks' calls, but I suppose someone's got to do it. She waited again …

'Hazel?'

'Hello Ron. We've struck gold with your pictures. Our eye-witness has identified Sidney Hammond as the one who struck the fatal blow and Barry McBride as his accomplice. He's one hundred percent sure on Hammond and ninety-nine on McBride.'

'That should have sorted your case then?'

'Well, we now know who killed the boy, but as there's no one to prosecute it can go no further – not unless your David Lucas has turned up? He must have a few answers.'

'He turned up Hazel but he's out of it now. He was found rolled up in a tarpaulin outside the station, stark naked and badly knocked about. There was a videocassette in with him, so we were able to see just what had gone on; course the villains were all hooded. It was harrowing to watch, obviously made as a money-spinner for the seedy end of the market: a genuine snuff movie. They've even called it, "Luke Learns a Lesson." He was dragged into this workshop where they stripped off his clothes. Then they fetched in the girl and made her watch while they spread-eagled him against a door and nailed him to it, a bloody great four-inch nail through each hand. He put up a hell of a fight, but they were just too many for him. They then took off her clothes and tied her to a chair. They told him he was to pay attention and watch carefully while they gave her a makeover. Then they lit a blowlamp and plugged in a soldering iron and forced him to watch as they burned off her eyebrows. God, it was all so sick. It's not something I'd care to see again Hazel. We're examining it to see if anyone can identify the location but it's just a lockup garage; could be anywhere. Lucas was supposed to be sedated and under guard in the local hospital; no hope of any useful information from that quarter I'm afraid. He managed to get up to the roof and jump. Six storeys. Nasty mess.'

'You say snuff movie. Who did they kill if it wasn't Lucas?'

'It was his poor bloody girlfriend. They've killed her. We saw it all on the video. I knew her slightly. She and her business partner ran a hairdressers and beauty salon. My wife has her hair done there when she can afford it. You sure you want to hear about it?'

'Your last story was enough to give me nightmares Ron. Go on.'

'It's pretty horrible. Once again, an anonymous phone call pointed us in the right direction. A woman called in to say she'd seen strange goings on in the local cemetery. She wouldn't give a name because she was with her friend's husband and she's afraid of being found out. Her husband knocks her about when he's had a drink.'

'Which is why she keeps her tryst in the cemetery?'

'Quite possibly. Anyway, she declined to give a name. Imagine it though. Trousers down in the cemetery in bloody November – got to be desperate.'

'I'm going to cover my ears if you're going to be coarse Ronald.'

'Well you'd never catch me doing that. Not in a graveyard and certainly not in the bloody winter.'

'I guess he's a lot younger.'

'What's that supposed to mean?'

'It means he had his love to keep him warm Ron. Come on. Stick to the story.

'It's pretty gruesome Hazel.'

'Worse than last time?'

'Well yes. McBride and Hammond were villains – knew what they were getting into – knew all about the high stakes, whereas young Michelle Elliot was an innocent. They were so cruel, she suffered horribly.'

'What happened?'

'Our anonymous caller and her man were snuggled down in the dark when they heard men's voices and a group passed by carrying something heavy. There was some stumbling and swearing as they went by. The couple kept very still and quiet. They heard digging going on and muttering, but they couldn't make out the words. Occasionally these blokes flashed a torch, and they were able to see that the object was blue. Eventually the men moved away, and our two lovers waited to make sure they'd gone and then fled having decided to keep their mouths tight shut. But then the woman's conscience got at her so she phoned in, telling us all this and explaining just where it had happened.'

'And?'

'We visited the location she'd described. There was no blue object but there was a newly dug grave. We got the vicar in and he told us it was the grave of one Maud Griggs at whose funeral he had officiated two days before. She was interred on top of her late hubby. He noted, that's the vicar not the late hubby, that the ground had been disturbed, it had been swept but not very well. There was fresh earth in the surrounding grass – it's a very well-kept cemetery. The sexton then confirmed that it was not how they had left it. They always lay plastic sheeting to prevent any spoil from getting on the grass.'

'Is this going where I think it's going?'

'Well we got a court order to open the grave and went back with some hefty constables, gumboots and spades. There she was about four foot down wrapped in the blue plastic tarpaulin, sealed in with duct tape. We knew what we'd found.'

'God how awful. Buried alive?'

'No. She was naked, tied hand and foot and sealed in. She'd suffocated before they'd buried her Hazel. She was alive when they put her in, but she couldn't have lasted long.'

The detective stopped his narrative quite suddenly and after a longish pause Hazel heard him take a shuddering deep breath.

'We watched the whole thing Hazel. I can't tell you the things they did to her.' There was another considerable pause. 'Those wicked bastards put her through all that just to make him watch. Every time he closed his eyes or turned his head away those evil bastards ran the blowlamp over his skin, saying, "You must pay attention Luke." Christ Hazel it was awful. She was screaming in pain. He was crying out for them to leave her alone, telling them she knew nothing, begging them to let her go but the more he pleaded the more those perverted devils made her suffer. They ran hot solder into her hair and onto her body. He was well out of it before they'd finished with her. She was whimpering and pleading for mercy as they sealed her inside the tarpaulin. How long have you been on the force Hazel?'

'Twelve years.'

'I've been fourteen and I've seen some pretty ghastly sights, but nothing to approach such sadistic brutality. I keep having flash-backs of the scene where we cut the tarpaulin open. We knew we were going to find her in there, we'd seen it on the video. But when I saw what they'd done to that lovely girl, I cried. I wasn't the only one crying. I never cry, not even at my mum's funeral. My name's down for counselling, I never thought I'd see the day.'

'It doesn't bear thinking about Ron.'

'I can't stop thinking about it. Lucas must have offended his big city paymasters but, like the other two, he knew what the score would be if he got it wrong. It's high stakes for those people. These killings are to encourage the others. But what could she have possibly done? She wasn't of his world. She was just in the wrong place at the wrong time. She was just a young innocent girl.'

'No one deserves to die like that Ron; but she won't be the last young woman to believe that she can reform her man. She must have had an idea he was a villain.'

'We'll never know now will we. He could have told her anything. Her business partner and the salon staff are inconsolable.

She was very popular – everybody liked her. They didn't approve of Lucas – too old for one thing and something shifty about him. But evidently, she was besotted with him. They've closed the place up, doesn't look as though they'll ever open it again. Her father has a history of heart trouble and has had a severe attack. He's in intensive care and not looking too good. Her mother's just sitting at his bedside looking old and lost. I guess they've given her something because she looks right out of it. There's a policewoman with her. Let's hope the old boy makes it, otherwise she'll have lost her whole family. She's looking pretty fragile herself. It's bloody hell here just now. The media crowd have caught wind of it and now we've got them baying at the door.'

★★★

CHAPTER SEVENTEEN

James Simms stood in the centre of the room, a defeated figure, head down like a whipped dog. The twins had stood by in awe as Robin worked himself into a frenzy, berating him for the way he'd been caught out at the car park.

'If you'd had your bloody wits about you instead of dreaming your way along the way you do, they'd never have caught you out like that.'

He'd shown not an inkling of sympathy for his unfortunate brother and his terrifying ordeal at the hands of the three men from London.

'Tell me this message again,' he barked, face contorted with rage.

'They said ... They said if the Driscoll's came to any harm, we would all be taken out,' stammered James, his gaze fixed on the patterned carpet. 'The number on the answer machine ... They're waiting for a call from us to say we'll back off from the Driscoll's ... If we don't call soon, they're going to start by killing one of the family ... I'm to make sure you understand it's a serious threat.'

'You said in forty minutes just now and that we'd vanish without a trace. Are you making it up as you go along?'

James stood, head down.

Alice Simms appeared in the doorway, drawn downstairs by Robin's hectoring tirade.

'What's this about the Driscoll's?'

'It's nothing to worry about Mother,' said Robin, his voice at once conciliatory. 'Come on. Let me take you back to your room. You look tired.'

'What's the matter with James?'

'He's all right. He's just had a bit of a shock that's all.'

'And the twins? They look as though they've seen a ghost.'

'Really Mother, it's nothing for you to worry about.'

He took her arm intending to lead her away. She shook him off.

'I want to know what's going on. I heard your ranting last night as well. Are you going to tell me what this is all about?'

'Just keeping things in order, the way Dad wants it.'

'It's more than that isn't it?'

Her persistence was beginning to rattle Robin. She'd never shown this sort of interest before or stood her ground with such determination. He could sense James and the twins following her every word and it was clear that she was not going to be easily diverted.

'There's a mob from Town trying to strongarm us. I'm just stressing the need for us to be together. Dad wants us to see them off. I didn't want to trouble you with it.'

'I think you mean you didn't want me to know Robin, but with all your bellowing I imagine the whole avenue is in on it. Is this why Justin was killed?'

Robin avoided her candid gaze, caught out by the directness of her question.

'It is, isn't it?' she pressed.

'We don't know that Mother.'

'I think you do Robin. You could have prevented it if you weren't so wrapped up in being the big macho man. I played their messages on the answer machine. They made no threats until you had ignored them twice. All you had to do was to pick up the phone to find out what they were after, but you thought it was clever to string them along – thought you'd win some kind of concession by making them wait. Well you misread it, badly didn't you? Now it turns out that all they want is for you to leave the Driscoll's in peace. They've killed Justin and put the fear of God into James because you have to be the great I am.

'You think, because you are a big fish around here, always one step ahead of the law, that you are untouchable. Well this is one small pond Robin and there's a whole ocean out there just filled with big fish indeed and unlike the police they are not bothered about the law. Going up against these people is extremely foolhardy. They might allow you to score a few points but that's all. They know your limitations. They can wipe us all out forever with one big punch. It seems to me that they would rather avoid doing so for some reason best known to themselves – they probably don't want the hassle of it all, but you take it from me; you don't bargain with these people, you do as they say when they say it. Show some sense man. If you take them on, we'll all come out of it badly. Just leave the Driscoll's alone. It really is that simple.

'That's not how Dad wants it,' replied Robin stubbornly, still unable to look her in the eye.

'He wants them dead of course.'

'Yes.'

'Why?'

'You know why.'

'Revenge?'

'Of course, it's revenge.'

'Absolutely senseless. Your father made her a widow. Isn't that enough?'

'It's what he wants.'

'Then he's an even bigger prat than I took him for.'

Robin's eyes opened wide and his jaw dropped with the shock of this last remark. He'd never heard his mother speak like this.

'Well you must just tell him no,' she continued. 'He doesn't realise what you're up against.'

'I'm not going against Dad's wishes because of a bunch of guys from London. If we don't see them off, they'll think we're a pushover and go on making more and more demands until they've got us by the short hairs.'

'This "bunch of guys" as you call them have already got us by the short hairs you dummy. You've seen what they can do. Your fathers locked up serving life because he's a headstrong prat. You're like him in so many ways Robin but up to now I've credited you with having more sense. I do hope you're not going to disappoint me.'

She turned away abruptly to leave them. They watched her walk away, their faces registering disbelief. She'd never spoken out like this before and her lack of respect for their father left them stunned.

At the foot of the stairs she stopped and looked back.

'The worst thing I ever did was to marry your father. I thought I could make him change his ways but that's how it is when you're young and silly. He corrupted my Justin just as he corrupted everyone who came in contact with him and I'm including all of us in that.'

Her shoulders slumped and she began to climb the stairs.

Robin gave James and the twins a hard look, all still standing there, shocked at their mother's outburst.

'She makes no difference,' he muttered. 'She's off to soak her head in vodka again. We're going to pick up Mrs. bloody Driscoll and her precious boy. If those London buggers are so interested in their welfare, I can use them to make a deal; if I've got them, I'll have the upper hand; I'll be the one to call the tune.'

'I don't think I'm up for this Robin. I really thought I was going to die this morning.' James, looking more determined than the tremor in his voice would suggest, kept his gaze straight ahead.

'You'll do just exactly as I say,' Robin shouted. 'Got it?' he thundered his face crimson with rage, 'Exactly as I say. We are going after them and you'll be with us James. You cross me in this, I'll make you sorry. You'll bloody be there and you'll be carrying. Now I've got calls to make.'

He winked at the twins as he left the room, cocking his head at James and rolling his eyes in a derisory gesture but felt a sudden doubt at their lack of response. Christ, he thought, they look as scared as he does.

★★★

The police were doing everything in their power to find Naomi but all their results so far were disappointingly negative. Such calls as they had received from the public were being checked out but so far had yielded nothing of any use. Arrangements were in hand for her parents and Philip to make a television appeal for information. Both families were desperately worried, but Mrs. Gibbs refused to believe the worst.

★★★

Naomi lay shivering under the pile of sacks as darkness fell. She dreaded another night of rodents scurrying in the darkness. Eventually her eyes grew heavy and she slipped into a feverish sleep. Several times she woke to find her symptoms had worsened and she drank sparingly from the second bottle to cool her tortured throat.

★★★

Police Constable Stephen Arnold wriggled his cold toes and wondered how his feet could have grown quite so cold while being tucked up inside the new pair of thermal socks and insulated from the frosty ground by his thick rubber soles. He breathed deeply, flexing his fingers inside the woollen gloves and he tried to stretch the mild ache out of his neck. Countless bright stars gleamed from a winter sky devoid of cloud and, despite his warm clothes; a sudden spasmodic shiver ran through his body. He stooped to pick up his thermos flask and was pouring the last of his mulligatawny soup when his radio crackled softly. Grateful for the break in the monotony, he keyed the answer button and spoke quietly.

'All quiet Sarge, bloody cold though. Still, only another half-hour or so.'

He listened a few moments, nodding vigorously, despite the fact that the Sergeant couldn't see him, he then returned the handset to its holster. The hot soup tasted good and as he sipped; his interested gaze followed a satellite as it tracked across the black void. Being thus occupied, he failed to detect the rubber-shod approach and so his balaclava clad assailant was able to pick his spot and, with a single, heavy blow, drop him, unconscious, to the freezing ground. Willing hands grasped his inert body, dragged it hastily into the back garden and rolled it under the hedge. Dark figures moved swiftly towards the house, fleeting silhouettes of black against the silvered lawn.

Maureen Driscoll woke suddenly, a gloved hand firmly in place across her mouth and cold metal against her throat. Terry's white face, illuminated by a small torch held under his chin, stared back at her and she saw the razor laid along the pale skin of his neck. A finger jabbed her shoulder and a hoarse voice spoke in the darkness.

'We're all leaving. You'll do exactly as you're told if you know what's good for you. First sign of trouble and we cut the boy's throat then yours. Now slowly, slowly out of bed.'

The hand was removed from her mouth and she swung her feet to the floor and stood, never taking her eyes from Terry's. She didn't trust herself to speak in case a tremor in her voice added to Terry's fears by betraying her own.

'Get your dressing gown and slippers then bring his. Don't do anything silly now Mrs. D.'

Her mind was racing as she walked through to Terry's room. The rush of cold air on the landing told her that a door or a window was open somewhere. Who were these men? Simms'? Why hadn't the alarm gone off? What were the police thinking of to let things go this far? She groped around in the dark for Terry's things, returned to her room where she and Terry were allowed to put on their dressing gowns and slippers: but the razors were never far away. The hoarse voice spoke again.

'You lead on Mrs. D. Downstairs, through the kitchen and out the back door. Then wait. Careful now eh.'

She led the way down to the kitchen and walked out through the open door into the garden to wait as instructed.

'So far so good,' said the same hoarse voice. 'No. Don't turn round. He'll be fine all the time you're a good girl. Now we're going to the back gate. Same again. Lead on and wait.'

She waited in the lane behind the house until the group caught up. A powerful hand gripped her chin roughly as she tried to look back for a sight of Terry.

'I said don't turn round. Don't make me cross Mrs. D', just do as I say. All right?'

She nodded.

'Good girl. Now, down the lane to the junction and turn right.'

They set off again, hidden by the tall fences and hedging, their footsteps making almost no sound on the frosted grass verge. As they turned out into the road, she saw a horsebox parked, the lowered tailboard forming a ramp.

'Inside quick.' A hand took her elbow and propelled her up and into the dark interior of the vehicle. She was pushed to the right as the tailboard was raised and she had the impression that she was separated from Terry by a central partition. It was silent but she was sure that their captors were in the box with them. She shivered, clad only in her nightdress and dressing gown, and she wrinkled her nose at the strong smell of horses.

'May I speak?' she asked, relieved to find that her voice was strong and steady.

'No,' came the unequivocal reply.

The engine rumbled into life and hands steadied her as the box moved off and picked up speed. After an uncomfortable ride, she had no clear idea of its duration, the vehicle slowed, stopped, and she heard the sound of heavy sliding doors. The horsebox jolted forward, and the sliding doors grumbled on their return journey as the truck stopped and the engine was switched off.

★★★

Billy stretched, yawned, and checked his watch. So far it had been an uneventful night, the only disturbance being the sounds of lusty passion issuing from Miranda's room where Andy, Billy's relief watcher, was finding out all about her lack of subtlety in matters of seduction. It had been quiet for a couple of hours and he smiled in the darkness remembering the frantic exertions he'd overheard despite the closed bedroom door.

Nothing was happening across the road.

He stretched again then, conscious of his heavy eyelids, rose to his feet stifling another huge yawn.

'Coffee time I think,' he said aloud.

He was conscious of a heightening of his senses as he made his way down to the kitchen. In the silence of the house sounds of running water and clinking of mug and spoon seemed inordinately noisy. Must be all that caffeine or all that humping, he thought, smiling in the darkness. Even the gentle rattle of bottles as he pushed the refrigerator door to seemed loud enough to wake the lovers. He heard no sign of life though as he padded back to his vantage-point at the window, his stockinged feet sinking into the soft pile of the stair carpet. He sipped his coffee and continued his vigil.

★★★

In the upstairs room opposite number twenty-one Grove Walk the two police officers were anticipating the end of their shift. They had the place to themselves as the owners had agreed that it would be better for all concerned if they moved out temporarily. In the dim light at the back of the room Detective Constable Kate Hewett contemplated her half-cup of cold coffee with disgust, before pouring it back into the Thermos flask.

'I must be losing it,' she sighed with regret. 'I went to finish my coffee and swallowed all that horrible skin.' She gave an involuntary shudder: 'Ugh, revolting.'

Her colleague, seated at the window, grunted, and shifted in his seat.

'Have some of mine. The flask's there next to you.'

'That's most kind of you Sergeant but as I've tasted your coffee before, I'll pass thank you. It reminded me of the stuff my dad does our fences with.'

'You're an ungrateful girl. There's folk who'd queue up for a cup of my coffee.'

'Well thanks all the same but I'll pass. We'll be off soon.'

'I keep telling you, keep the milk separate and add it after you've poured the coffee. You put too much milk. That's why it skins over.'

'You sound just like my dad. I make it milky because that's how I like it. It's just that I let the last cup go cold. God, what a life, come to work in the dark, sit here in the dark, go home in the bloody dark.'

The Sergeant at the window stretched his arms wide and yawned.

'Less than half an hour to go now. Stop moaning. Thank your stars you're not out there with old Steve. There's a real thick frost. He must be freezing.'

'I wouldn't mind being out there with him. He's a real hunk. I bet we could melt some frost.'

'It's time he called in. Give him a shout.'

'Why're you laughing?'

She heard chuckling and could make out his shaking shoulders against the pale background of the net curtain.

'Come on. What did I say?'

'Never mind. Just call him up,' replied the Sergeant, managing to stifle his mirth. 'Go on it's time.'

'Don't tell me, he's gay.'

'I'm saying nothing. Call him up now.'

She depressed the 'send' key and called Constable Stephen Arnold. Nothing.

'He's not answering Dave.'

'Try him again. He's probably doing a pee. It's that bloody cold out there.'

She repeated the procedure but again with no success.

'This is not like him Dave. He always responds immediately.'

She felt a sudden pang of apprehension – a cold intuition.

'Dave?'

Her short utterance was charged with anguish. He was irritated by her sudden show of fear and the implicit question: What are we going to do now?

166

He turned in his chair and saw the fear in her face.

'Get a grip Kate,' he said gently. 'It's probably just a glitch with his radio. Try again and if you still can't raise him, call in. You know the procedure.'

He watched as she called Constable Stephen Arnold again and once more failed to get a response. Something in her demeanour reached out to him, seemed to flicker on his skin like the splash of a mild electric shock. She seemed on the verge of going to pieces and, for an instant, he felt a stab of foreboding – a sudden concern for the wellbeing of Steve Arnold.

'Come on Kate. Call in and explain. You know what to do.'

'Something's happened to him Dave. I know it. I just know it.'

Her voice betrayed her anxiety. She was almost wailing, her lip trembled, and she was obviously close to tears.

'Do it now Kate,' he said firmly.

Kate's professionalism saw her through the next few minutes as she followed correct radio procedure and explained the situation. She concluded her report and stood the radio on a chair.

'They're checking on him. We're to hang on.'

The voices on the radio, punctuated by bursts of static interference, held their undivided attention. They listened in disbelief to the discoveries that Steve Arnold and the Driscoll's were nowhere to be found.

'The back-door's wide open and there's no one in the house. There must have been at least three or four of them, there's footprints in the frost – loads of them.'

Then they recognised Danny Prior's breathless voice. 'He's here, under the hedge, rambling on about hot soup and cold feet. He's concussed I reckon, not making a lot of sense. I'm calling the ambulance. Still no sign of Mrs. Driscoll and the boy.'

'I said we should have more than one officer out there,' muttered Dave, his face clouded with concern. 'Let's hope he's going to be okay and the Driscoll's of course. Right under our noses eh. What can you expect? We're undermanned every time it seems to me. You okay? I've never believed in woman's intuition – not until now.'

He stopped, at a loss, aware that he was talking too much. He put a hand on Kate's shoulder.

'I was laughing, Kate, because he said he didn't half fancy you.'

Kate made no response. She sat with folded arms, head down, a picture of total dejection.

***

Billy remained at the window listening with half an ear to the routine police messages. The time dragged by. He was thinking about rousing Andy when he became aware that the constable behind Mrs. Driscoll's house was not answering his radio. He listened with interest as Kate Hewett failed to contact P.C. Arnold and he followed with some amusement her repeated attempts to contact him. You're going to get a right bollocking when you do answer he smiled to himself. As it became clear, however, that the constable was not going to reply, Billy began to feel edgy. The ensuing radio traffic soon left him in no doubt that the police operation had gone badly wrong and, like the watchers in the house opposite, he listened in disbelief to the news that Maureen Driscoll and her son had been taken.

He seized the phone, jabbed in the digits of Mr. Edmonds' number, and waited impatiently for him to pick up. After what seemed an age Mr. Edmonds' sleepy voice announced, 'It's three a.m. Billy.'

'I'm sorry Mr. Edmonds but it's happened. They've got Mrs. Driscoll and the boy.'

'Okay Billy. I didn't expect them to make their move in daylight. You're sure?'

'Just listened in on the whole thing. They've nobbled the copper round the back and taken the pair of them. Coppers are in a right old state. One lot's shot off to the Simms' place and two cars have just pulled up across the road. The ambulance has just arrived for the injured copper. He's had a whack on the head, got concussion they reckon.'

'Now Billy, call the others and fill them in on it. I want you all in a state of readiness. I'm going to phone round to see if I can get an angle on where they might have been taken. It's a long shot but someone might know something. In the meantime, be ready. If I hear anything useful, I want you lot on the road double quick. I don't suppose the police know any more than we do?'

'They haven't got a clue. There's messages flying to and fro' but they're baffled right now. They're just turning the Simms family out of bed, but they'll know nothing of course.'

'If the police had been on the ball Mrs. Driscoll and her boy would be safely tucked up in bed. What a bloody mess. Our people are going to be extremely disappointed at this turn of events. The Simms have taken one liberty too many this time. It's all going to turn very nasty now. Remember Billy, ready at all times eh, anything happens, get on the phone. This line will be kept open.'

The phone went dead.

Miranda's bedroom door opened, and an indignant Andy stood blinking in the landing light.

'What's all the racket Billy,' he demanded, 'it's gone three.'

'Put some clothes on mate. Christ, I've seen more meat on an Oxo cube. I can see your mum never made you eat your crusts. They've just snatched the Driscoll's from under the noses of the boys in blue.'

Ignoring Billy's personal remarks, Andy stepped across to the window and peered out through the net curtain.

'Who'd be a copper,' he muttered. 'Look at them. They'll be manoeuvring some poor sod's head onto the chopping block. They'll have their scapegoat.'

'My money's on the poor bugger who got hit on the head,' replied Billy. 'Will you get dressed? We have to be ready to move when Mr. Edmonds phones. Evidently the governor's going to be really pissed off when he hears so let's do as we're told eh. I'm just going to phone the others – fill them in like.'

'Hey,' whispered Andy. 'What a woman eh. A week-end with her would kill you I reckon.'

'Funny you should say that. When that door opened, and you stood there like two eyes on a stick I thought you were on your way to Heaven.'

'No mate. That's where I'd just come from. There's a warm bed in there. You going to have some?'

'No, I'm not. Now move your bony arse Andy. The sex Olympics are on hold. If you're not ready when he calls, we'll go without you and then you'll be in the deepest shit.'

Andy crept into the bedroom to retrieve his clothes and Billy groaned as he heard Miranda enquiring about the time. To his relief Andy reappeared with his arms full of clothes and made for the bathroom.

'Ooh,' he giggled, 'I thought she'd got me.'

As the bathroom door closed behind Andy, Miranda appeared in the doorway of her bedroom.

'What's going on Billy?' she asked petulantly. 'It's gone three in the morning.'

'God it must be a nudist convention,' exclaimed Billy. 'Mind, you're a lot nicer to look at than that specimen in there,' he said, casting a glance at the bathroom door.

'Leave him alone,' she pouted. 'He's lovely. Not too heavy see.'

'We're waiting for a call from Mr. Edmonds. He wants us ready to go. The filth over the road have been outflanked and the parties they were supposed to be guarding have been snatched. They're in a right flap. I'm just going to phone the others and bring them up to date. A cup of tea would be nice.'

'Right.' Miranda slipped into a housecoat then paused at the top of the stairs. 'I'll miss you Billy. Maybe you'll come back after?'

'I might just do that,' replied Billy, winking as he picked up the phone.

CHAPTER EIGHTEEN

Early Wednesday morning

Naomi huddled beneath the filthy sacking, enduring the gritty unpleasantness, grateful for the odorous warmth. Her fever seemed to be subsiding, but she felt so dirty and longed for something to drink. She drained the second bottle. She stared into the darkness. It's Wednesday, the second morning, she thought as the rectangular window gradually turned pale and details of her surroundings reappeared as the early light intensified. She felt drained, defeated. The hopelessness of her situation was all too real.

Holding her breath, she pushed the sacking to one side then clambered to her feet, yawned, stretched, made her way to the window, and peered out. It had turned milder during the night, but the overcast sky threatened rain and gave the new day a cheerless aspect. The derelict house appeared even more forlorn in the early light. The once bright windows seemed to gape like dark, hollow eyes returning her gaze in a doleful stare of resignation. She wondered about its past, imagining how in times gone by the household would have been waking to another day, an interdependent community of family and servants interacting within those stout walls, secure in their enduring permanence. Where are you now? She wondered, continuing to regard the desolate monument to wealth and class divisions.

She was jolted out of her reverie by the sight of a scruffy looking man standing in a ground floor window. He stepped out over the windowsill looking furtively to his left and right, making it obvious that he did not wish to be seen. Naomi wondered just how long he'd been standing there as she began to kick at the wooden boards and pound with her fists, calling out as loudly as she could.

'HELP! HELP ME. PLEASE. UP HERE!'

The man, startled by this sudden outcry, turned, and looked towards her, then fled across the back of the house and beyond her field of vision.

'Please,' she sobbed, her voice hoarse but loud enough. 'Please come back. HELP ME!'

She continued to shout and hammer at the wall until at last her voice cracked and she could shout no more. Suffering with the stinging rawness of her throat and the aching of her bruised hands and feet, she gave up and slid to the floor sobbing in despair, cursing the wretched man for running off, for abandoning her so cruelly.

***

The detective constables had been sitting in the unmarked car for several hours watching the Simms family home. The Simms had of course denied any knowledge of the disappearance of the Driscoll's or that of Naomi Gibbs. Robin Simms had objected most strongly to the early morning visit and threatened the police with legal action for harassment, all his usual bluster in fact. The police knew very well that the Simms gang was responsible, not only for these recent abductions, but also for several that had happened previously but knowing is not proving. The Crown Prosecution Service prefers to back certainties.

Each investigation had either drawn a complete blank or led to the discovery of a body. As far as it could be ascertained, no kidnap victim had ever survived and in each case the criminal fraternity had remained tight lipped. The victims had either disappeared completely or had been found dead; two found in builders' skips, badly mutilated, and one at the bottom of a swimming pool, hands tied, pockets filled with gravel. It was clear from the way information on the whereabouts of these bodies was brought to the attention of the Police that those responsible for killing them wanted them to be found with due media coverage: a lesson for those who might be thinking of diverting funds or business to their own advantage.

The missing persons investigated so far had all been petty criminals known to be involved in various ways in drug trafficking and no doubt their deaths had been brought about by transgression of the Simms' rules. Phrases like "Gangland Killing" and "Gang Execution" always featured in media reportage of their passing.

For all their efforts, the huge numbers of man-hours expended, weary footslogging monotony, interviews with recalcitrant or frightened witnesses, the police came up with little in the way of useful leads. They were unable to assemble a body of hard evidence that might, with at least some degree of certainty, pointing to likely perpetrators of these heinous crimes.

This was different though because Maureen and Terry were well known to the Force, several officers were personal friends, and Naomi Gibbs was the daughter of a respectable, local family. The Chief Constable was beginning to demand regular updates on progress and to show his disappointment with the poor results achieved thus far, but despite his intervention and everyone's best efforts, the enquiry was losing momentum. There were simply no more leads to follow. To their chagrin, the police found themselves once again without the means to connect the Simms family to these abductions.

★★★

Oblivious to the passing of time, desperately disappointed at the man's failure to help her, Naomi remained slumped against the wall in a state of abject misery until the faint noises beyond the door impinged upon her hearing. She looked up thinking at first that her tormentors had returned. But these were sounds of stealth. The twins would simply march up the stairs and throw back the door. They had no reason to creep about. The stairs creaked again, closer this time, and then there was silence. She waited. Then, after an interminable pause, she heard, as if it were guided by a shaking hand, the metallic sound of the key entering and then turning in the lock. Again, an endless pause before she heard the padlock lifted from its staple. The door swung back to reveal the man, whom she now saw, was quite elderly, standing timidly as though waiting to be invited in.

'You came back,' said Naomi hoarsely, almost choking with emotion.

The man stepped inside and paused.

'I've seen you before. You were on the railway that night.'

His cultured voice came as a surprise; he sounded just like her bank manager, Mr. Tomkin.

'Yes, I was. Please get me out of here before they come back.'

She was suddenly anxious that the twins would return to thwart her escape and wanted to tell the man that had he come in straight away she would be safely out of harm's way by now. Recognising his nervousness, however, she resisted her shrewish urge and sat still, trying to appear composed.

The man stepped across to her, pulling a face as he caught the smell of the bucket, then knelt in front of her. She held out her arms as he produced a penknife, cut through her bonds, unwound the stiff white spiral from her cold wrists and dropped it to the floor where it lay like a broken spring. She saw his tears and felt her own eyes filling up.

'Oh,' she sighed, getting to her feet, chafing her wrists, 'thank you so much. You've saved my life. She hobbled across and grabbed the phone but then cried out in anguish as she saw that the battery was dead. 'We must hurry before they come back,' she said. 'My car's just out there. I've got spare keys. Quick, come on,' she cried, pulling at his sleeve, 'We'll go straight to the police.'

'They'll recognise your car and block the drive. It's a long way to the gate for a start and then you've got several miles of narrow lane to negotiate before you get to the main road. If you meet them, they'll run you into the ditch. You'll never get past them.'

'But they won't be expecting to meet me. They think I'm locked in here.'

'It's a very lonely route my dear. Your car would most likely be the only one they'd see. They're hardly likely to overlook it, are they?'

'What if we could make it to the gate then turn the other way, to the left? Where does that go?'

'It peters out after about half a mile. There's no way out that way, not by road anyway.'

'Oh, what are we going to do?' she cried in frustration, conscious of the prickle of yet more tears.

'First thing to do is to get out of here and into concealment. I've got the very place. Then you stay safely out of sight while I go to the police.'

'Have you got a car?' asked Naomi, thinking it most unlikely.

'No. I'll walk.'

'It's miles.'

'Oh, I'm an accomplished walker. I come out here at least twice a week. I cut through the wood as the crow flies and it cuts off miles. I get to the main road in no time. An hour later and I'm back in town. Now let's get out of sight.'

He paused as they turned to leave.

'These are new,' he observed, fingering the shiny galvanised bolts on the door. 'I suppose they don't want anyone walking in on them at the wrong moment.' He looked thoughtful as he worked the bolts to and fro.

They walked out to the landing where she waited nervously while he locked the door. Then they descended the stairs and he reached down to return the keys to their hiding place. Keys in hand he looked up at Naomi. She paused then shook her head. He crossed the path, scraped away at the base of a large tree, dropped the keys into the depression and dragged leaf mould back over them.

'Those two have been around a lot lately,' he said, looking back to the top of the stairs. 'I don't know what they do up there, but I've heard girls screaming. I must say they strike me as a particularly unpleasant pair. Now, follow me.'

He led the way across to the house and helped Naomi in over the windowsill where she'd first seen him.

'It does seem rather odd going in through the window like this but the floor's in much better condition here. It's so rotten at the back door, one could fall through into the cellars you know.'

They crossed to the doorway, turned into a passage then entered an enormous room that still retained its air of elegance despite decades of neglect and pale fungi growing on the crumbling plaster. Naomi gasped at the sheer size of it. The windows were from floor to ceiling and she could see remains of the elaborate plaster cornice still clinging to the walls and ceiling. At the furthest end, there was a huge opening where a large fireplace had been removed.

'This was the ballroom,' he told her, pointing to the opposite end. 'There was a lovely staircase there and as a child, I used to sit on the landing behind the bannisters and watch all the ladies and gentlemen dancing.'

He stopped and Naomi saw happiness in his face as he recalled the scene.

'They were grand affairs you know,' he went on. 'All the ladies in their beautiful gowns, sparkling with their jewellery, all the gentlemen in black tie, some in dress uniform, the musicians playing so beautifully, chandeliers, laughter, what an atmosphere that was. I used to love it. Mummy always allowed me to watch. She knew it made me so happy. All gone now though,' he said with a sigh.

This shabby old man who sounded like an old-fashioned BBC announcer intrigued Naomi no end.

They reached the fireplace.

'Here we are,' he said. 'Up there.' He pointed to the chimney.

'What?' she said. 'Up the chimney?'

'You'll find a stone shelf up there. There's lots of room, bone dry, amazingly comfortable. Come on. I'll show you. Need a leg up?'

'No thank you,' she replied, conscious of the shortness of her skirt. 'But I do need to wee before I go up there.'

'Ah,' he paused, somewhat embarrassed. 'You'd better be quick then. I'll wait here.'

Naomi clambered out through the nearest window and disappeared into the dense shrubbery. She soon reappeared.

'All done,' she smiled, returning to the hearth.

She watched his nimble ascent into the chimney, surprised by his agility, then followed.

'Give me your hand,' he said, and drew her up into the dark void where she found herself standing beside him on a platform. He lit a candle stub, placed it into a niche in the brickwork and the dim light was enough to show her that the surroundings were relatively clean. It became obvious though that her companion's personal hygiene was rather rudimentary.

'I expect you're hungry.' He handed her a sandwich in a transparent triangular package. She looked doubtfully at the labelling wondering about the "sell by" date but was unable to find it in the feeble light from the candle.

'It's all right,' he said, producing a large bottle of mineral water. 'I never get meat or prawns, only salad with cheese, they keep better. They've never made me unwell. Now how about a drink? Not too much at first mind.'

'Marvellous,' she answered, accepting the proffered bottle with gratitude. She tipped back her head and allowed the water to trickle into her mouth, enjoying the cool cleansing of dust from her throat and the easing of the soreness.

'Oh, you've no idea how good that is,' she gasped, taking a second swig before handing back the bottle.

The sandwich was wonderful too. The bread being soft, the cheese wonderfully tangy and the limp salad kind to her throat. She chewed slowly, relishing the first half, postponing her enjoyment of the second.

'I only got these on Monday,' he said, opening one for himself. 'They're usually very nice. Why don't we sit down?'

They sat on a roll of hessian that was placed along the back of the shelf and ate in silence, taking turns with the water and she felt much better as the nourishment began to revive her spirits. She would have enjoyed another sandwich but didn't like to ask. As it was, she was wondering whether he'd already given her half of his food supply.

'Did you live here once? She asked. 'You seem to know all about it.'

'I was born here, grew up here, know every inch of it. I know every path through the wood – every last bit of it.'

'What happened?' Naomi was eaten up with curiosity. The man was a puzzle to her.

'That would be an awful long time in the telling.'

'What's your name?' she asked, sensing reticence on his part, wishing not to embarrass him, 'I'm Naomi.'

'Mummy always calls me Matty.'

'Is that for Matthew?'

'That's right.'

'What does your dad call you?'

She knew at once that she had ventured too far. Matty made no answer and she sensed the change in his demeanour.

'Sorry,' she said, placing her hand on his arm. 'I always chatter too much.'

'Father called me Matthew or Sir,' he mumbled at last, 'Matthew or Sir.'

There followed an awkward pause during which she could hear him drawing deep breaths, trying to regain his composure.

'I'm sorry Matty,' she said again, filled with regret that she had caused him discomfort.

'It's all right my dear,' he sighed at last, 'just unpleasant memories – they stay with one forever it seems.'

'I guess I'll have my own share of those then,' she replied.

'I'm afraid you will … I'm afraid you will. But you'll find you can keep them in check after a time. They do fade to a certain extent.'

He shushed her suddenly and pinched out the candle. They sat still in the dark and her heart went out to him as she realised that this was how he lived his life, on edge the whole time like a wild creature, always in fear of discovery.

'I think I hear a car on the drive,' he whispered.

★★★

CHAPTER NINETEEN

As the two police officers waited and watched their colleagues were working very hard to find a lead. All the usual villains and their associates – anyone who might know something – had been rounded up and subjected to intensive questioning, but so far without success. None of those under suspicion looked as if they might cooperate. Initial optimism was fading as the police found themselves looking at yet another dead end.

'Not a lot of action so far,' said the policeman in the passenger seat. 'Just James going off to work nice and early.'

His colleague grunted and stretched his arms.

'An example to us all.'

They became alert as they saw the front door of the house open and Robin Simms, wearing a long dark coat and a tweed cap, come out and placed a holdall in the boot of the dark blue Jaguar parked on the drive. He paused, looked all around, then gave them a wave before re-entering the house.

'Cheeky bugger,' said the policeman behind the wheel.

***

'Here we go,' replied his partner as the door opened a second time and Simms strode across to the car, climbed in, settled himself comfortably and drove out onto the road and away. The policeman grabbed the radio, gave their call sign, and reported that Simms was on the move. A second car would follow the Jaguar while they continued to watch the house. They listened with interest as their colleagues reported the Jaguar's progress.

A third unmarked car took up the pursuit and reported that Simms had pulled into the Railway Station where a tall dark woman had joined him. Simms was by now on the A12 heading in the direction of Ipswich.

'Looks like he's off for a dirty week-end,' said the policeman behind the wheel.

'On a Wednesday?' replied his partner. 'It's all right for some eh.'

'They can't go on like this you know,' replied the driver. 'They've got to come unstuck sometime. They must involve a lot of people when they organise these abductions and killings; people who do their dirty work for them. It just needs one of them to talk and they'll be well stuffed. All we need is to find a chink, a starting place. It's got to happen sometime; law of averages says so. They've flouted the law a long time now and the longer they go on doing it, the more likely it becomes that someone'll foul up. Then we'll have the bastards – I know we will.'

'Get real mate. Look at what happened to Inspector Driscoll. Why do you think they've been getting away with it for so long? Nobody's going to cross that Simms lot. They all know what will happen if they grass.'

'I still say it can't go on forever. I can't tell you how it will end, but I reckon it will before much longer.'

'Let's hope it's soon then, not too late for Mrs. Driscoll and the boy.'

'And the girl.'

'No. She's a goner mate. I guess they're all goners by now.'

'Let's hope not eh.'

★★★

The police car, having tracked Robin Simms along the lanes, drove slowly into the car park of the Ashton Grange Hotel and parked at the far end, away from his Jaguar. The driver, Detective Sergeant Brian Mayhew, switched off the ignition and applied the handbrake.

'I think we'll sit a while, see what transpires. Very posh eh. Get on the radio and tell them where we are.'

His partner, Detective Constable Dennis Hill, gave their call sign, explained their present position, and leant back in his seat.

'What do you think he's up to then Sarge?'

'I guess he's establishing his whereabouts at 11.00 this Wednesday morning and he'll have several witnesses including you and me.'

'We just going to sit here 'til he makes a move?'

'Sit tight, I'll go in and have a nose round, see what's what.'

Dennis watched his colleague stroll across to the hotel entrance and walk inside.

A few minutes later he came back in hurry, almost running, his face pale and anxious. Dennis opened his door as the Sergeant drew near.

'What's up?'

'We've been done mate. That's Bill Bayliss and his missus in there. They've worked a right flanker.'

'You sure?'

'Course I'm sure. I showed the receptionist my warrant card and asked to look at the register. She pointed to where they'd signed in and as I was reading it, she says, "He's just coming out of the lift now." I turn round for a look and there he is. Bill bloody Bayliss with his wife large as life.'

'Christ, Robin Simms could be anywhere then,' exclaimed Dennis.

'Damn right he could. Let's break the bad news.'

Brian took the radio and reported the situation. He started the engine and let in the clutch.

'It makes me so fucking mad,' he fumed, driving towards the exit. 'That bloody git Simms is always a jump ahead. You know they'd registered as Mr. D. Aylesbury and Ms K. Campbell.'

'Can't we have them for giving false particulars?'

'Maybe. Right now, we have to be concerned about Simms whereabouts and the safety of Maureen and Terry.'

They drove back along the country lanes in silence.

'They're having a laugh,' said Dennis at last.

'Who?'

'Bayliss. D. Aylesbury. What if the D stands for Donald?'

'So?'

'What do you think of when you hear the word Aylesbury?'

'Ducklings, ducks I suppose.'

'Yeah … So?'

'Ducks … Donald? Oh no, Donald bloody Duck. What a bloody wind up.'

'I reckon so. What about Ms. K. Campbell? Khaki Campbell is a breed of duck you know.'

'They really are taking the piss eh.' The Sergeant looked peeved as he drove on in silence.

★★★

Robin Simms kept a close eye on his rear-view mirror as he and James drove along the narrow lane towards Kingsfield Park. The old Vauxhall hummed along sweetly enough, and he laughed out loud at the success of his ruse. He'd simply walked out to the car and placed the bag in the boot, waved to the policemen then gone back inside where he'd divested himself of the overcoat and cap. Bill Bayliss had put them on, walked out to the car and driven off. Then he'd simply left by the back door, made his way through the gardens to where James was waiting in the Vectra three streets away. He chuckled at the thought of all those policemen tracking the wrong man.

'Like bluebottles on a dog turd,' he laughed.

James joined in but with rather less enthusiasm than his brother. He didn't think that Bill would appreciate the simile, but he wasn't about to point it out.

Checking the mirror once again, Robin steered the car in through the leaning gateway, pulled up beneath the thick canopy of trees and waited. Satisfied at last that no one was following, he continued along the driveway finally coming to a stop near the hayloft. He hummed a tune as he climbed the steps feeling in his jacket pocket for the large key, but the tune died on his lips as he gazed in disbelief at the heavy-duty padlock.

'What the bloody hell's this?' He muttered, pulling at it to check if it was unlocked. It was locked of course – left so by Matty.

'I don't believe this,' he grunted. 'James,' he called. 'What's this bloody padlock?'

'No idea,' his brother replied. 'I don't remember there ever being a padlock.'

Robin, his lightness of mood swept aside by the anger swelling in his chest, produced his mobile phone, grim-faced he flipped it open and scrolled through the phone book numbers.

'Ah,' he said, his voice thick with malice when Joshua answered at last. 'I'm out at Kingsfield Park looking at a fucking great padlock. You and that bloody sister of yours had better get out here with the key and an explanation P.D.Q. You really don't want me to have to come looking for you. The Old Bill will be watching to see where you're off to. You lose them. Don't you dare lead them out here. I've got something big going down and you two have really fucked up my timing. Get going. I'm in a murderous mood.' He stood listening: the phone held tightly against his ear. 'James,' he called. 'Joshua says the keys are under the bottom step. Fetch them up to me.'

James knelt and felt around under the step but found nothing. He lay on his belly and peered into the space. Nothing.

'There are no keys Robin,' he said nervously. 'They're not here.'

Robin stamped his way to the bottom of the stairs, cursed James for a useless idiot, shouldered him aside and felt around under the step. There were no keys to be found.

He stood, his face like thunder and spoke into the phone. 'We have both looked under the bottom step Joshua. There are no fucking keys. You're really trying my patience. I repeat, get out here double quick if you know what's good for you.' He dropped the phone into his pocket and looked at his watch. 'About half an hour I reckon,' he said quietly.

James simply nodded anxious not to be the butt of his brother's fury. Leaving the stairs, Robin climbed back into the Vauxhall and drove in under the overhanging foliage where he was surprised to find Naomi's Peugeot parked.

'Just what the hell have they been up to this time?' he fumed. 'There'd better be a good explanation for all this or I'm going to get very heavy.'

James looked most uncomfortable; wishing heartily he were elsewhere.

★★★

Matty took Naomi's hand.

'Stay here quiet as a mouse. I'm going to see who's out there.'

'Are you sure that's a good idea,' she whispered. 'What if they see you?'

'I'll be careful. They won't see me. I know my way around too well.'

'Be careful then. I don't want to be stuck up here forever.'

'Don't worry. I'll be very careful.'

Quietly, he moved across to where three or four bricks had been removed and peered into the opening.

'I can see most of the ballroom through here,' he whispered. 'I always have a peep before I climb down. It wouldn't do for someone to see me leave; give the whole game away.'

He patted her hand and climbed down without a sound. Naomi could only sit hugging her knees, and hoping he knew what he was doing. She knew that if the twins caught him, he would come in for some pretty rough treatment. God only knows what they'd do to him to find out where she was, she thought. She snuggled down in her dark corner, worried about Matty but so grateful to be away from that filthy loft and its scurrying vermin. Drowsiness settled on her and, hoping that there were no rats or mice in the chimney, she allowed herself to doze, her mind filled with thoughts of Philip and her family.

★★★

James remained in the car while Robin, his face set in anger, paced up and down the drive waiting for Joshua and Rebecca to arrive. Matty circled round to where Naomi's car was hidden intending to use the dense vegetation as cover as he looked out towards the drive to see where the new arrivals had parked. The presence of the second car under the trees surprised him. He backed up as he caught sight of James sitting in the front passenger seat and melted away on a different tack and as he neared the drive, he heard Robin's footsteps. He moved forward as Robin once again produced his phone. Matty listened.

'Change of plan. I've got to sort something out. Everything okay your end?'

Matty watched as Robin nodded several times, seemingly reassured by the answers to his questions.

'Right, keep them there 'til I give the word to move. You're clear on how to get here?'

Again, he nodded, obviously satisfied with the answer.

'Good. I'll be in touch A.S.A.P.'

He dropped the phone into his pocket and Matty, about to creep away, froze as he heard the tyres of an approaching car crunching on the gravel drive.

★★★

CHAPTER TWENTY

Chief Superintendent Douglas Jessop strode across the car park heading for the main entrance to the police station, his brow furrowed in thought. Things had developed so damn quickly. The murder of the Simms boy, the abduction of the Gibbs girl and then the Driscoll's and now the hunt for Robin Simms. Then there were the two villains from Kent, identified as having murdered the Simms boy and then themselves being murdered. Now a third one was dead, having jumped off the hospital roof after being forced to watch the brutal torture and murder of his young girlfriend. Sergeant Blissett had reported her conversations with the D.S. from Kent, and it seemed that his force was up against a degree of brutality even more malevolent than that of the Simms gang. Douglas' priority now, however, was to track down Robin Simms and prevent him from harming the Driscoll's. Like the majority of his officers, he believed Naomi Gibbs to be already dead.

'All this and not a single solitary lead,' he muttered, as he preserved the high gloss on his shoes by sidestepping the large puddles. 'The Chief Constable's going to be demanding results, shouting the odds about teamwork and competence in his inimitable way.'

Feeling very hard done by, Chief Superintendent Jessop entered the station.

'Sergeant Ellis,' he called as he strode through to his office. 'I'd like a word with Inspector Moss. See if you can round him up will you. I'll be in my office.'

Without waiting for an acknowledgement, he swept through the swing doors and was gone, leaving the rather miffed Sergeant staring after him.

'Hmmm,' he rumbled to himself. 'Team building's off today then. What happened to "please" and "thank you" Mr. bloody Jessop?'

Chief Superintendent Jessop was surprised to see Inspector Browning, his face pale and tense, waiting at his office door.

'You look like a bearer of bad tidings Bob. You feeling okay?'

'I need a word Sir. I think I know where they're holding Maureen and Terry Driscoll.'

'Come on in then. If you're right, it'll be the first thing to go our way in a long time. Running this station has become exceedingly tricky; not unlike trying to contain an octopus in a parrot cage. Bit early for a snort so it'll have to be coffee, sit down. Milk and no sugar. Right?'

Inspector Browning sat miserably while Douglas busied himself arranging kettle, cafetiere, cups and saucers with deft movements before dropping into his chair and placing his large white hands flat on the desk before him.

'There we are. Won't take a minute. Now Bob?' he said expectantly.

'The Inspector cleared his throat at last. He then spoke quickly but so softly that Douglas had to lean forward to catch what he was saying.

'When you've heard what I've got to say Sir I don't think you'll want to drink coffee with me.'

'Bob? I don't like the sound of this at all. Nothing's that bad surely. I bet it's nothing we can't sort out between us. What is it? Crown jewels? Bank robbery?'

This clumsy attempt at humour sent a spasm of pain across Bob's taut features.

'You'd lose your bet Sir. What I've done can't be sorted between us or by anyone else. I'm a bent copper, and there's no way out of that except my dismissal from the force. I don't know how I'm going to face my Judith with this. She'll take the boy and go. I've made such a bloody mess of everything.'

He covered his face with his hands and remained slumped in the chair.

Douglas, not at all sure what to say next, relieved to hear the rising note of the kettle, rose to his feet to pour boiling water into the jug and arrange the filter while simultaneously producing a bottle of whisky from a desk drawer. He poured a generous measure into each cup.

'Just a little booster Bob. I've a feeling we're both going to need it.'

He returned to his chair and leant back with folded arms.

'Now you're a good officer Bob. You've earned much respect during your time here by your diligence and integrity. Christ man!' he cried, banging his hand on the desk, 'You're an example to us all.'

It's all a sham Sir,' came the unhappy reply, the voice so low that Douglas could hardly make out the words. 'I guess I was trying to make it right – trying to pretend it wasn't serious – hoping it would go away.'

He sat with downcast eyes, a study in abject misery. A long silence hung between them. Douglas, though conscious of the seriousness of the matter, waited with some impatience for the Inspector to resume.

'I've been accepting bribes Sir,' he managed at last.

Douglas waited again.

'Arthur Simms set me up and I was too arrogant, too wet behind the ears to see it coming. They got me drunk. I must have made it so bloody easy for them.'

Inspector Browning then related the whole sorry sequence of events while Douglas listened, his face as neutral as he could make it.

'I went to his home to put an end to it. I was so sure that I could just finish what I believed had become an inappropriate relationship – just walk away a wiser man. It wasn't 'til they showed me the video and Simms explained what I would have to do in return for his silence that I saw what an utter fool I'd been, how completely I'd been sucked in.'

'What did you have to do for your money?'

Douglas' voice was cooling, distant, and the Inspector was reminded of the change in Arthur Simms' manner when he'd dropped all pretence at friendship and stated the terms of his arrangement.

'Just supply information when they asked for it.'

'What sort of information?' Chief Superintendent Jessop's voice was now very cold.

'He would tell me about little jobs he had on the go and ask if I knew of any reason why he couldn't go ahead safely, whether any police action was planned that might to jeopardise him or his people. Stuff like that.'

'And you told him what he wanted to know?'

'Always. He had me right where he wanted me in every sense.'

'Did your information ever contain details of a police operation?'

'Yes.'

'Care to elaborate?'

'No Sir. Not at the moment.'

'Where you instrumental in any way in the murder of Frank Driscoll?' The voice was now positively stony.

'Absolutely not. It was because of the abduction of Maureen and Terry that I finally found the backbone to own up to all this.'

'I'm not following you.'

'When I first became friendly with Arthur Simms I overheard a telephone conversation. He was shouting angrily about someone who'd crossed him, and I heard him say, "Get him out to Kingsfield and keep him there. I'll fucking flay him when I get there." Someone shushed him then, reminded him that I was close by and he reappeared, all smiles and good humour. I believe Maureen and Terry might well be out there.'

'Go home Bob and stay there. I'm suspending you from duty. I can't discuss your future – there will be an enquiry into your conduct. It'll be as fair as we can make it. You must of course tell Judith the whole story, clean slate and all that. You've tried the other way and look where that's got you. I hope she stands by you. She's a good woman.'

The Chief shook his head. 'You of all people, Bob.'

★★★

Douglas sat staring at the door after the departure of his disgraced colleague.

'What a bloody bombshell,' he muttered, 'and what a time to drop it.'

He depressed the plunger on the cafetiere, drank the two shots of whisky and poured himself a cup of coffee before reaching for his telephone and placing a call to the Chief Constable.

★★★

Chief Inspector Jessop nodded slowly as the Chief Constable re-iterated his instructions.

'I'm sorry Sir I'm still a bit baffled. Wouldn't it be better to get out there now and then if we strike it lucky, set up a negotiating team – get on with it?'

He listened again, pinching the bridge of his nose in an effort to forestall the headache he could feel building up.

'No Sir,' he said, still puzzled by his chief's reaction to the news. 'I certainly am not questioning your judgement. Yes Sir: that's how we'll do it. I'll assemble the appropriate teams and stand by for your go ahead.'

The Chief Constable cut the connection and Douglas sighed with relief, glad that the one-sided conversation was at an end. He resented his superior's brusque manner and the ease with which he was able to make him feel such a bloody fool. At least this verbal mauling had taken place in the privacy of his office and there'd been no one to witness his discomfort.

'Bloody man,' he exclaimed, slamming the phone down into its cradle.

★★★

Judith Browning, surprised to see her husband's Audi parked on the drive, climbed out of her car, and allowed the door to slam behind her while she selected her front door key. She pushed open the heavy door and was surprised again by the sight of her husband standing there looking somewhat dishevelled, holding a well filled whisky tumbler.

'Bit early for that Bob,' she remarked, hooking her coat on the hallstand.

'I've got to talk to you,' he replied, refusing to meet her gaze.

'How many have you had?'

'Just the one. Would you come in here please?'

He turned and led the way into the dining room. She followed and was surprised yet again when he thrust a tumbler of whisky into her hand.

'Really Bob! What's going on?' She was now thoroughly alarmed.

'I'm going to tell you how I've betrayed you Judith. I haven't the guts to face you. I'm going to stand here and look out at the garden.'

'Bob? I'm frightened. Please sit down and talk to me. Whatever it is we can share it – it's no good holding it all in the way you do. You'll become ill, depressed.'

'I'm going to begin Judith. I can only do this once and if you're not here when I've finished, that'll be no worse than I deserve. I'm not worthy of you. I never have been.'

She watched him turn away, take a long pull at his drink and then he began to speak. He omitted none of his follies and made no attempt to excuse his behaviour. He simply talked on in a dispirited monotone, sparing neither of them. She listened in silence, eyes welling with tears, taking large gulps of whisky while he unburdened himself of the guilt and the shame, he'd been carrying for more than a decade.

When at last he finished the silence hung between them ...

'I'm still here Bob,' she managed at last.

He continued to stare out of the window.

'I shall understand if you take Chas and go. I've been an absolute shit. I've ruined all our lives for want of a bit of courage.

Really, I should be the one to go. It would be fairer. No need for you two to uproot yourselves. It's me that's thrown it all away – let everyone down.'

She stepped forward, seized his arm, and turned him to face her.

'Bob. Look at me,' she commanded.

'I've made you cry,' he mumbled. 'I'm so sorry.'

'You know if you'd told me about all this at the time, I'd have been back to mother like a shot.'

'I know you would. That was why I couldn't tell you. I couldn't face up to it.'

'Not to mention the loss of your job as well.'

'That was less important Judith. We were young. I could have found something else. I'll have to now anyway.'

'What will they do to you?'

'A dishonourable end to my career on the force at least. Goodbye pension too, I expect.'

'If you'd told me this sordid story at the time Bob Browning, I'm quite sure I would have left you and I would have been one hundred per cent in the right to do so – you'd have got what you deserved. But life isn't so simple, is it? If you'd done the honourable thing – owned up, I would never have found out what a good man you are and what a wonderful father you are to Chas – he adores you. It's all out now. If I could put the happiness we've shared into a scale, your misdemeanours, for want of a better word, couldn't even begin to balance it. I've had the happiest years of my life with you and Chas. You're the one who's suffered all that time. Well, no longer! If this … this … this bloody video turns up, we'll destroy it together and … and … and they can all go to bloody hell. We won't even look at it.'

She took a long pull at her drink. 'What can they do?' she went on, 'I know. Your boss knows. You've pulled their teeth Bob. If they've got more copies, what the hell! we can see it through together.'

'I've never heard you swear like that,' he said, surprised at her vehemence.

'I often feel the need to let fly,' she replied, grinning at him but failing to get a reaction, 'and now I have. Perhaps I should drink more of this stuff.'

'I can't believe you're not disgusted with me Judith,' he said, his voice tremulous with remorse.

'That's because you've been scourging yourself all these years, it's been eating away at you. It's grown out of proportion. Yes, it's a serious situation and I can't pretend I'm not hurt, but we have to deal with it. I've tried to tell you how I feel Bob. It will never go away but we've got to overcome it. It can only harm us if we let it. Come on man, we've got each other. We can manage on my salary and the pension scheme is pretty good. You'll find something and you're not too old to salt away a bit for the future. What happened to your ill-gotten gains by the way? I don't remember you flashing your money around.'

'It's all in a bank account in my name. It's not really a lot to show for all the grief that came with it. I shall surrender it anyway, but I don't know how to go about it yet.'

'Not a good hourly rate then,' she joked, and was pleased to see the beginnings of a smile playing round his lips. 'Come on man, smile. That's it, have another drink.'

She uncorked the bottle and poured a small measure into his glass.

He found himself able to look her in the eye at last. 'You've turned this wretched business into a celebration Judith. I can't believe you still want me. I don't know what to say.'

'I'm so relieved Bob. I've watched you drawing further and further away from us and now I know why. Now it's off your chest I hope you're going to let it go. That's what I want.'

She reached up and kissed him on the lips. They held each other for a long time.

'I've got so much to be grateful for Judith,' he murmured at last.

'We both have,' she whispered. 'We both have.'

He held her to him, overawed by her generosity of spirit.

Owning up was proving to be cathartic thus far but he had not lost sight of the danger he would face when the Simms discovered what he'd done. They'd be out to get even. He thought back to what had happened to poor Frank Driscoll and was in no doubt about the magnitude of the risk he was facing.

He decided to keep this side of things to himself for the time being although he guessed that Judith would soon work it out for herself. It would all be out in the open soon enough – be in all the papers. They'd have to move away of course – make a fresh start somewhere new – somewhere where he wouldn't be known as that disgraced ex-copper.

★★★

CHAPTER TWENTY-ONE

The black BMW pulled up just short of where Robin stood waiting and after a moment's delay Joshua and Rebecca climbed out, neither of them willing to meet his eye.

He stood in the middle of the drive, feet spread, hands on hips, glaring at the discomfited pair.

'You two!' he exclaimed with contempt; his stare hateful. He waved a hand towards the loft. 'Get that fucking door open now then bring all the keys to me.'

The twins hurried to do his bidding, Joshua pausing to check under the bottom step while Rebecca ran up the stairs, unlocked the door using her own keys and pushed it open. She remained motionless on the threshold, holding out a warning hand as he joined her.

'She's gone Josh,' she whispered. 'So's the phone. She's climbed out through the bloody window.'

'Christ Becks! What do we do now?'

'Not a word. Take my key down to him while I get rid of that rope and the bottles. Don't hurry yourself. Give me time to sort things,' she continued, handing over the keys.

As Joshua turned to go, she gathered up the severed rope then, having replaced the bucket in the adjoining loft, along with the empty bottles, stood at the top of the stairs listening as Robin tore a strip off Joshua.

'Are you quite certain you weren't followed,' Robin demanded.

Joshua nodded but regretted doing so immediately as a painful spasm wracked his neck and shoulders. He stood pale faced and uncomfortable as Robin continued to upbraid him.

'I've got a lot to think about at the moment but when I've sorted it you two are going to give me chapter and verse on just what it is you've been up to out here. We'll start with who owns that bloody Peugeot over there. Got your mobile with you?'

'Yeah. It's here.' Still avoiding eye contact, Joshua pulled the phone from his breast pocket and held it up.

'I suppose you charge the battery from time to time?'

'Yeah, last night. I always keep it charged up.'

'There's a surprise. Now get your idle arse down to the gate and keep your eyes peeled for a horsebox. When it turns up ring me and direct the driver up here. Then get out of sight and watch the gate. Anyone comes in I want to know about it. Think you can manage that little job?' Robin's voice was thick with sarcasm. 'Get going,' he continued, giving Joshua a hefty push that jarred his neck and made him gasp with pain. 'Get on you bloody big tosser,' he jeered, as Joshua stumbled then trudged away towards the gate.

Robin ascended the stairs as the rain began to fall and Rebecca retreated nervously into the loft. 'I guess you heard all that?' he said. So you won't be surprised when I start asking questions will you? For now, get this place swept out and get those covers back on the window.' He paused as he caught sight of the bolts on the door. 'What's all this then?' he asked, sliding one of the bolts in and out. 'Didn't want to be disturbed eh? Rolling about on the floor with your kit off I shouldn't wonder,' he laughed, as Rebecca flushed and refused to look at him.

He stood at the door watching the raindrops bounce on the wooden stairs, listening to the clatter as Rebecca applied the broom vigorously to the dusty corners. James was nowhere to be seen. Robin assumed he was keeping dry in the car.

He took out his mobile, thumbed in the number and put it to his ear. 'Right,' he said, as he heard the answering voice. 'All set here. Quick as you can eh. Make sure you're not followed. You'll be met at the gate, expect you within the half-hour. Oh, and bring some sandwiches and something hot to drink. We're all a bit peckish.'

He returned the phone to his pocket and started down the stairs taking care not to slip on the wet surface.

Matty took a cautious, step backwards into the shadows and continued to watch and listen.

★★★

Billy and Andy stood at the gateway to Kingsfield Park, Billy cursing as the rain settled into a steady downpour. Ned and the others had been sent back down the lane to park the cars behind a tumbledown barn and wait instruction.

'God Almighty, this is all we need,' grumbled Billy, gazing resentfully at the leaden sky. 'It looks as if it's in for the day; bloody marvellous eh?'

Andy shrugged, turned up his coat collar and held his rifle inside the coat doing his best to keep it dry.

'I don't know why you have to bring that bloody great awkward thing.'

Billy's anxiety about the viability of carrying out their task successfully with so little to go on was apparent in the foulness of his mood. Failure would not go down well. His acceptance of the job implied that he was able to see it through to a successful conclusion – any other result would probably be a personal disaster – excuses would count for nothing.

'We're really up against it Andy,' he went on. 'Out here in the middle of bloody nowhere, no bloody idea where they are, it's pissing down, we're really up against the bleeding clock and you have to bring that bloody musket. It'll get in the way, be a bloody nuisance. It's twelve fifteen already,' he added, checking his watch.

'This musket as you call it is a marvel of technology Billy,' replied Andy with a smile. 'It's got an unbelievably high muzzle velocity and with this scope I can kill at five hundred yards, no problem. It's incredibly quiet too. If I can see 'em I can kill 'em. It's a bloody masterpiece. You'll be glad of it before the day's out.'

'I don't need a fucking lecture Andy. Let's get on with it eh. We haven't got very long.'

He checked his watch again as he moved in through the gate, Andy following, and they proceeded along the drive, alert, ready to conceal themselves amongst the dense vegetation at the first sign of any approach.

They advanced steadily beneath the dripping branches until Billy gripped Andy's wrist.

'Listen!'

As the sound of approaching footsteps drew closer, they stole aside into the undergrowth and waited.

'Praise the Lord,' whispered Andy as the heavy rain ceased quite suddenly.

'There's more to come by the look of that sky,' replied Billy, eyeing the low cloud, and running his wet hands across his face.

They waited in silence as the trudging footsteps drew closer.

'That's Joshua Simms,' whispered Billy, as the plodding figure appeared round the curve in the drive. 'Look at him. He's injured I reckon – he looks all stiff, like he can't turn his neck. I'm going back to that big tree by the bend. Let him go by and when he gets to the tree give him a shout. I'll stick him when he looks back, okay?'

'Got it.' Andy's smile was positively wolfish.

Billy moved away quickly and was soon lost to sight amongst the dripping trees. Andy remained perfectly still as the hunched figure of Joshua plodded past, wet hair plastered to his scalp, rain beaded on his eyebrows.

Joshua was preoccupied with the problems raised by the unexpected turn of recent events. What would Rebecca tell Robin to save her own skin? What had happened to the keys they'd hidden under the stairs? How had Naomi been cut loose? Someone had rescued her. What was going to happen when she brought the law swarming all over the place?

Too miserable with the pain in his neck and shoulders to focus fully on the outcome of these events, he trudged on, his mind dulled by the rhythmic crunching of his feet in the wet gravel. The sudden sound of someone calling his name shook him from his reverie and he stopped in surprise. Turning awkwardly, being careful not to jar his neck again, he peered at the tall, beckoning, fair-haired man but failed to recognise him. As he hesitated, Billy stepped behind him, seized his wrist, and spun him round then thrust a dagger into his upper chest. Joshua cried out with pain and fear, staggering back under the force of the blow which, although intended to be fatal, merely opened a long, shallow wound below his left armpit. He aimed a vicious kick, catching Billy just below the knee, sending him sprawling then turned and ran back the way he'd come.

'Stop him!' cried Billy, scrambling to his feet, snatching up his knife and hobbling after the wounded man; the pain in his knee making him stumble. Joshua was running back along the drive, his blood mingling with the fallen rain, dribbling between the stones. 'We've got to stop him,' cried Billy in desperation as he continued the chase. 'Andy! Come on man!'

Joshua left the drive and ran in between the trunks of two large trees and Billy lost sight of him amongst the tall shrubs beyond. He stood at the spot where Joshua had run into the woods, listening, trying to ascertain Joshua's whereabouts but heard nothing. Wary of an ambush, he limped forward following the path taken by his quarry and was relieved to see blood beading on the glossy laurel leaves where Joshua had passed. He listened again and he could hear sounds of someone moving stealthily through the heavy growth. Joshua had to be stopped from alerting his family to the presence of Billy and Andy but the sound of a shot in that quiet place would just as surely betray them. Billy listened as the rustling noises receded, annoyed that he was without a silencer for his pistol, worrying at the prospect of Joshua taking him by surprise amongst that chaotic growth of vegetation. His own prowess with a knife was limited to a sneak thrust with no warning and he knew enough about Joshua, with or without his wound, to be wary of engaging him in any kind of fight. He might even have a gun: he might even have it aimed at him right now. Billy's fingers closed around the butt of his pistol. Where the bloody hell was Andy?

He moved forward again following the trail of blood with extreme care, aware of his racing pulse and the growing dread inside himself – a fear that threatened to make him turn tail and dash back, to the comparative safety of the drive. Away from this overwhelming, threatening tangle of roots and branches that hemmed him in on all sides, this jungle that offered Joshua countless hiding places from which to strike at him. He wiped his sweating palms on his trousers, took a fresh grip on the haft of his knife and, his skin prickling in nervous tension, moved forward again, somewhat reassured to see the increased amounts of blood where Joshua had passed. He must be badly hurt, thought Billy, bleeding heavily now all right. Mustn't get careless now, the bastard could still jump out from anywhere. He moved on, hoping fervently to find Joshua's body lying face down on the sodden ground.

Joshua's injury had begun to slow him down, the loss of blood and the pain of his wound draining him of the strength he needed to continue his flight. His mobile phone had been damaged by Billy's knife thrust; so he was unable to summon help. Billy continued his cautious pursuit but pulled up suddenly when he saw that Joshua had stopped with his back against a tree and was waiting to face him with a long-bladed knife of his own. Billy held back, dismayed at finding himself facing Joshua alone and feeling at a serious disadvantage. The two stood, eyes locked, each assessing the other, the sound of water dripping from the trees slowing like a clock running down. Where the hell was Andy?

Despite the paleness of his face Joshua looked dangerous. His crouching stance and the belligerent way he held his knife thrust forward made it clear to Billy that Joshua was much more accustomed to fighting with knives than he was. Even wounded and having lost a great deal of blood he looked confident, well able to strike a deadly blow, and Billy didn't fancy his chances if they came to close quarters. He moved his hand towards his pistol. The sound of the shot might alert members of the Simms family who could well be nearby but that was now unavoidable. There was no way he was going to engage in a knife fight with Joshua.

'Come on big man,' jeered Joshua. 'See if you can finish it before your weedy mate catches up. You won't find it so easy this time.'

Billy found Joshua's penetrating stare unnerving. The challenge in those vivid, blue eyes and the beckoning hand decided him. He changed the knife to his left hand and his fingers of his right were closing round the grip of his pistol when Joshua lunged suddenly and before Billy could step back or draw the weapon, stabbed him through the forearm. Caught out by the speed of the attack, Billy staggered back, his injured knee threatening to buckle, his left-hand fumbling to grasp his knife more securely but managing only to drop it in the process. He tried to draw his pistol, but his injured arm was sluggish – too weak to do his will. He tried to shoot through the fabric of his pocket, but his fingers were equally useless.

Joshua grinned and raised the shining blade, holding it before Billy's eyes.

He reached forward grasping a fistful of Billy's jacket, screwed it round in his powerful grip and drew Billy towards him, leering into his face.

'I know what's in your pocket city boy but it's not much use now is it?' he sneered. Billy's eyes followed the gleaming blade in helpless fascination as it was raised to strike, when Joshua uttered a breathy moan, staggered, and began to sink to the ground. He rotated as he collapsed and came to rest sitting with his back to Billy before slumping forward onto his face.

Billy spun round to see Andy hurrying towards him holding the rifle across his chest. 'Clean head shot eh?' smiled Andy, reaching to support him. 'You've gone quite pale mate. Let's have a look at that arm. What do you think of the old musket now?'

'Wicked,' replied Billy much relieved, sinking to the ground as his shaking legs gave way beneath him. 'You saved my bacon, there mate. I never even heard the shot. He just went down – stone dead – unbelievable. It seemed a bloody long time coming though?'

Andy reached down, grasped a handful of Joshua's hair and pulled him round to face them. He pointed to the trickle of blood running pinkly down Joshua's wet forehead from the tiny wound above his eye.

'What about that then?' he asked proudly.

'Doesn't look much does it?' replied Billy. 'Didn't even go right through did it?'

'That's not how it works mate,' said Andy. 'These rounds disintegrate when they hit, and each little bit will have carved its own channel through his brain. It's more of an explosion really – much more deadly than a single hole. You can survive those with a bit of luck but this way you're gone – no question.'

Andy tied a handkerchief round Billy's wounded arm.

'I had to wait for a clear shot Billy. All these branches criss-crossing all over the place, I lost sight of you altogether a couple of times. Then he stepped out of the shadow and bang! Like magic eh? That's the best we can do with that for now,' he went on, making sure the handkerchief wasn't too tight. 'It's bled a good deal, which is good – helps to clean it. Let's hope he's missed any nerves. You feel okay? You're a bit pasty looking, going into shock I reckon.'

'Thanks Andy,' said Billy, trying to flex the fingers of his injured arm and scrambling up, 'that feels much better. I owe you. Now let's get him out of sight. We've still got a lot to do.'

They moved towards the body, Billy cursing the pain in his knee as the rain began again.

'Hang on a mo',' he said, as they prepared to roll the dead man out of sight. He pulled the mobile phone from Joshua's breast pocket. 'Look at that. That's what saved the bugger. I stabbed his bloody phone.'

He checked the offending phone, switched it off and pushed it back into the pocket.

'Nice one Andy,' he said, pointing to the small hole in Joshua's forehead. 'I reckon you're an A1 assassin,' he laughed, cleaning his blade in Joshua's wet hair.

The dead Joshua presented a gruesome sight. One of his eyes had rolled back into his head and was showing mostly white with a tracery of fine, red blood vessels, the other, unblinking in the rain, held them in its empty stare.

'He was a dangerous sod,' said Andy reaching to draw the eyelids down before they rolled the body out of sight.

'I could say the same about you, Deadeye Dick,' laughed Billy, opening the hand of the dead man in order to help himself to the knife. 'Nice one eh?' he grinned holding it up for Andy's approval.

'Would have stuck you with that all right,' replied Andy. 'That's almost a bloody sword that is.'

'Come on,' said Billy, recovering Joshua's scabbard. 'That's one less of the bastards to worry about.'

'There's a bit of a path here,' said Andy. 'It looks as though it leads back towards the drive. It'll make easier walking than struggling through this soaking bloody jungle.'

They set off grateful not to have to fight their way through the dense, saturated undergrowth.

'Well spotted young Andy,' said Billy. 'It's quite a highway isn't it? Someone must walk here pretty regular for it to be so open. Hello. What's this, a well or something?'

They found themselves in a partial clearing in the centre of which stood a stone wall forming a circle about two feet high and four feet in diameter with a solid looking wooden cover on top.

'Looks like a well to me,' said Andy. 'Want to look?'

'Yeah,' replied Billy, 'Why not.'

Andy moved forward then stopped as he detected the first whiff of decay. He screwed up his face in disgust.

'My God what a fucking awful pong. There's a body down there I reckon.'

'Maybe more than one,' said Billy, who was also familiar with the foul smell of decomposing human remains.

'We could put old Joshua down there,' he continued. 'No one's going to trip over him if he's down there out of the way. They'd never find him. Let's see if we can shift that cover.'

Despite Billy's injuries they slid the cover to one side without much difficulty then stepped back quickly, gagging at the noxious stink that emanated from the depths.

'They won't need dogs to find this,' choked Andy, 'just follow their noses.'

'It'll do nicely,' said Billy. 'It couldn't happen to a nicer bloke. Come on.'

They hurried back to where they'd rolled Joshua's body out of sight and Billy suggested that he could help Andy hoist it into a fireman's lift, while he carried the rifle.

'No way mate,' said Andy. 'Dead folk lose control you know. He's not pissing down my back, or worse. Loop his belt round his ankles then you can take his feet one handed, and I'll do the heavy end. I'll come back for the rifle.'

This method worked reasonably well, and they made their way back to the well where they toppled the body into the hole then ran back to escape the sickening stench. They heard a loud splash as the body hit the water and then went forward to replace the cover.

'There's a lot of water down there then,' said Andy. 'Must be all this bloody rain.'

'Now he's really out of sight,' said Billy. 'I'm beginning to enjoy this. 'Let's go and get the next fucker.'

They continued along the path, making their way back to the drive.

'How's the knee?' asked Andy.

'It's better now I'm on the move. It's freed it up a bit.'

'You wait til tomorrow. Then you'll know all about it, won't be able to move when you wake up what with that and your bleedin' arm as well.'

'Thanks mate. You're a real bloody tonic you are You know just how to cheer a bloke up; got the bloody gift for it.'

★★★

Joshua's body bobbed on the foul, viscous surface where the putrescent, bloated corpses of Rebecca's victims jostled and bumped it, as if resentful of its rude arrival in their midst.

★★★

Rebecca propped the broom by the door, put on her coat and descended the staircase to where Robin stood waiting impatiently for the arrival of the horsebox and its luckless passengers.

'Ah. See if you can raise Joshua will you,' he said crossly. 'Use your phone – he might answer to you.'

She pressed the keys and listened.

'His 'phone's switched off. Do you want me to leave a message?'

'No give him a few more minutes to make sure he's reached the gate. He should switch it on then. He'd better bloody switch it on. God, he's such a perverse sod. Why has he got it switched off now after all I've just said to him?'

'At least the rain's left off,' said Rebecca, a futile attempt at appeasement.

Robin grunted contemptuously.

'Is that supposed to be funny?' he growled as he turned away and began to pace up and down impatiently on the drive.

'About bloody time,' he said loudly as his phone jangled suddenly in his pocket. He pulled it out and held it to his ear.

'Joshua?' he said.

'No Robin. It isn't Joshua,' said a voice he failed to recognise.

'Who is this?' He demanded, striding rapidly away from Rebecca. 'How did you get this number?'

'Calm yourself Robin,' the voice answered. 'It's a simple matter to get hold of telephone numbers. We shouldn't waste precious time discussing something so mundane.'

'What do you want?'

'That's more like it Robin. Straight to the point eh. I suggest that you listen carefully. It's important after all. You still have time to deliver the woman and the boy to a safe place of your own choosing. Then when you've done so you phone the number I'm about to give you and we see them safely home. You have until one o'clock plus ten minutes for shall we say reflection. If we haven't heard from you by then we shall kill a member of your family. Simple enough? We want the woman and the boy unharmed and we're prepared to go to great lengths to achieve that. Understood?'

'If you want this woman and the boy so badly come up with a deal,' said Robin. 'Don't try and get heavy. The police are watching the house. Dad's safe in prison, he just about runs the place, and you don't know where I am. All your threats are so much bullshit.'

'Your naivety disappoints me Robin. Here is the number …'

'Bollocks to that,' Robin interrupted. 'Come up with a deal I might find interesting.'

'The deal, Robin, if you must call it that, is unchanged. Release the woman and the boy unharmed in exchange for the lives of the remaining members of your precious family, yours included of course. Your intractable attitude has already led to the demise of your little brother Justin. You surely don't want to lose anyone else, do you?'

'It's all a big bloody bluff. You want them? You pay!'

'As I say, your naivety disappoints me. You are out of your depth and certainly in no position to make demands. One o'clock plus ten minutes. The number is on your answering machine,' the voice said coldly. The line went dead.

'Wanker!' fumed Robin, returning the phone to his pocket.

'Who was that?' asked Rebecca, who had followed Robin and listened to his end of the conversation with growing concern. 'What woman? What boy? The Driscoll's? You said something about threats too?'

'Nothing for you to worry yourself with Rebecca,' replied Robin. 'It's something Dad wants cleared up. I'm dealing with it. That's all you need to know.'

'But what's that about the police watching the house and Dad being safe in prison? It all sounded bloody scary to me.'

'I've just told you!' he shouted. 'I'm dealing with it! Now drop it will you!'

Rebecca, realising there was nothing to be gained by trying to talk to Robin in his present mood turned and walked away. Like Joshua, she was worried about how Naomi had managed to escape. Someone knew we had her up there she mused, and they knew where to find the keys. She stopped walking, sobered by this disturbing thought. Had someone been watching when she and Josh had brought Naomi to the loft? Worse still had they seen what had gone on before? If so, why hadn't they told the police? Come to that, why had Naomi not told the police?

Suddenly she felt exposed, felt threatened – as if eyes were on her – tracking her every move – interested in what she might do next. A sudden gust of wind buffeted the trees and flurries of raindrops splashed down making her cry out and jump back in alarm. She ran back to be near Robin afraid to look right or left, afraid of what she might see there. Matty narrowed his eyes as she fell into step with her pacing brother, her eyes fixed on the gravel, her smooth face pale as a church candle.

'What was that all about then?' asked Robin gruffly.

'All what?' she answered innocently.

'You cried out back there.'

'Oh, I was miles away when some water nearly splashed me, it made me jump, startled me.'

'Why did you call Josh then? Isn't he down at the gate?'

'I didn't know I'd said Josh,' she replied. 'I don't know what made me say it.'

Robin shot her a suspicious glance, as he continued his pacing. 'He'd better be at the gate if he knows what's good for him.'

'I don't know where he is Robin,' she replied, wiping away the tears which had appeared inexplicably to trickle down her cheeks.

Robin shook his head.

'I'll never understand you two,' he muttered, hunching his shoulders as the rain began again. 'Your behaviour's beginning to worry me Rebecca. I hope you haven't been sampling the merchandise. You've seen how users go downhill fast. You do remember Dad's law? You remember what he said he'd do if any of us broke it?'

She nodded her tearful face a picture of abject misery.

'Oh Josh,' she whispered plaintively, as Robin turned away and resumed his restless pacing.

★★★

Billy and Andy remained in concealment in a spot well back from the stable block from where they could observe the distant figures.

'That's Robin Simms and his sister,' whispered Billy, 'Rebecca, Joshua's twin.'

'She is a cracker,' breathed Andy. 'Hope I don't have to shoot her.'

'Looks from here as though they're not happy, they're rowing about something.'

Billy raised his hand suddenly.

'Listen!' he hissed.

They heard the engine of an approaching truck labouring in a low gear, its transmission whining in short surges, as if complaining about the unevenness of the drive. At last the lurching horsebox came into view and drew up next to Robin and Rebecca.

'Can't tell what they're saying,' said Billy, 'but they don't look too pleased to see each other. Ah, that's James Simms,' he continued, as a figure came out of the woods beyond the drive and joined the group by the horsebox. 'Looks as though they're all out here except for their Mum.'

'That must be Mrs. Driscoll and her boy then,' said Andy as the ramp was lowered and the sorry looking pair were led out and made to wait while Robin held a heated discussion with the driver.

After a short while Robin waved his arm in a dismissive gesture, the horsebox turned, set off to grind its way back towards the gate and the two captives were taken up the stairs to the loft.

'We're going to have to get them out of there somehow,' said Billy. 'Any ideas?'

'Not at the moment,' replied Andy. 'We need to get a bit nearer – see if there's some way we can get the drop on them.'

'If we could lure them out you could knock 'em over with that easy enough,' said Billy, indicating the rifle.

'Yeah. If I can see 'em they're goners,' said Andy, a trace of resentment creeping into his voice. Truth was he was extremely pleased with the shot that killed Joshua and felt that Billy had not been fully appreciative of his timely pressure on the trigger.

'Right then. Let's get a bit closer,' said Billy.

He was in the act of switching off his mobile when it vibrated in his hand. He rolled his eyes at Andy as he placed the instrument to his ear.

'Hello,' he whispered.

'It's me Billy. I'm told that Simms has tried to make a deal over the release of the Driscoll's. There's no way our people will do that – absolutely no way. He's been given 'til one o'clock plus ten minutes to hand them over. It rather looks as though he won't do that, it's ten to one already, so it's down to you Billy. We're depending on you to get them out if you can. Whatever you decide, you'll have to act quickly. I'm told that the police will certainly be with you before much longer.'

'We've found where they're holding them Mr. Edmonds. They're in a loft over some old stables. Robin, James, and Rebecca Simms are with them. We're just moving in closer to see if we can do something.'

'Where's Joshua Simms? You need to know what that cunning bastard is up to you know. He could wreck your plans.'

'He's dead Mr. Edmonds. Andy shot him and we've dropped his body down a well.'

'Well you've got off to good start then. Well done Andy. I'll wait to hear from you then Billy. Good hunting.'

Billy switched off his phone and checked his watch as the pair moved stealthily towards the stable block.

'You know we've only been here about half an hour,' he muttered. 'Feels like a bloody lifetime.'

'Well we have been busy mate,' replied Andy. 'It's not every day we get to knock off someone.'

★★★

CHAPTER TWENTY-TWO

Naomi started as she heard someone climbing up into the chimney. She reached out her arms into the thick darkness in a defensive attitude then heaved a sigh of relief as she recognised the sour smell and saw Matty lighting the candle.

'Oh Matty, where have you been?' she whispered. 'You were so long. I thought perhaps they'd caught you.'

'Get up. Get up,' he said, pulling at the hessian seat. 'Quickly now. Come on, get up,' he repeated, pulling her to her feet.

She was alarmed by his attitude and bullying manner.

'What is it?' she asked, bewildered by the change in him. 'Don't you dare pull me about like that.'

'No time for niceties. Come on. Help me. Come on,' he muttered impatiently.

He was on his knees trying to unroll the hessian, so she knelt beside him and began to unroll her end.

'Take your time,' she said, trying to calm him. 'More haste, less speed you know.' She reached across and straightened his end of the roll. 'Come on now. Both together,' she said, unrolling her end, relieved to see him becoming less agitated.

They worked in unison turning the bulky roll, forming a second as they went, this being the only practical way to do it in the limited space. The roll diminished as they continued to turn it and it began to assume a boxy shape as the layers were peeled away.

At last they drew away the end of the hessian to reveal a long brown leather case. Matty grunted with satisfaction and hugged it to his chest for a moment before opening it to expose a long heavily wrapped object. His excitement now under control, he stripped away the layers of white cloth and laid before her with careful reverence the twin barrels of a twelve-bore shot-gun. She gasped with surprise as she regarded the dark lustre of oily metal gleaming in the yellow candlelight. In no time, he had unwrapped the stock and fore end and laid them on the cloth. She watched as he wiped the excess oil from the barrels and pulled them through with clean lint. The pungent smell of the discarded cloths stained yellow with gun oil was over-powering in the confined space but did much to mask Matty's body odour.

'Father's gun,' he muttered at last, attaching the stock and snapping the fore end into place with practised skill. He rubbed his hand lovingly across the smooth, dark wood.

'What are you going to do Matty?' asked Naomi, alarmed by the look on his face as he nursed the gun in his lap.

'French walnut you know,' he said, ignoring her question. 'Specially selected; they only use the absolute best for guns of this quality.'

'Matty I'm frightened. Please put it away.'

'Has to be perfectly clean you know. Father inspects it and woe betide Matthew if he finds a speck of dust or a smidgen of oil in the wrong place.'

He picked a handful of reddish, orange cartridges from the case, dropped them into his pocket, broke the gun and gave it to her to hold while he climbed down.

'Tell me what you're going to do Matty,' she begged. 'Who's out there? What's got into you?'

'Pass the gun down,' he said, ignoring her questions as be-fore, as he began to descend.

'I won't,' she said, close to tears, 'not until you tell me what you're up to.'

Matty's expression became angry as he snatched the gun from her grasp with surprising strength.

'He'll hurt Mummy,' he said. 'You stay here out of harm's way until I come for you. Understand?'

He enunciated this last word with such vehemence that she simply nodded and sank down onto the hessian.

'Put out the candle,' he said and was gone.

***

One of the many special advantages enjoyed by Arthur Simms was that of having his meals brought to him in his cell. His absence from the canteen suited the prison officers very well because that was often where the hard men, envious of Simms' seemingly untouchable status, chose to confront him. Inevitably riotous violence would ensue involving damage to the furniture and fittings and to those officers called upon to quell the uproar. So, a blind eye was turned each time Huw Jenkins appeared at the hotplate to collect the meals for Simms and himself. Huw had elected himself to this role and Simms had taken a liking to him – the arrangement was working very well.

Simms smiled to himself as he heard Huw's approach, the fine baritone voice rendering the carol, *Good Christian Men Rejoice*; he put aside his magazine and waited for Huw to appear at the open door.

'Ah, the voice from the valleys, very Christmassy,' he said with a smile, as he accepted the tray from Huw who then made himself comfortable on the lower bunk with his own. Huw never sang while in the cell.

They ate in silence for several minutes.

'Not bad today,' said Simms at last. 'I'm quite fond of corned beef.'

'Yeah, it's okay,' replied Huw. 'They can't really spoil corned beef, can they?'

'Salad's a bit past it though,' Simms continued. 'Still it's green so I suppose it's good for us even if it is a bit dried up.'

'I picked out the best there was,' said Huw. 'You should have seen some of it – you wouldn't feed it to a bloody goat.'

Simms signalled the end of the conversation by reaching across and turning on his radio in time to catch the tail end of the weather before World at One. The two men finished their food in silence then lay back listening as a correspondent described the gruesome aftermath of a car bomb explosion in Tel Aviv.

Simms became aware of a man standing in the doorway but ignored him, preferring to listen to the radio.

The newcomer was Darren Rossiter, a hard case Liverpudlian. He continued to lean against the doorframe, his eyes never leaving Simms' face. Rossiter had the dark blue chin of one who needed to shave twice a day and though half a head shorter than Simms he was of a similar build – broad, deep chested – a powerful physique. He remained at the door, hands in pockets, staring insolently at the reclining Simms.

'I want a word Simms,' he said at last in his thick Liverpudlian accent. Simms, though irritated by this intrusion, continued to ignore him. 'I said I want a word,' he repeated, louder now.

'I don't want a word as it happens,' replied Simms. 'Bugger off Rossiter.'

'I'll wait. We need to talk.'

'Yeah? I don't think so. Now fuck off. Don't make me angry you scouse prat. It's well gone one o'clock,' said Rossiter.

Simms ignored this as Huw, sensing the rising tension between the two, made sure that he was well to the back of the bunk – out of harm's way.

Rossiter, failing to get a response, entered the cell, picked up the magazine from Simms' bunk, tore it slowly and deliberately down the middle and tossed the two halves onto the recumbent Simms.

The big man swung his legs off the bunk and stood up. Rossiter tensed ready to evade the blow that would surely follow but even though he had prepared himself and was ducking away it caught him high on the temple knocking him back through the doorway and into the opposite wall with bruising force. He picked himself up and ran away along the deserted landing.

Simms, still slightly off balance after throwing the mighty punch, experienced a moment of bewilderment as he saw Huw, his face contorted in a silent scream, come off the bunk like a sprinter out of the blocks. It was over in a trice. Huw's weapon, a long, pointed scissor blade, pierced Simms' exposed chest high on the left side and he wrenched the handle savagely from side to side as Simms, his expression frozen in shock, folded and flopped to the floor. Huw stood over the body, his chest heaving from his efforts, cold sweat tracking down over his ribs. It had all gone off without a hitch. Simms was dead. The once so powerful body lay lifeless on the floor and Huw had done it. It was not the first time he had killed but he had never attempted to take on anyone as physically powerful as Simms and he felt grateful towards Rossiter for the way he had distracted Simms for those critical seconds.

He thought about the additional generous payment that would soon be transferred to his account. He would have almost four hundred thousand by the time of his release: not enough to last a lifetime, particularly when Miranda got her sticky fingers on it but still a tidy sum and the house in Grove Walk was all paid for. He thought of Miranda by a Spanish pool, a yellow bikini to emphasise her wonderful tan, her long dark hair falling to her smooth shoulders, men's eyes ogling from behind their dark glasses. But the job was not yet finished: more to do.

As instructed, Huw withdrew the scissor, wiped it on Simms' shirt then backed to the door offering it behind his back: a precaution to protect the identity of its recipient. Consequently, Huw never knew whose hand it was that received the blade then plunged it into his neck, severing his spinal cord at the base of his skull. His inert body lay slumped in the doorway.

Huw's killer left the scene quickly, the immediate task being to clean and reassemble the scissors and return them to the tailors' shop. His aim was to achieve this before the bodies were discovered and the prison became an echoing bedlam of shouting and searching.

After the sound of running footsteps it was unusually quiet, just Simms' radio playing 'World at One' to the cooling bodies on the floor: a double murder scene surprisingly devoid of blood, but then both victims' hearts had stopped almost at once.

There was no doubt that the ensuing media frenzy and the fact that the two murders were to remain unsolved would lead to disciplinary measures, dismissals and resignations all the way up to the Prison Governor and that the Home Secretary himself would find his tenure under serious threat. It was after all a case of gross mismanagement and the indignant clamour for remedial action and reassurances that this must never happen again, would echo and re echo for as long as it made good copy or until the next spectacular event swept it from the front pages.

But before any of this, word of Simms' demise would spread throughout the prison. A new top man would emerge. Those who were able would align themselves quickly with the new order, while those whose loyalty to the late Simms had been rather too overt, would be uncomfortably aware of the settling of scores yet to come.

★★★

CHAPTER TWENTY-THREE

Matty made his way stealthily through the trees towards where he had seen James Simms sitting in the Vectra. The car was empty. He kept the gun muzzle up as he picked his way with care towards the loft then paused in the last of the cover as close as he could get to the foot of the staircase. All seemed quiet, just a gentle breeze stirring the waving branches. Keeping his eyes fixed on the door at the top of the stairs, he placed two cartridges between the first three fingers of his left hand.

Just like it used to be he thought, remembering the pheasant drives and the frantic excitement when the birds flew over thick and fast. He and his father had refined their teamwork – shooter and loader – into a polished sequence of slick moves and the boy Matthew had revelled in it, receiving the hot, empty gun, reloading in a trice, then the double explosions as his father brought down yet another pair of birds, thrust his empty gun at him and took the newly loaded one.

Bang bang! Bang bang! Bang bang! ...

It had seemed to go on for an age as all around, guns banged, ejected cartridges arced through the air in smoking pairs, loaders, like himself, cartridges held between fingers and between teeth, sweated, handling the hot gun barrels as bird after bird crumpled and fell to earth.

Then, when the sky was clear of flying birds and the dogs were released to pick up, his father would say, 'Well done Matthew. We'll make a loader of you yet.'

Those were the only times he could remember when he had enjoyed the approval of his father and even then, timid

Matthew had learned not to become over familiar with that cold, distant man.

He wiped tears from his weathered cheek and suppressed a sob as the horror came flooding back to him as he remembered how he had found his beloved mother dead.

'Mummy,' he said aloud, beginning to move towards the staircase.

Slowly and silently, he ascended, checking each stair then returning his gaze to the door, gun held ready before him.

At last he reached the top and paused to listen. He could hear Robin Simms' voice raised in anger. His thumb slid forward, making certain the safety was off as he opened the door, slipped inside, and slid the bolt home behind him. The occupants of the loft stared at him in amazement, Robin cut off in mid sentence.

'You mustn't hurt Mummy,' said Matty, moving the muzzle in a narrow arc to cover the two men and the girl.

White faced; Maureen began to inch surreptitiously to one side drawing Terry with her.

***

'You're not going to believe this.'

Andy stood, the rifle propped in a forked branch, trained on the distant loft, his eye to the telescopic sight. Billy, beginning to feel severe pain in his injured arm, nursed it close to his chest and sat leaning back against a tree trunk, distress etched on his drawn features.

'Billy!'

'Yeah?'

'You deaf or something?'

'I heard you.'

'I said you're not going to believe this,' said Andy, pointing at the scope. 'Come on. Come and take a butchers.'

Billy grimaced in pain as he got to his feet.

'Christ Andy, I'm lightheaded,' he said, steadying himself against the tree, 'bit dizzy like.'

'You stood up too quick mate. Give yourself a minute. You are looking a bit rough though.'

Billy moved across to where Andy held the rifle ready settled behind it and put his eye to the lens.

'Well?' said Andy, at last.

'It's some scruffy old geezer with a bloody great shotgun. He's listening at the door like. Christ! He's gone in. What's his bloody game? This is all going pear shaped Andy. Anything happens to those two and we're right in the shit.'

Billy continued to peer through the scope and was panning slowly right when he uttered a gasp of surprise.

'Oh my God.'

★★★

Chief Superintendent Jessop ran into his office and snatched up the ringing phone. 'Jessop,' he said his voice tight with tension.

'Good man,' said the Chief Constable. 'All fixed at your end? Ready to go?'

'We certainly are,' replied Jessop, 'and have been for over half an hour,' he added smugly, allowing his voice to carry his criticism of the delay.

If he detected this implied rebuke, the Chief Constable chose to ignore it.

'Just get your people out there Jessop. Quick as you like.'

The line went dead.

The negotiation personnel and the armed response unit, together with a squad of police officers were en-route for Kingsfield Park in a fraction over five minutes.

★★★

'What's up?' asked Andy in alarm.

'You're right. I don't believe it. The fuzz has turned up mob handed.'

He handed the rifle to Andy.

'Take a gander. Start at the foot of the stairs and pan right. There's at least half a dozen coppers there in the trees.'

Andy focused on the policemen.

'There's more coming up. It's an armed response unit taking up positions. What do you want to do?'

'I want to bugger off out of it Andy, go home and get into a hot bath with a bloody great scotch in my hand. As it is though we've got to stay put and see what goes down. First thing is to tell Ned to keep the guys out of sight until the fuzz have gone home. If he tries to get down to the main road with all these coppers coming and going, he'll be stopped and that'll be big trouble too, with all them shooters in the cars.

Andy continued to observe the developing police operation as Billy thumbed Ned's number.

★★★

'You mustn't hurt Mummy,' Matty repeated, still covering the three Simms.

He had identified Robin as being the dangerous one. The girl and the second man were genuinely frightened by his arrival while Robin was obviously angling for a way to seize the advantage. Maureen and Terry were out of the line of fire and had continued to edge further away from Robin, while his attention was focused on Matty.

'Tell me what it is you're after,' said Robin. 'I'm sure we can come to an arrangement.'

'Keep you're hands still, just as they are,' replied Matty. 'You and these two, he indicated James and Rebecca, are to leave now. I shall step over there away from the door,' he nodded to his left, 'and you will go, drive off in that car of yours.'

He took a step away from the door, alert, watchful, gun barrels trained unwaveringly on Robin's chest.

Nobody moved.

He took a second step.

'Can't be done old man,' said Robin at last. 'Look, there's no need for the gun. I'm sure we can talk this out.'

'I want you to get out,' said Matty, his features taut with concentration. He took another step saying, 'Go on,' jerking his head towards the door. 'Leave us now.'

The girl seemed eager to go and had begun to move towards the door when Robin stepped behind her suddenly and pushed her directly at Matty. In the same movement, he drew a handgun and got off two badly aimed shots well wide of the mark, simply punching two small holes in the planking of the wall well to Matty's left.

The double boom of the shotgun in that confined space was prodigious beyond belief: a stunning blast of destruction that ripped the air like a thunderclap. Maureen's screams went unheard as Rebecca's body, thrown back by the heavy impact of the lead shot fired from close range, cannoned into Robin, her chest a ruin of blood, bone, and tissue. In the same moment, he joined her in death as the second barrel blew away the left side of his face in a flying spatter of crimson.

Matty stood, powerless, caught by the cold gaze of Rebecca's vivid blue eyes, like a staring rabbit helpless in the beam of a poacher's lamp. Overwhelmed in the interminable ringing silence and caught fast in his bloody nightmare, he became aware, at last, of distant sobbing.

James, down on his knees, slid his weapon across the floor to where Matty stood white faced, shaking in reaction to what he'd done. James's frightened eyes were fixed on Matty's hands. He could see the number 5 stamped on the ends of the cartridges held between Matty's fingers.

'Please. Please don't shoot,' he begged, not knowing that for only the second time in his life Matty had neglected to reload.

Ignoring him Matty turned to where Maureen had thrown herself on top of Terry. She was crying, holding the boy down with all her strength. As he went towards them, they heard heavy footfalls on the stairs.

A voice called, 'Police! Stand away from the door.'

The door rattled as someone tried to push it open. Matty looked questioningly at Maureen. She wiped her tear-streaked face with her hands leaving a dirty smear across her cheek then nodded. He moved back to the door and was reaching to draw the bolt when the battering ram struck with a loud crash, smashing the brittle old boards, bursting the door inwards in a shower of splintered fragments.

★★★

The sounds of gunfire had brought Billy to his feet again.

'God, I wish we knew what's gone on in there Andy,' he said anxiously.

They had watched as the police personnel, in response to the shooting, had rushed the stairs and battered their way inside.

'It'll be bloody mayhem in there now that lot's gone in,' replied Andy, shaking his head.

'It wasn't exactly peaceful before, was it? At least the shooting's stopped,' said Billy.

'For the moment anyway,' replied Andy. 'Mind, coppers can get a bit trigger-happy too: all that excitement, adrenaline and that. They're panicky before they go in. Then with all the shouting and screaming going on, they might let fly in the heat of the moment.'

'Yeah. Well all we can do now is hang on – see who they bring out eh. Let's hope the Driscoll's have survived.'

'That's where my money is,' said Andy. 'Four shots right, and the twelve-bore fired the last two. I reckon that old boy was after the Simms not the Driscoll's.'

'Yeah but the first two shots might have got the Driscoll's.'

'It's possible but I don't think so Billy.'

'I hope you're right.'

'We'll find out soon I reckon.'

* * *

Matty was knocked down by the inrushing policemen. His shotgun was knocked away by an overweight, red-faced officer shouting, 'You! On the floor now!' his voice cracking under the strain.

There were policemen everywhere – such a confusion of shouting and thumping of big boots. James was thrown down and held by a panting officer, his discarded weapon collected and bagged.

Maureen got to her feet, helping Terry up and keeping a protective arm around his shoulders. They smiled, holding each other tightly.

'Cavalry,' Terry shouted, but Maureen only shook her head, unable to hear him for the din. There seemed to be uniforms, Kevlar jackets and black and white checked caps everywhere. Then she realised that a Police Inspector was addressing her.

'Mrs. Driscoll. Boy, are we glad to see you're both okay.'

'Oh, thank God,' sobbed Maureen, sagging with relief. 'Get us out of here please,' she continued, averting her eyes from the bodies on the floor.

'Come along Ma'am,' he said kindly. 'It's all over. You're quite safe now.'

He placed a gentle hand beneath Maureen's elbow and began to guide her and Terry towards the door. A woman police officer draped blankets around their shoulders and gave Terry a smile and a friendly pat of reassurance.

'Soon have you in the warm,' she said, falling into step beside him and adjusting his blanket as they went.

Maureen stopped suddenly.

'Come along Ma'am,' said the policeman. 'We're rather in the way here. Crime Scene Officers have a lot to do and we want to get you to hospital where they can look after you both.'

'Thank you for your concern, but we're not moving from this spot until you release that man.'

She pointed to where Matty lay face down pinioned by the large red-faced policeman who was now sitting on him.

'He was armed Ma'am,' replied the officer. 'We shall hold him for questioning.'

'Let him up and take those handcuffs off,' said Maureen. 'He won't be able to answer your questions if that fat oaf suffocates him. There's your killer,' she continued, pointing at the body of Robin Simms. 'He was going to murder us but Matty saved us. He's a hero. Can't you see that?'

'We have to act on what we do see Ma'am. As we entered the premises he was in possession of this shotgun and we could see bodies on the floor. Disarming him was our priority.'

'Well now he's disarmed so you can let him up, can't you?'

The police officer picked up the shotgun in gloved hands and broke it pulling his head away involuntarily as the ejected cartridges flew close to his ear and fell to the floor with a clatter.

'Well that's a relief but we couldn't know that when we came in. How did this old tramp come to be in possession of a shotgun?' he mused. 'This looks a valuable gun too: worth a lot of money I should think. Get him on his feet Bradshaw. One of you should have ascertained the status of this weapon immediately,' he admonished those closest to him, giving them a frosty stare.

'Well take care of the gun,' he began, but was taken aback when Matty sidled close to him thrusting out his side pocket and looking down at it meaningfully.

'He wants you to look in his pocket,' said Maureen.

The Inspector recoiled, obviously less than eager to discover the contents of Matty's pocket and beckoned to Constable Bradshaw.

'Just check his pockets would you.'

225

Constable Bradshaw looked uncomfortable with this but eventually eased his hand into Matty's pocket and retrieved four red cartridges.

'And those,' said Matty, pointing to where the two cartridges he had held between his fingers had rolled across the floor when he had been knocked down.

'Make sure you get them all Bradshaw, including the two that've been fired,' said the officer testily as he turned back to Maureen.

'What about the handcuffs?' she asked.

Matty looked from one to the other, as the policeman debated with himself the best answer to Maureen's question.

'I can't fetch Naomi 'til you take them off,' said Matty at last, his voice hoarse and shaky.

'What's that?' said the policeman. 'Are you referring to Naomi Gibbs, the missing girl? What do you know about her?'

'She didn't tell me her surname, just Naomi. They had her tied up in here. She called to me from the window this morning. I was frightened at first – she was shouting and banging – making such a fearful racket that I'm ashamed to say I ran off and hid in the wood. Then later when she'd quietened down, I crept back, took the keys and let myself in. They'd thrown a rope over that beam and tied her wrists. The other end was tied to the ring on the wall.'

'Who's the 'they' you keep referring to?' asked the police officer, eyeing Matty with suspicion.

'That one and her fellow,' answered Matty, indicating Rebecca's blood-soaked body but not looking at it directly.

'How did you come to have the keys to the door?' asked the policeman, obviously still sceptical, 'and where are they now?'

'I saw where they hid them. They came here quite often and always hid them in the same place: under the bottom step. They used to bring girls here. I don't know exactly what they got up to, but I heard screaming. I heard it several times.'

'But did nothing about it?' the officer said pointedly.

'I didn't fancy tackling them myself and I've always been chary about going to the police I'm afraid. One never knows how it might turn out you know. They said I'd done something before.'

'So where are the keys now?' asked the policeman, determined to stick to his line of questioning.

'When I released Naomi, I hid them somewhere else.'

'Can you show me where?'

'I most certainly can. So could Naomi. She saw what I did with them.'

Maureen moved to Matty and took his hands in hers.

'Thank you Matty,' she said, tears welling up in her eyes. 'I was so sure that he would kill us. It all seemed so hopeless, then you came through that door. It was like a miracle.'

Terry joined his hands with theirs and smiled at Matty. Matty was embarrassed but he returned their frank gaze as all about them, police officers busied themselves with their various and necessary procedures.

'I can't stop this silly trembling. I don't think I'll ever be warm again,' said Maureen, withdrawing her hands at last and chafing them together. It was an awkward pause. All three of them were shaking.

The Inspector cleared his throat.

'The ambulance Mrs. Driscoll? Perhaps you and your boy would like to go down now?'

'What are you going to do with Matty?'

'This is an extremely serious situation as I'm sure you're aware Ma'am. There are laid down procedures that must be followed – of which I am sure you are also aware. I can assure you that he will be treated with consideration. We'll take his statement at the station for a start but first I need to know the whereabouts of Naomi Gibbs.'

'I can take you to her,' said Matty, holding out his wrists again.

'Bradshaw,' called the Inspector. 'Get these cuffs off him will you.'

Maureen and Terry stood back and watched Matty lead the Inspector and two constables down the stairs and over to the house before she allowed the smiling policewoman to conduct herself and Terry down to the waiting ambulance.

★★★

CHAPTER TWENTY-FOUR

Billy and Andy watched as the two ambulances parked near to the loft, followed a few minutes later by a well-polished, black panel van.

'Undertaker I reckon,' said Andy, as the van manoeuvred into position alongside the ambulances. 'Discreet see: no name on the side.'

Billy simply grunted, keeping his eye to the telescopic sight.

Soon, the two men from the van unloaded a stretcher then carried it upstairs and into the loft.

Andy stood up to the eyepiece as Billy took out his phone.

Both concentrated on the distant doorway.

At last the two men reappeared bearing a bagged body strapped to the stretcher and proceeded to carry it down the steep stairs and load it into the van.

'That's the first dead 'un loaded up,' said Andy. 'Wonder who it is?'

'Was,' replied Billy tersely. 'Pray it's not Mrs. Driscoll or the boy.'

'They've gone back up with the stretcher,' said Andy. 'There's more to come I reckon.'

★★★

Billy returned to his resting-place, sat down, and leant back against the tree with a sigh of relief.

'Well that turned out okay. I was bloody glad when they both came down safe. God Almighty this bloody arm is giving me some real gyp now Andy,' he groaned, 'and my knee. It's really beginning to ache.' Billy took out his mobile phone and thumbed in the familiar sequence of digits.

'They'll all be gone soon mate,' said Andy, 'then we'll get Ned to pick us up and get you to the doctor. You'll just have to hang on. It shouldn't be too much longer now. I reckon the coppers'll leave someone at the scene, so we'd be best off meeting Ned down at the gate, out of sight like. What do you reckon?'

Billy held up a hand as he heard Mr. Edmonds pick up.

'Yeah, they're both okay Mr. Edmonds. Looked a bit pale, bit stressed out like but no injuries as far as we could see went off in the ambulance: no bother: they put a young girl in with them: early twenties, I guess. James Simms came out in cuffs and was put in the second ambulance. They fetched out two bodies,' he continued, 'and we saw the old guy go off to the house with three coppers. Then they fetched him back and put him in the other ambulance with James Simms and his escort.'

'So, the bodies have to be those of Robin Simms and his sister?'

'That's how we reckon it Mr. Edmonds. How did you know they were out here?'

'I have my contacts Billy. You should know that by now.'

'You mean you've got a nark on the inside? A bent copper who keeps you up to date.'

Billy was surprised to hear Mr. Edmonds' outburst of laughter.

'Very shrewd of you Billy,' he said at last. 'Very shrewd. Right on the nail but he's not just any copper – he's a big fish who finds it's in his best interests to keep me informed of developments.'

'You've got the negatives then.'

'Something like that Billy. You are sharp today. So, to get back to your end of things it was your rustic chum who saved their bacon then?'

'Eh?'

'The old chap with the shotgun Billy.'

'Oh yeah. It was him fired last, so he must've I guess.'

'Well let us be thankful for that eh. You know that James Simms is the only one left now, apart from his mother that is. You did say Joshua is accounted for?'

'Yeah, that's right. What's happened to their old man then?'

'There's been an incident at the prison Billy. Two dead and one of them was Arthur Simms. I'm told there's a right flap on there now. Robin Simms died without knowing about his father's demise, pity in a way but I suppose it makes no difference really. At least the grieving widow has one son left to conduct their business affairs; I mean their legitimate business affairs of course.

'There'll be opportunities now Billy – fair bit of dealing just waiting to be picked up. Of course, there'll be other interested parties ready to horn in on it: you'd need to be forceful if you wanted to come out on top. Very forceful actually. You get my drift?'

'I hear what you're saying Mr. Edmonds. I could count on you for some heavy help?'

'Most certainly Billy, usual arrangement.'

'Sounds like my cup of tea Mr. Edmonds.'

'Thought so Billy; thought so. When can I expect you?'

'We have to hang on 'til all these coppers bugger off before we can make a move, but it shouldn't be too much longer. Then I need to get to the doctor. I'll phone you after I've seen him.'

'What's happened to you Billy? Why the doctor?'

'Joshua stabbed me through the arm. It bled a lot, but I think it might be infected.'

'Get it seen to as soon as you can then let me know how you are. Tell the doctor to bill me for your treatment.'

'Thanks very much Mr. Edmonds. That's very good of you.'

'Can't have you out of action Billy but I think any thanks are due to the old guy with the shotgun eh?'

'Sure Mr. Edmonds. He certainly saved the day for us.'

'For you Billy: for you.'

The phone went dead.

'What's up mate?' asked Andy. 'You've gone really pale. What did he say to you?'

'Told me I've had a lucky result Andy; more or less said that the old tramp saved my bacon: yours too I suppose.'

'They don't mess about do they. You ever wish you'd never joined?'

'It's too late for that mate. Once you're in you're in – no way out of it.'

'Unless you get on the wrong side of someone like Mr. bloody Edmonds and disappear,' Andy said bitterly.

'He's all right is Mr. Edmonds. He was in the same boat as us I reckon. That's why he was so worried. It's not him, it's the buggers in high places – fuckers with hand-made suits and big cigars: decision makers that the likes of us never get to meet.'

'Don't get bitter mate. Life's too short. Can't say I'd want to meet any of 'em myself,' said Andy. 'Bit high powered for me I reckon. I'm just an Indian, not a chief. Best off without all that stuff – Just get on with it eh?'

'Yeah, keep your nose clean as my old man used to say. Mind you it was hard to keep it clean today, wasn't it? I mean we couldn't have stopped that bastard from shooting the Driscoll's, but we'd have been right in the shit if he had, wouldn't we?'

'Yeah, we would've. Serious shit all right.'

'That's what you don't realise when you start this game. Bit of this, bit of that, a few easy quid then before you know it, you're in up to here,' said Billy, holding his hand across his eyebrows.

'That's how they do it Billy. But they're never short of blokes, are they? There'll always be young guys willing to take what seems like easy money. We never saw what we were getting into did we?'

★★★

Philip hesitated at the entrance to the hospital ward, unsure if it was the right one. There were people all coming and going and who seemed to know their way around and he was about to ask for directions when he spotted the sign bearing the name of the ward he was looking for. He moved towards a second door and was relieved when he saw Mr. and Mrs. Gibbs leaning over a bed, obscuring the occupant from view. He almost ran down the ward in his excitement and when he reached her bedside gripped Naomi's hands and stood there unable to speak. The two of them looked at each other, each acutely aware that up until a short while ago neither of them had dared to believe they would ever see the other again.

'I thought I'd lost you Naomi,' he managed at last, his voice thick with emotion.

'We all did lad,' said Mr. Gibbs, wiping tears from his eyes and gripping Philip by the arm; a simple action but one that made it obvious that he was pleased to see him there.

Philip and Naomi continued to hold hands and gaze at each other, and so neither of them saw her mother tweak her husband's sleeve, nor did they notice her parents move away and make their way out of the ward.

'Good idea love,' murmured Mr. Gibbs as they passed through the door, 'I could do with a coffee.'

'I could do with a large gin,' she replied, 'but hot coffee will have to do for now.' She looked back. 'I don't believe they've said a word yet.'

'Plenty of time for that now. I've never seen young Philip lost for words. Did you see the way he came rushing in?'

'They'll find it difficult for a minute or two. They've been through the mill all right. That bloody bunch of bastards has a lot to answer for,' his wife replied angrily. 'When I think of what they've done to our little girl, of what they put us all through, of all their filthy threats and what they did to her poor little cat. Well let's hope that this time the law shuts them down for good, locks them all up and loses all the keys.' She paused, dried her eyes, and blew her nose.

They set their polystyrene beakers down on the green, metal tabletop, disposed of the previous occupants' rubbish and said nothing more, each lost in their own thoughts. Each dwelling on what might have been; each grateful beyond measure that their prayers had been answered and that their precious daughter had been restored to them.

'Look,' said Mrs. Gibbs suddenly. 'It's Philip's parents. Quick Brian head them off and bring them in here.'

CHAPTER TWENTY-FIVE

Alice Simms sat alone in her large sitting room, her hands in her lap, her face in repose, the bottle of vodka and a glass on the occasional table by her side. The Police Inspector who had brought the shocking news to her door had been kind and sympathetic and her colleague had gone to the kitchen and brewed tea as they spoke. Years after the event she would remember sipping that hot, sweet tea. She'd asked no questions but simply listened as the good woman, holding Alice's hands between her own, broke the news as gently as possible. The tea was strong and very sweet. It was the best cup of tea she could remember.

The police officers, having made sure she contacted someone to come and stay with her and was fit to be left alone, offered their condolences once more and left.

'I'm not your grieving widow,' she exclaimed emphatically, addressing the empty room at last. 'I don't miss that bullying bastard that much,' she said, clicking her finger and thumb together in a gesture of contempt. 'Cup of tea? It should have been vintage champagne! Never mind, there's plenty of this – Russian ruin,' she laughed bitterly, held up the crystal glass at eye level and poured herself another large vodka.

'I've still got James,' she said, after a long contemplative silence. 'We can't stay here though. We'll have to move away and make a fresh start. James will be all right now without that bastard Robin getting at him at every turn. Robin's dead, Rebecca's dead, Arthur's bloody dead and Joshua's missing. Well, he'll turn up dead too I expect. Arthur Simms eh. What a bloody fool of a man you turned out to be: a stubborn, pig-headed, bloody fool of a man. Threw it all away just so you could take your petty, stupid revenge on a dead man; as if having him murdered wasn't enough for you. Well now you're gone too, the world's a better place and bloody good riddance to an evil bastard.'

She put down the glass, stood and walked across to the wide bay window where she stood looking out, reflecting on the events that had shaped her life, her ill-judged decisions and how they had always led her false.

'You always heard what you wanted to hear,' she berated herself, thinking back to the days when Arthur had come courting, filling her head with romantic dreams of a rosy future together. Then her eyes filled with hot tears as she thought about her parents. She heard her father's harsh voice, recalled the last words she had ever heard him say, saw the wagging finger as if it was yesterday: saw again the finality in his face, the determined set of his jaw.

'Now you just listen to me my girl. If you take up with that bloody thug, that hooligan, then you'll cease to be our daughter. We'll disown you, and don't think I don't mean it.'

'You can't stand it because Arthur's a real man,' she'd screamed at him, 'not one of your pin-striped, middle-class mummy's boys. He's worth ten of any of them and I love him, and he loves me. As for being your bloody daughter, where's that got me then, you bloody bully? He's not out to impress you because he doesn't care a damn what you think and that hurts your precious pride doesn't it. You're nothing, and I can't wait to get away from you and your pathetic, snobby little values.'

He'd simply pointed at the door, overwrought, too angry for more words.

She remembered the last time she had looked at her mother standing meekly by, wringing her hands, wanting them to stop before it went too far, but lacking the strength to stand against him.

She'd defended her man, thrown in her lot with him; cut herself off from her family to be with him and love him and he'd turned out to be an absolute bastard.

Her thoughts turned to her baby Justin. That had been a good part. It hadn't lasted long enough to call it an affair, but she remembered the kindness, the gentleness of her lover, Justin's father.

'Just that once for me,' she whispered. 'Some women get to spend the rest of their lives with a man like him.'

She hugged herself and cried quietly, as the light continued to fade and shadows of winter stole across the carpet, enveloping her in the evening gloom.

'You worked it out though, you bastard,' she muttered, remembering every slap and punch as Arthur had beaten her. 'You never said how you found out. I guess you saw it in his little face. But you did your best to make me regret it. You stole my lovely boy away from me. You made him worship you, ape your cruel ways, made it your business to ruin him, turned him into a brutish thug like yourself, like the others, and he's gone too; a victim, just like all the rest.'

★★★

CHAPTER TWENTY-SIX

Miranda sat before the locked desk weighing the hammer in her hands. Huw's financial affairs had never been an open book. He'd been so secretive about his money, but she'd always believed that their joint current account was different. He was never mean. She'd had access to it at all times – cheque book and debit card – and he'd never objected seriously to her spending, just the occasional, good natured jibe when she'd been particularly extravagant. He'd consulted quite freely with her on how she wanted money paid into the account during his absence and he had agreed readily when she'd said she'd like a cheque through the post each month. She would pay it in herself. It was, she'd said, safer than electronic transfer, direct debits and all that stuff. And, being a realist, she had diverted £500 each month into a building society account in her own name. At first, she hadn't intended to deceive Huw but realised she needed to look after her own interests, so she'd gone ahead without asking. She had meant to surprise him with the money when he came home. But now he was dead and the cheque for November had not appeared. Up to now the cheques had arrived on the front doormat on the same day of the month.

She remembered how she had objected so vociferously that evening when he had broken the news that he was going to be tried on criminal charges of fraud and money laundering and would have to serve a long prison term. He'd made it clear to her that he was not guilty of these charges but had come to "an arrangement" whereby he would take the blame for someone else, someone higher up who had promised to show appreciation in the form of a large lump sum.

They'd had the most tremendous row.

'You're bloody mad!' she'd cried. 'You'll have a criminal record, you silly bugger. And you never even talked to me about it? My opinion, my happiness doesn't count then?'

'I've already got a criminal record you silly cow!' he'd shouted back. 'Where do you think all the bloody money comes from? My job at the pub? Aunt Fanny's will? Father Christmas? Eh? I'm getting big bucks for this so it's going to be worth a spell in the nick. It'll set us up proper. We'll go abroad and live the life of bloody Riley.'

The disclosure had been a complete shock, but she'd been unable to talk him out of it even though she'd shed copious tears.

'These people don't mess around love,' he'd said, reaching for her hand. 'I couldn't back out now even if I wanted to. They'd find me and that would be the end of us.'

The finality in his voice and the expression on his face had disturbed her deeply. She knew that he'd had no choice really. She'd put on a brave front but had all along remained concerned for his safety.

Now he was gone, murdered on the say so of some distant, evil bastard, someone she'd never heard of, about whom she knew nothing. Someone "higher up" who had decided that her Huw was expendable. She'd grieved for him. She was still grieving in her smart, black trouser suit and fashionable, black shoes. But her grief was tempered by concern for her own future. For a start there was a funeral to be paid for.

She wanted details of the Swiss bank who sent her cheque each month and she examined the desk front with care.

'This desk is an antique,' she said aloud. 'Don't bust it up more than you have to girl. You'll probably have to flog it before long.'

She put aside the hammer and, after rummaging through the toolbox, came up with a pair of wide bladed paint scrapers and a sturdy screwdriver. Placing the two scrapers together she slid them in under the edge of the roll top near the lock then, using the hammer, tapped the screwdriver gently, forcing its wedge-shaped tip between the scrapers. She continued to tap gently, listening as the increase in pressure caused each successive tap to rise in pitch until there was a sudden, sharp crack as the brass lock gave way and the roll top shot open a few inches.

Pleased with the success of her method, the precious desk was almost unmarked, she gave a cry of delight, reached forward, and opened the roll front to its full extent.

'Damn!' she exclaimed, on finding that all the interior drawers were locked. There was no way she could insert a blade in the drawers without causing serious damage to the beautifully veneered cabinetwork.

She ran her hand along under the top of the cabinet and gave another little cry as she dislodged a small brass key which fell almost silently onto the leather desktop.

Picking up the key she addressed the double doors in the knee-hole and soon had these open. Removing the documents from the lower shelves, she searched through them thoroughly, but neither the information she sought, nor a second key was forthcoming. Going back to the upper drawers, she studied the interior of the desk intently. Then she dragged it away from the wall and examined the back.

'Bloody hell!' she exclaimed at last, defeated by the locked drawers. 'This old furniture often has a secret mechanism,' she mused, allowing the screwdriver to fall into the toolbox.

She dropped to her knees and studied the drawer fronts at eye level. The gilded ormolu decoration attracted her attention. It was fixed to the front of the narrow shelf above the drawers in the form of a miniature balustrade and reminded her of an altar rail. There were little posts at intervals, each surmounted by a tiny sphere. She tried, without success to unscrew one. She tried another then another and experienced a moment's hope when one of them turned in her fingers. But it simply continued to rotate without releasing a secret latch. After pressing down on it without a result she gripped it from above using her long nails to apply upward pressure and she became excited when the ball lifted between her thumb and middle finger enabling her to withdraw a long metal rod. It resembled a knitting needle with no point. Once this was extracted, she discovered that the three left-hand drawers were now unlocked. Each had a little brass socket with a vertical hole to accept the rod that simply passed down through the aligned holes to prevent the drawers from opening. Each was fitted with a lock as well but, fortunately, these were unlocked.

'There's clever,' she marvelled, pulling on the corresponding ball above the drawers on the right. It was the same locking device and so all six drawers were free to open.

She found what she was after in the third drawer, a letter from a bank in Switzerland quoting the number of the joint account. The remaining drawers yielded nothing to do with Huw's trial, but she did find details of two high interest deposit accounts held at the same bank and under the last drawer she found a second small brass key taped to the bottom. The drawers returned smoothly into their slots and she reinserted the two rods to lock them, marvelling at the ease with which she could slide them home.

'Perfect alignment that,' she murmured in admiration, inserting the key, and locking each drawer in turn. 'Real workmanship that is. Just need to get a new lock for the front now and it's all tickety-boo,' she chuckled, feeling pleased with herself. Without the two paint scrapers, the screwdriver would have caused considerable damage to the delicate cabinetwork.

She gathered the papers together then picked up the phone and made an appointment to see her bank manager.

'I've been broke before, seriously broke,' she muttered, looking up the number for her solicitor. 'At least I've got a few quid in the building society this time; and the house is all paid up. It'll come to me if those evil buggers haven't got at that as well, fingers crossed eh.'

Smiling to herself, she rummaged in her purse and found the scrap of paper bearing the number of Billy's mobile 'phone.

★★★

CHAPTER TWENTY-SEVEN

Maureen, sounding somewhat flustered, called from the kitchen as the strident double chime of the front doorbell rang through the house.

'Would you get that Terry?'

'Certainly, Madam,' he answered, rising from his chair, and inclining his head to an imaginary employer. He paced majestically towards the front door, gliding across the hall carpet, his face bearing the benign expression of a butler in full flow. He kept this up until he drew back the door and was even prepared to issue a formal greeting, butler style. As it was his mouth dropped open in astonishment, as he recognised the woman standing there. They regarded each other for a long moment.

'You're Terry, aren't you?' she said at last, with a wan smile. 'I was hoping to speak with your mother.'

She looked ill at ease and had obviously been crying.

'Come in,' he managed to say, standing back from the door.

'I think you'd better check with your mother first,' she replied, making no move to enter.

'Who is it Terry,' called Maureen.

He stood tongue tied, feeling awkward, conscious of the tension in the woman and of the likely outcome when Maureen realised who was at the door.

'Terry?' called Maureen, approaching along the hall, a perplexed expression on her face. 'Didn't you hear me?' she snapped irritably then stopped in surprise as she recognised the caller.

The two women stood in silence for what seemed a long time until Alice Simms spoke quietly. 'I wanted to explain. I just ... I wanted to talk to you. I t ...' she stopped and stood looking woe begone.

'God you've got a bloody nerve coming here,' said Maureen at last. 'I can't imagine what you and I might have to talk about. Unless it's what your murderous bloody family has done to us. I have absolutely no wish to talk to you. Just go away.' She turned her back. 'Shut the door Terry.'

'Please,' cried Alice. 'I can't bear it. I can't bear thinking about everything that's happened. I can't bear what they did. I want to tell you ...' she stopped again, holding a handkerchief to her face, her shoulders heaving as she cried silently.

'I told you to shut the door,' grated Maureen, her voice taut with anger. Terry remained holding the door open. 'Close that door. Now!' she snapped, reaching across to do it herself. Terry put up a hand to stop her.

'We can't leave her out there in that state Mum.'

'You don't understand. I can't talk to her.'

Terry continued to hold the door open. Alice, looking absolutely wretched, blew her nose, dabbed at her eyes, and stood waiting submissively.

'You don't know what you're asking,' Maureen hissed at Terry. 'You know as well as I do that, they murdered your father. They entered our home and took us out at knifepoint and were going to kill us too. But for Matty arriving when he did, we'd both be dead. You know all this and yet you expect me to allow this person to enter our home. She has no business coming here like this. What is the matter with you boy?'

'Please,' said Alice. 'I couldn't come before. I've been so unhappy, so ashamed, all that guilt – nothing I could do about it – nothing I dared do about it. But now they're gone I can start again in my own way. I want to make amends if I can. I want you to know I'm not like them. You don't know what it's been like for me being part of that family. You can't know what it feels like to have given birth then watch your children schooled into such evil ways. I want to tell you about my Justin. He was my lovely boy. Then my husband turned him, made him like that. At least

I've still got James, he was always the gentlest.' She stopped; head down, emotionally drained by her outburst.

'Mum?' pleaded Terry. 'You can't just turn her away. Look at the state she's in.'

Maureen met Terry's unyielding gaze and capitulating at last to the resolve she saw there, stood aside from the door.

'You'd better come in and say whatever it is you want to tell us,' she said resignedly. 'Come through.'

Alice stepped over the threshold and placed a hand on Terry's shoulder.

'Thank you,' she breathed, still dabbing her eyes. 'You're a good boy.'

She followed Maureen into the lounge, took the seat that was offered and the two sat regarding each other.

Terry, conscious of the high tension in the room, decided they were best left alone for the present and went through to the kitchen. He couldn't explain why, but he felt an attachment to Alice. He liked her. Her distress disturbed him. He wanted to offer her comfort if he could and was hopeful that his mother would become less severe towards her.

'He's such a lovely boy,' began Alice.

'Yes, he is. Can be very stubborn though as you've just seen for yourself,' replied Maureen. 'He's so like his father. Once he's decided on something, he follows it through no matter what. He's just the same with his games – competes right up to the last whistle and finds it so hard when they lose. He soon gets over it though – bounces back, ready for next time.'

She stopped, realising that she had talked more than she intended, perhaps giving her unwelcome visitor the mistaken impression that she had begun to thaw.

'He must have been an adorable child,' said Alice.

'I'm sure you didn't come here to talk about Terry,' said Maureen dismissively, attempting to re-establish distance between them.

'No. That's true. I've decided to move away. I'm selling up and I've found a place where I think James and I can be happy. I'm told he'll very likely receive a custodial sentence. He's never been in trouble, but the solicitor says the charges are serious enough. People died after all and he was present, and he did have a gun even though it wasn't used. At least I can get the place ready so that he'll have a chance to make a new start when he comes home. I felt I couldn't just disappear without saying sorry for the dreadful wrongs you have suffered at the hands of my family. If only there was some way I could make amends. I feel so responsible.'

'What's done is done Mrs. Simms. You can't give me back my dead husband, can you? You can't erase my son's memories of how he suffered at the hands of your thug of a son can you? You can't make up for the fact that I was woken in my own bed with a razor at my throat, can you? You can't begin to understand my fright on seeing a shining razor at my son's throat and the terror in his eyes, can you? You can't eradicate our nightmare of being held at gunpoint in the certain knowledge that we were about to be shot, can you? I'm glad they're dead Mrs Simms, the whole brutal, bloody, murderous crew of them. When I heard what had happened, I thanked my maker for his justice. So, don't come to me looking for understanding, looking for sympathy. You have no idea of what we've been through Mrs. bloody Simms!'

Maureen's voice had become louder and harsher until she was bellowing in her fury. She found herself on her feet wiping spittle from her lips, almost overcome with blinding anger and wanting to strike out at Alice when Terry backed into the room carrying a tray of tea, which he set down then turned to go.

'No. Stay,' said Maureen. 'You pour the tea; I'm too shaky, too upset.'

Alice sat with eyes downcast, shocked, and deeply affected by the emotional ferocity of Maureen's outburst. She'd come there with a naïve and muddle-headed notion that merely by talking woman to woman, that she and Maureen might see each other as kindred spirits, perhaps even be ready to come together in a cosy, sisterly bond. She'd believed she could smooth away the dreadful events perpetrated by the members of her family – even assuage her own conscience in the process; atone for the wrong she herself had done to this woman and gain for herself at least some small measure of absolution. The truth, now so apparent, was that she'd had no real grasp of the depth of suffering that had been inflicted upon the Driscoll's and that she herself was nothing more than a painful reminder to them.

She accepted the proffered cup of tea, nodding her thanks as Terry added sugar and stirred it for her.

'Thank you, Terry,' she said, so quietly as to be almost inaudible.

Maureen had begun to regain her composure by this time but was feeling some embarrassment after her emotional outburst. Alice, speechless, dwelling on the litany of horrors she had just heard, sat huddled, both hands around the teacup. It was Terry who broke the lengthening silence.

'It wasn't your fault Mrs. Simms.'

She looked at him, her lip trembling, about to weep again. She wanted to cry.

'You don't understand. It was my fault. It all comes back on me. I allowed it to happen because I was lonely, so unhappy and so bloody selfish.' But she knew now that the burden she carried, the words she had wanted to say, to share, must always remain unsaid. Putting down her cup, she stood ready to leave. 'I'm so sorry,' she said, holding out her hand. 'I shouldn't have come here. I wanted to put things right between us, but I've made you so angry.'

Maureen took her hand and the two women studied each other briefly then walked together to the front door.

Inside, Maureen embraced Terry and cried.

Outside, Alice let in the clutch and drove away, tears running freely down her cheeks. She'd wanted more than anything to hug Terry, to hold him tight and never let go.

★★★

EPILOGUE

Periodically, on this warm, spring afternoon comes the double clack of the church gate as people come and go, most to tend the graves of departed loved ones, some few to pray inside. Footsteps crunch in the gravel until the walkers turn aside, follow the grass pathways between the ancient yew trees to where the familiar plots, unkempt after a winter of neglect, await their attention.

A promise of spring: thrusting green shoots pierce the damp turf, lifting the spirits of those kneeling there, working so busily. Maureen and Terry work side by side, gathering and discarding detritus from the year gone by and washing the dusty grime from Frank Driscoll's gravestone, happy to feel the sun on their backs, they rejoice in their togetherness.

The author

Sean Maple was born in April 1936 in Wimbledon, London. At the end of the war, his family moved down to Kent. As a youngster in the 1950's Sean took jobs which allowed him to continue playing the jazz trombone in the evenings not giving much thought to the future. Between 1972 and 1975 Sean trained as teacher. He taught in a county primary junior school until his retirement in 1996 at the age of 60. Sean played in various jazz bands, mainly in East Kent, until 2019. He has done weekend tours in Belgium, France and Germany. These were great times for him especially after the fall of the Berlin wall. Sean's favourite activities are walking, reading and mainly jazz music from the 1930s to present day. Sean has acquired skills in carpentry and has only stopped playing the trombone recently. He published a short story in a local newspaper as well as some poetry. Sean is married and has three children the youngest being 55. Sean currently resides in Kent. A Conflict of Interests with Murderous Intent is his first crime novel.

Lightning Source UK Ltd.
Milton Keynes UK
UKHW010952081121
393605UK00001B/213